T5-BQB-076

LOVE SONGS

$4.00
SIGNED

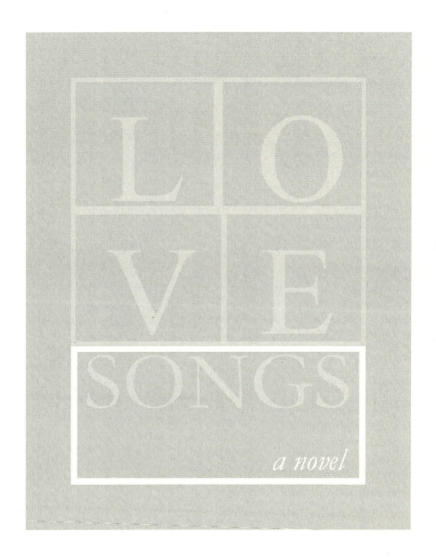

LOVE
SONGS

a novel

Gwen Harmon

Copyright © 2008 by Gwen Harmon

All rights reserved.

This is a work of fiction. Names, characters, places and incidents are used ficti-
tiously and any resemblance to actual persons, living or dead, business establish-
ments, events, or locales is entirely coincidental. All characters contained in this
book are copyrighted creations of Gwen Harmon.

No part of this publication may be reproduced or transmitted in any form or by
any means, electronic or mechanical, including photocopy, recording or any information and retrieval system, without the permission in writing from the copyright holder/publisher, except in the case of brief quotations included in critical
articles and reviews.

Cover and interior design by: Gwen Harmon

Publisher: Gwen Harmon

ISBN – 978-0-6152-1174-9

Printed in the United States of America via Lulu Press
(www.lulu.com)

For all of the Sonja's, Gail's, Evelyn's
and the men who love them!

Rose!
Thanks so much
for supporting me —

Acknowledgements

This started as a typical romance novel written by someone who had experienced typical romances. As my life evolved into its more defined purpose, this book took on much more substance. I hope this book reflects the many ups, downs and detours we experience as we navigate through life as daughters, wives, mothers, sisters, lovers and friends.

Many thanks to my sister Diane who always propped me up even when I didn't believe I had the talent to pursue my childhood dream.

Many thanks to my high school friends, Doris, Gwen, Mildred in heaven, Pat and Olean who used to wait impatiently as I hand wrote short stories in class and let them read my work page after page!

Many thanks to Betty and Cassandra who read the first draft in its infancy and were so kind in your critiques. Because of you, it's a much better final product. Many thanks to my Jackson State University sisters Teresa, Debbie, Mearl, Janice, Vivian, Gloria, Francis, Kathy and Gwan who gave me enough material for a hundred books to come!

Many thanks to my dearest friends Dorothy, Norma, Valerie, Jackie, Karen, Gladys, Rhonda and Arnetta who bugged me, nagged me and never stopped asking, "Where is the book?" My sincere thanks to Charlesetta, Tangela and Beverly who always offered support and encouragement.

Many thanks to my son Jeremy who says I'm one of the smartest people he knows. *I raised that boy right!* Many thanks to my niece Yolissma who represents the challenge of the future generation and who reminds us older folks to just relax and let love do its thing.

And finally, I must acknowledge my love of God and his son Jesus Christ who blessed me with the eerie talent to "see the words" that I write and "hear" the characters that I write about on every page. Without their divine guidance, I could be deemed just plain crazy.

Chapter 1

SONJA

Santa Baby

Santa Baby, slip a sable under the tree for me.
Been an awful good girl, Santa baby,
So hurry down the chimney tonight.

There is only one industry in Texas that rivals the oil business. Sex.

The secluded Dallas Baron's Club looked stately and impressive. The red brick, three story, colonial structure with its circular driveway was competing with the Bentley's, Mercedes-Benz's, Ferrari's and Porsche's parked on the property.

A passerby would have simply thought it was a very wealthy, respectable gathering of the very wealthy and respectable. They would have been right but very shocked at what actually brought these men to the private Club. It had a lot to do with wealth, but very little to do with respectable behavior.

Entering the mansion, one couldn't help but be impressed by the immaculate glass like Italian marble floors, the curving massive staircase and the priceless artwork adorning the walls. The attractive blonde hostess with her 1,000-watt smile was waiting to seat the guests. Would it be dinner first or entertainment followed by dinner? She already knew the choice most of the club members would make. It was always entertainment followed by dinner. No matter how young or how old they were. No matter if they had old money or new money, it was always the entertainment first.

The blonde hostess would smile, nod, and discreetly signal for an equally gorgeous blonde, brunette or redhead to show the gentlemen to a table.

Tonight's special guest was the longest living member of the elite club; eighty-two year-old Senator Earl Simmons. He was celebrating retirement from the Texas Senate after 50 years of service and passing the mantle of his Senate seat and political legacy to his 28 year-old grandson.

Most of the voters in the Senator's district knew the election was just a mere formality. The young Simmons only had to utter the words, "My granddaddy says," and wishes would be granted. He had been uttering those words since he was six years old at a private boys' school.

He brashly used them while at Harvard, and after a while the Dallas Police Department ignored his speeding red Ferrari, tired of hearing those words and seeing their law enforcement efforts derailed where the rich Simmons kid was concerned.

Tonight was his right of family passage. He was sharing a Simmons man's family secret. His grandfather had gotten him a membership into the Dallas Baron's Club and he took it quite seriously. He would not disappoint the old man as his father had, first refusing to enter politics and second becoming a Democrat. A bleeding heart liberal! Earl Simmons, III however was going to wear the family crest right on his forehead and make his granddaddy proud as he worked his first job ever as a Texas State Senator.

The elder Senator Simmons always had the best table at the Dallas Baron's Club. His server, Denise, a pretty young redhead, was standing at attention with her personal data blackberry connected to her Blue-Tooth, ready to respond to his every command. The menu consisted of more than the best Texas beef and bourbon, but the best women.

As the music started, the stage lights dimmed and the cavernous room seemed to glow. The white linen tablecloths provided a stark reflection against the Brazilian walnut wood paneled walls. The hardwood stage was polished to resemble a copper penny. The music surrounded the patrons with its state of the art sound system, and it actually felt like an orchestra was playing at each table.

The young Simmons was as giddy as a kid on his first pony ride.

"Granddaddy, this is awesome! When do I get to meet my date?"

The elder statesman smiled and leaned in closer to his grandson. In a fatherly tone, he started to educate the young lad on the rules. He pointed to the tables in the room, each with a beautiful "assistant" poised at attention, holding her personal data phone as though it were a weapon. A set of headphones with a nearly invisible microphone curved around their elegantly styled tresses.

"You see my boy, you have to bid on 'em. Now this one coming out now is just like an appetizer. She's good and all, but not very filling. My assistant here, Denise will let me know what the starting bid is and if I want to counter, I let her know. It goes on like a silent auction until the music and her dancing ends. The highest bidder wins."

As if on a magical cue, he looked up at Denise, who politely smiled and lit his Cuban cigar.

The young dancer was good and the young Simmons wanted to bid on her right away. These were the prettiest women he had ever laid eyes on. Each could be Miss America, Miss Universe, Miss World, a super model or the Playmate of the Year.

What he didn't know was that many of these women had indeed walked those very same famous pageant stages and runways, but fell short of receiving the crown. They were now part of an elite and more financially rewarded group than those who had won those pageants. It seemed like an eternity, but dancer after dancer performed and got rave reviews from the filled room. Each dancer was better than the last but as the finale act grew closer, the room took on an electrical charge.

Denise the assistant leaned down to Senator Simmons ear and whispered. His eyes sparkled and he nudged his grandson.

"Now here comes the main course. This one is the headliner and is the one everyone wants to spend time with. I'm gon' bid on her for you. Now when I win, understand it's up to you and her what happens next. She is something else. She's the best and you deserve the best. Just wait until you see her."

The stage lights glowed lavender and white as the music slowly started to build. The Senator looked up at Denise.

"We are starting Lovely Lena at $8,000 tonight Senator." She adjusted her earpiece to listen to an incoming transmission.

The red velvet stage curtains slowly opened revealing the silhouette of a woman in a white trench coat and white fedora. Slow sultry lyrics enveloped the room sung by Phoebe Snow asking,

Did you say I've got a lot to learn?
Well don't think I'm trying not to learn,

Since this is the perfect spot to learn.
Teach me tonight.

The woman, billed as Lovely Lena, sensually walked the length of the t- shaped stage and slowly unbuttoned the coat.

Starting with the ABC of it,
Right down to the XYZ of it,
Help me solve the mystery of it.
Teach me tonight.

The coat slowly dropped to the floor to reveal a snow-white lace and satin g-string with matching bra. The fabric molded the tanned and taut body of the woman who shielded her face with the oversized white fedora.

Her legs were bare and perfect and seemed to glide across the floor in the three-inch silver stilettos, as she swayed to the music. Each man in the room was sure she was asking only him to teach her tonight. The table assistants became frantic as they tried to keep up with the bidding.

The young Mr. Simmons was getting concerned. His grandfather had not placed a bid yet. "Granddaddy, we should bid, shouldn't we?"

"We will. And we will win. Don't worry, Denise here always takes care of me." He winked at Denise, who politely smiled and winked back.

The sky's a blackboard high above you.
If a shooting star goes by, I'll use that star to write,
I love you a thousand times across the sky.

Lovely Lena did a perfect spin and split down to the floor, keeping the hat dangerously low over her eyes as her body undulated showing a tight abdomen with round and inviting breasts trying to burst from the confines of the satin bra.

One thing isn't very clear my love,
Should the teacher stand so near my love?
Graduation's almost here my love.
Come on and teach me tonight.

Phoebe Snow was getting more impatient as she growled out the lyrics and the dancer matched her urgency with steady, rhythmic undulating moves as she positioned herself on her knees. Like a caged tiger, she started to crawl and pace the stage as though looking for her prey.

Each strain of the song's guitar accentuated her movements and as the crescendo built with Phoebe Snow's voice, the dancer grabbed the hat with one hand and flung it into the audience, revealing silky blue-black hair that fell to her breasts. Her other hand artistically released the bra at the same time to let her hair cover her chest.

The sky's a blackboard high above you.
If a shooting star goes by, we'll take that star and write I
love you.
One thing isn't very clear my love.
Should the teacher stand so near to me my love? Gradua-
tion's almost hear my love.
Come on to my house and teach me!
Yeah teach me teach me tonight.

The face was that of a sex goddess. Dark smoldering eyes. Full and passionate pouty lips. As she swiftly turned her back to the audience and slowly sauntered away, she cast a lingering look over her shoulder to invite the one who was man enough to teach her tonight.

Senator Simmons nodded to Denise who professionally keyed in his bid. He always did one thousand dollars more than the highest bid. Lovely Lena was now at $15,000, and the Senator had made it $16,000. His grandson was impressed. Finally catching his breath, he looked at his grandfather with a newfound pride.

"She is damn gorgeous. I mean she looks like Salma Hayek, Marilyn Monroe and Halle Berry all rolled into one." He gushed and took a swig of his bourbon.

"Well, it's before your time, but she got that stage name because she looks a lot like the movie star Lena Horne, except our gal is prettier. Now we have to go and wait for her in the dining area."

The old man was slowly getting up from the table as Denise placed his ticket on the table. He signed it and gave it back to her.

All transactions were done on personal accounts or by cash. The younger Simmons' face showed disappointment.

"Can't I have dinner with her alone?"

"Oh you will. I just want her to know you're someone special. Then I'll leave you alone. Remember, do not ask her anything on these premises. You got it? You make arrangements to see her on your own and don't ask her anything about money. This is just like a real date, except we paid for the whole herd instead of the steak. Don't be a dumbass and get caught up either, she's a businesswoman and don't forget it. This ain't about falling in love and getting married. It's about having a good time. Let's go to the dining area."

Sonja Davenport was in her dressing room with only the white g-string still on, removing her makeup. There was a soft knock at the door and she gave permission to enter.

Denise the assistant jubilantly came in with a small piece of paper and handed it to the performer.

"Sixteen thousand dollars! Congratulations. Another top night. You are a great performer!"

Sonja looked at the receipt and signed it to confirm she was having dinner with the patron. She looked at the name on the ticket. Senator Earl Simmons. He hadn't been around in a while.

"Senator Simmons? That's a blast from the past," Sonja mumbled.

Denise answered quickly, "Oh it's a special night. His grandson is with him, and the date is for him. He is sooo cute, too. One day I'll be cashing in like you instead of living off the tips. I can't wait."

The dressing room suddenly became ice cold as Sonja glared at the eager assistant in training, "First of all, never compare yourself to me. You will never be as good as I am. Secondly, I don't need you to give me a babe report on any client. I don't care how cute they are. I am not your BFF and we don't share any secrets. I am your boss! Take this ticket and get back to work." Sonja pushed the paper towards the stunned young woman.

Stammering an apology, Denise quickly exited the dressing room. The insistent ringing of her dressing room phone brought Sonja out of her rage.

"What?" she snapped into the receiver.

"Sonja, sorry to bother you. This is the reception area. I have an emergency phone call for you from your message service. The hospital in Birmingham, Alabama called. Your mother's had a stroke."

GAIL

Someone To Watch Over Me

There's a saying old, says that love is blind.
Still we're often told seek and ye shall find.
So I'm going to seek a certain lad I've had in mind.
Looking everywhere, haven't found him yet.

Gail Emerson sat up on the side of her bed slowly, hoping the slower movement would decrease the throbbing sensation in her head and behind her eyes. She squinted and looked at her alarm clock. Once again it had betrayed her, because it was reading 7:18 a.m.

She had overslept and would be late for work at the hospital. That would make three times in this month. Before even justifying needing to get a new clock, her common sense spoke loudly and criticized her for drinking too many margaritas with Larry Coleman. Slowly picking up the phone she dialed the hospital nurse's station and prayed the supervisor wouldn't answer. Her mind was too slow to think of a good lie this time.

"Methodist Hospital. Nurse's station, fourth floor. Mrs. Kennedy."

Gail's heart leaped. She was in luck. It was her close friend Laura Kennedy who covered for her most of the time, especially since Gail's second divorce. They had a running private joke of excuses like, Gail was sick; the kids were sick; the car was sick; and if she had owned a dog or cat, they too would have been sick.

"Laura, it's Gail. Look, I'm running really late. Has anyone missed me yet?"

"Not yet, only because Sandra has been in a meeting all morning with the Board. I hear today is the day girl. Get your butt in here quick and in a hurry. I can only cover for you for a little while longer." Laura whispered. Gail hung up the phone and ran to the shower.

Sandra Moore was the nursing supervisor who was resigning today to move to Florida with her ailing husband. Sandra Moore had been nursing supervisor for 10 years and controlled the entire promotion process for the nurses on the fourth floor and the trauma center. She made no secret about the influence she wielded. If she didn't like you, forget any peace at work. If she did like you, you were treated as an outcast by the rest of the staff out of either fear or resentment.

Gail had been one of five nurses applying for the supervisors' position once it became known that Sandra was leaving. There was never any specific date given, just the month of May for naming the replacement.

Today was May 27th and it was expected that Sandra would name an interim replacement until the Board hired a permanent head of nurses. That procedure was only a formality, since Sandra's interim choice was expected to be named the permanent replacement.

Gail quickly shampooed her recently cropped hair and reviewed her history with Sandra. No major fights. No major reprimands. In fact, no major conversations either, except for the time Sandra suggested that she go to medical school and become a doctor. Gail was that good at her job. There was another time right after Gail divorced jerk #1 that Sandra had complimented her on how well-behaved Jonathan and Jessica were when they came to get movie money.

Sandra was a good-looking brunette, with bewitching green eyes. She didn't have any kids and was married to a man who was twice her age, which made him close to seventy-four years old. The staff felt she worked even though he was wealthy just to intimidate and exercise control. She had met her husband when he was a patient at the hospital, deathly ill with terminal cancer. He fell in love, and ignoring the vehement protests from his children of the same age, he married the attractive and aloof nurse.

Gail smiled to herself, remembering the day Jonathan and Jessica had visited the hospital. She did have wonderful kids. Jonathan, Jr. was 13 and so smart it made her dizzy. He looked so much like his father it was frightening, with the same light brown skin, light brown eyes and a very tall slim frame. They had only been gone a few days for summer vacation with their father, but she missed them terribly.

Jessica was nine years old and precious, a daddy's girl who wrapped her Daddy around every finger. She looked a lot like Gail, with thick long hair and almond shaped eyes. Gail knew she and Jonathan could make gorgeous babies if nothing else. In fact, that was all they made together in 10 years of marriage that was good. Everything else concerning the marriage was a disaster.

Gail married him because he was good looking, and destined to make it as a professional basketball player. He married her because she was his hometown sweetheart, considered too naive to be a threat to his money or other women he might desire … and she wasn't bad looking either.

Jonathan's professional basketball career ended after eight outstanding years and a serious knee injury. His desire for other women, however, did not end. Gail always referred to him as a great father but a lousy husband. He provided well for the two kids, but sent Gail through hell financially, demanding an accounting of every dime of the child support he paid. She felt she was still under his thumb, even though she was free of him.

Coaching at Alabama State University provided Jonathan with a high profile career and, Gail suspected, a classic venue to select from a wide range of college ingénues and attractive professors.

Gail dressed in twenty minutes and dashed to her car. The drive to the hospital would take about fifteen minutes, which would put her at the hospital by 8:15 a.m., only fifteen minutes late.

Gail really needed this promotion. The salary would be at least a $15,000 increase, and for once she would have some financial flexibility in planning for the kids. They needed a real summer vacation, and she had lied about the ill condition of her eight-year-old Saab so often, it was becoming true. Every month there was a mechanic under the hood. A new car was long over due.

Just as she was starting to dream about new clothes and furniture, she heard the police car siren. Glancing in her rear view mirror, she saw the police cruiser gathering speed on her bumper.

"No way! I was only going 50. No damn way was I speeding." Gail mumbled as she pulled over and started rummaging through her purse for her driver's license.

Then she heard a familiar voice, "If you promise to handcuff me, I'll let you go."

15

Gail turned and looked into the face of Officer Larry Coleman, her drinking buddy and the bed warmer she had chosen the night before. For a moment, last night's image of him handcuffed to his four-poster bed, naked and spread eagle, flashed into her mind.

Aside from being handsome and one of the best lovers Gail had ever had, Larry had a special large organ, his mouth. He loved to brag about his sexual conquests and Birmingham was a very small town.

"Larry what in the hell did you stop me for? I'm late for work." She tossed her wallet into her purse.

"You're always late Gail and a dollar short. What else is new?" He ran his fingers through her moussed hair, until she slapped his hand away.

They had nothing in common except casual sex. Even more annoying was his persistent insecurity about her first ex-husband. He and Jonathan used to play poker, along with Charles, her second ex-husband. Birmingham was too small.

"I've got to go! Call me later," Gail was starting to pull away.

"Wait just a minute! I've got something funny to tell you. This other woman I'm kinda messing with, called me this morning pissed as hell because I wasn't with her last night. Because you know, I was with my real baby. Anyway, I think this babe is serious. She's talking marriage. Can you believe that? I might be getting married." He peered at her over his reflective sunglasses, watching her intently for a reaction.

"The young lady has my condolences Larry."

"I could be a good husband. I'm ready. You just didn't give us a try. I don't make as much money as Mr. Slam Dunk and didn't whip your ass like Charles, so I didn't stand a chance huh?" Larry's insecurities surfaced again.

"Good luck Larry, and take care. I've got to go." Gail sped off. He would have to bring up Charles, her second husband. Charles and Larry played poker every Friday night with a group of about 15 men. It was ironic that when Charles hit Gail for the first time, Larry and his partner responded to the call.

She didn't press charges that first time, nor the second, but when the third beating happened, Jonathan, Jr. was home and grabbed a kitchen knife to defend his Mama. She knew then that Charles would have to go.

She called the police and this time Larry took his poker-playing buddy to jail. Later that night he came by to check on her and the kids. The day Gail's divorce became final, she and Larry celebrated in bed, and yet he and Charles still played poker every Friday night.

Walking down the hospital corridor, Gail felt her co-workers were extra friendly to her, or was it her imagination? She had to find Laura first, to get a read on what was going on. She met Laura coming out of a patient's room, with a stressed expression on her face. "Laura, what's wrong?"

"A new pain in the ass patient. Some construction worker with a severe case of hypertension. He has a real attitude problem and I hope he gets discharged real soon. I can't even finish reading The National Enquirer 'cause his ass keeps buzzing the station!" Laura was breathing hard, as she usually did when she was upset. Being overweight only added to her strained breathing.

"Never mind that man girl, what's the word on the position?" Gail asked impatiently.

"That's no way for a nursing supervisor to be talking about a patient." Laura started doing the happy dance.

"Oh God, please say you're not kidding. How do you know?" Gail's heart was beating so fast she had to cover chest with her hand.

"Well all I know is that Sandra came by the station, said to tell you she wanted to have lunch with you today in her office, not in the cafeteria." Laura whispered.

"But that could mean I didn't get it! I mean she could be warning me about being late." Gail was trying to prepare herself for the worst case scenario, possibly another disappointing chapter in her life.

"Please child. Sandra is leaving in a week. She could care less about who shows up late. And why would she have to tell you over lunch that you didn't get the position? She hasn't said more than 20 words to you all month. Look Gail, you are the smartest nurse—no, the smartest person at this hospital. I always tell Ted, that you should have been a doctor. He even said so, and you know my husband rarely agrees with anything I say or do. You deserve this. Enjoy it and be blessed. Come over to the house after work for dinner." Laura grabbed her purse. Her shift was over.

Seconds later, the patient in room 409 buzzed. Laura rolled her eyes and sighed.

"I pity you with this one, but you're well rested, so go check on Mr. Pain …" Laura silently mouthed the words, *"in the ass,"* before waddling down the hall.

Room 409 had at least a dozen flower arrangements. There were magazines and newspapers on the floor and on the patient's bed. He was one of the best-looking men Gail had seen. Laura was definitely falling down on the job. She never mentioned this brother was so attractive.

Gail picked up his chart and read his name. *Maceo Sloan.* His frame sprawled in the bed made Gail guess that he was at least

6'4. His medium brown skin was slightly glistening from perspiration. Even the top of his shaved head had a slight glow to it. His moustache and beard were trimmed and shaped as though an artist had been commissioned to perfect it.

"Hi Mr. Sloan. I'm Gail Emerson. What can I get for you?" Gail asked in her best smiling nurses' voice.

"Miss, Ms., Mrs. Emerson, I have been asking for a phone for 24 hours, and that other person who says she is a nurse was supposed to check on it for me. But no one seems to take me seriously. I need a phone to conduct some important business. Now if I have to, I'll call Paul Monroe. You do know Paul Monroe, I assume?"

Gail read his chart closely. Yep. His doctor had adamantly instructed no access to phones. Even though he was only 51 according to his chart and in good physical shape, his blood pressure was dangerously high. He was brought in two days earlier complaining of dizziness and severe headaches.

Why would a construction worker think he could threaten her by contacting the hospital's Chairman of the Board of Directors?

"Mr. Sloan, respect and courtesy are mutually received and given. And as far as service? This is a hospital not a restaurant. We are here to keep you alive. When Dr. Goldstein makes his rounds I will personally ask about your phone request, but until then, no phone. Now, how about some juice or …" Gail's nice little speech was interrupted by Sloan's glare.

He lowered his voice to barely above a whisper, "Do not patronize me. Until I get what I want nurse, this hospital is no longer authorized to take blood, urine or spit. Now if you don't mind, please leave my room." He replaced his reading glasses and dramatically snapped the newspaper up to block his view of Gail.

Gail thought, "Brat!" But then for some reason she felt sorry for him. Acting out like this for a grown up was pretty pathetic.

"Mr. Sloan, is there someone I can call for you? I have orders and if I go against your doctor I could be in serious trouble."

"Ha! That's a joke. I get the feeling that people at this hospital never have to worry about getting into trouble. I'm tired Nurse Emerson. Think I'll take a nap." He kept the newspaper in front of his face, blocking her sight of him.

Gail quietly left the room and instantly felt this was not going to be such a good day after all. Supposed he complained to the Board Chairman, or even worse made such a fuss that Sandra had to get involved? That could mean her promotion would be in jeopardy.

EVELYN

Killing Me Softly

I heard he sang a good song. I heard he had a style.
And so I came to see him to listen for a while.
And there he was this young boy, a stranger to my eyes.
Strumming my pain with his fingers, singing my life with
his words.
Killing me softly with his song.
Killing me softly with his song.
Killing me softly.

Evelyn Jones Williams looked at the ceiling of the five star hotel in Paris. She then examined her new five-carat pear shaped diamond wedding ring, and she estimated that her entire observation of the ceiling and wedding ring took thirty seconds.

She checked her Piaget watch. *Yes, thirty 30 seconds.*

In exactly one more minute, her newlywed husband would stop making love to her, moan and climax, then dash to the bathroom for a vigorous shower. It had been that way for the past 6 months. Sixty seconds from start to finish of actual intercourse,

20 to 30 minutes of foreplay. Why, she wondered, did she ever think their extravagant honeymoon would be any different?

"That was good. Real good honey." Kevin breathed hard. Too hard for so little effort, Evelyn thought. It was amazing how he could play racquetball and tennis for hours and barely need to catch his breath, but sixty seconds with her was exhausting. She must be some kind of woman! Even that bit of private sarcasm made her laugh out loud. She used to cry afterwards, but not anymore. Instead, she shopped.

Kevin was already in the shower. Afterwards he came to bed and fell into a deep sleep. Even though she kept telling herself not to cry, Evelyn felt the hot tears of frustration streaming down her face.

Everything with Kevin had been quick. They met, courted and got married after nine months of dating. He actually wanted to get married after three months, but Evelyn just couldn't go through with such a hasty decision. She hesitated as long as possible until her family, or actually her mother, kept threatening her with the idea that this wonderful, handsome, successful lawyer, was going to get away if she didn't say she'd marry him.

The only thing Evelyn had wanted from Kevin was his company and to use him to make an old boyfriend jealous. He was always such a gentleman that she practically had to rape him the first time they had sex. But it had been so good! He had spent an eternity kissing every inch of her dark chocolate body, building her passion up to a boiling point.

Looking back, she realized that the act of intercourse was just as quick then as it was now, she was just too worked up to notice. Or maybe she was in too big of a hurry to remove the hurt and pain Larry Coleman had caused her with the announcement of his intention to get married. She wanted to deny she married Kevin on the rebound from being dumped, but her wounded feelings told her otherwise.

Even though Larry was the town whore, she had fallen under his spell and for years had waited for him to ask her to be his wife. She waited through countless other women. Older women, younger women, black women, white women, rich and poor women. But no matter how many others were there, he always came back to his "Hershey Kiss."

She figured by marrying Kevin, a successful lawyer, she would prove the point to Larry that she was still desirable to a man who was just as good looking and who made a hell of a lot more money. Kevin was an attorney at a prestigious Birmingham law firm, the first African American to make partner. As with everything he desired, success seemed to come quick and easy for him. He accepted the law firm's offer and moved back to Birmingham after living on the west coast for most of his adult life.

One year after joining the firm he landed a major corporate account based on the west coast that brought in millions for the firm. That made him partner. It was the talk of the Birmingham business community.

Evelyn went to community college to study marketing and fashion merchandising with the hopes of owning her own women's clothing boutique. She was learning the inside tricks of the trade by managing one of Birmingham's finest women's boutiques.

That was how she met Kevin. It had been a very slow Friday when this gorgeous, tall and high yellow brother walked in wearing a Brooks Brothers suit. His posture was so erect he could have been a model, his swagger so confident, he could have been royalty. He didn't have the pretty boy look, like NBA star Rick Fox, but he was close. Evelyn remembered how clean he smelled.

Not a trace of after-shave or cologne. Just a good old-fashioned soap scrubbed clean.

A stunning and equally tall woman was hanging on his arm, looking completely bored, and Evelyn thought, *Snob*. In fact, she was the biggest snob Evelyn had ever encountered and being from the deep south, she had waited on some of the best racists in the world. But this woman was a real piece of work. None of the merchandise was "right," none of the jewelry "fit right" and the perfume didn't smell "right." Evelyn was about at the end of her rope.

While the "Barbie doll" was trying on the 15th or 16th outfit, Kevin started a conversation

"Don't take it personal. She's a model from Chicago and this is her first time in the south. We have a special dinner tonight and I felt she should wear something a little more...."

"Conservative?" Evelyn interjected. She took Kevin's silence as a sign of agreement, so she continued.

"Well, you do know what we call Chicago in the south don't you? ... North Mississippi." Evelyn purred, carefully picking up the Barbie dolls lime green spandex mini dress draped across the chair and holding it with her thumb and index finger as though it could bite.

"Well, this is the place if you're looking for a makeover. I haven't lost a patient yet. Some of the richest women in the south shop here." Evelyn continued to hold the spandex dress away from her body as if it was contaminated before placing it in the dressing room.

"I've been here a year and I've heard that a lot of well dressed women come here. Where are my manners? I'm Kevin Williams." He extended his hand.

"I'm Evelyn Jones. So you've been here a year? Where from? Chicago?"

His handshake was firm and he held Evelyn's hand a little longer than necessary, "No, California. The bay area, around San Jose. Actually, I was born here. My parents are still in San Diego but my grandparents live here. Virgie and Henry Williams."

He was looking intently into Evelyn's face, as though he was searching for something familiar.

"You're kidding! Mr. and Mrs. Williams go to my church. They are the nicest people." Evelyn really liked this guy. He was down to earth and obviously friendly. How did he end up with such a Barbie Doll? Thinking of the devil, she re-appeared wearing her lime green spandex dress.

She wore lots of gold bangles, beads and chains, which clanked every time she moved. This might have worked on a fashion shoot, but not for everyday living. Fluttering her false lashes and tossing her *weaved?* shoulder length hair, she cooed to Kevin. "I just can't wear any of this! My frame is just not built for off the rack. Let's just pass on this dinner thing, pleeease?"

Her cuddling and whining up to Kevin irritated Evelyn more than her insulting the merchandise. He looked at her with a stern expression, "No we can't pass. It's a dinner to celebrate my being made partner. I am the guest of honor. My family will be there. The firms' partners and spouses will be there." He spoke to her as though she was mentally challenged.

Evelyn pretended not to be listening. Glancing at Evelyn, Kevin continued, "Now com'on. Out of all of these clothes there has to be something you like. Evelyn is the assistant manager. Rely on her expertise. Evelyn, in your opinion, what would you wear to an ultra conservative dinner at the Southern Acres Country Club?"

"Well, you can never go wrong in a Chanel or Escada collection. We have several that just came in the back. I was holding them for a special order, but I'd be happy ..."

Barbie Doll interrupted, "I really don't wear suits well. What do you have in a really sexy dress? My best features are my long legs."

Evelyn shot a glance at Kevin.

"I think the Chanel would go over nicely. Is that what you would wear Evelyn?" He gave her a sly wink.

"Oh, no. My hips, which are my best feature, are much too full for Chanel. It's more for the slim to no hips woman." *This was going to be fun.*

"Evelyn, your hips are just fine. Chanel is missing a real treat." Kevin leaned closer to Evelyn.

She couldn't believe he was such a willing partner in disrespecting his upset, insignificant other. But then, she deserved it. They left the shop without buying anything and several hours later, Kevin called Evelyn at the shop to invite her to his law firm's dinner. Miss Barbie Doll was on a plane back to Chicago.

The dinner at the Country Club was the typical boring upper class affair, with everyone being much too polite, especially to Evelyn. It was her first time there, even though a majority of her customers were members. The white women at the firm's table were obviously caught off guard at seeing Evelyn.

The only fun Evelyn had at the dinner was seeing some of the waiters and servers who were from her neighborhood. They paid extra special attention to her and would often ask her by name if she needed anything.

After dinner, the men all sat in a mahogany paneled cigar smoking room, while the women all freshened up in an overly decorated powder room. So very *"Gone With the Wind,"* thought Evelyn.

Stephanie Parker, married to the founder and president of the law firm, was the first to speak as they entered the ladies room.

"Evelyn, you sneaky thing! How long have you and Kevin been dating? I've tried to fix him up for a year without any luck."

"Stef, this is just our first date. He sort of needed an emergency escort." Evelyn noticed the other women pretending not to listen as they applied lipstick.

"Listen honey, this is not just a date. This is the kind of evening you spend with someone you really like. Someone special. And the way he was eyeballing you during dinner, you are special."

Too much wine at dinner accentuated Stephanie's southern drawl, and while she spoke she dramatically adjusted her push up bra, accenting her curvaceous figure in a black strapless gown, which hugged every inch.

The former Miss Alabama had been nipped, tucked and liposucked to death and was never seen looking less than beauty pageant perfect. She was Evelyn's best and favorite customer at the boutique. Her commissions on Stephanie alone had paid for her new Miata. They had attended high school together and had a decent friendship. Stephanie was the kind of white girl who was so honest, that you had to like her.

Her husband, Simon Parker, had left his wife of twenty-seven years for Stephanie. In fact, she was only 23 years old, the same age as one of Simon's children, when they met during the Miss Alabama pageant. Ironically, the first Mrs. Parker was the chair of the pageant committee and used to host receptions for the contestants and sponsors. It was at one of these celebrated receptions that Stephanie met Simon.

Stephanie was viewed as white trash, not poor trash, just brazen, for destroying one of the town's most elite marriages. Even though the upper class whites did not like her, she was tolerated. The 60-year-old Simon Parker had millions of dollars and lots of influence. He didn't like his 25-year-old beautiful wife being made unhappy by anything or anyone.

Stephanie told Evelyn that marrying an older rich man was the smartest thing she had ever done, almost. It ran a close second to entering the Miss Alabama Pageant.

"Well, Evelyn, I always told you to marry an old man with money. You seem to be taking half of my advice. That's a start." She was preening and posing in the mirror, lifting her waist length flaming red hair over her head and letting it cascade down her back. The other women stared in stone silence.

Evelyn knew Stephanie's show was for them. After applying cherry red lipstick, Evelyn slowly brushed her thick wavy hair. She had recently cut it to just below her ears.

"That is such a pretty shade! May I try it?" Stephanie asked. Evelyn handed her the lipstick.

Smoothing down her white raw silk dress, which draped dangerously low in the back, Evelyn turned to Stephanie. "Well Mrs. Parker, it ain't easy finding old black millionaires in Birmingham. So give me a break. Anyway, Kevin and I are hardly close to marriage. We just met! Right now I'm more concerned with getting my business off the ground."

"Well honey, you just have to know where to look! And all is fair in love and war. That's right! You always did want to be an entrepreneur. You should talk to Simon. He's always looking for a good investment. I always brag about how smart you are and what a good buyer you are. He just loves the stuff you sell me from the shop. And now with Kevin in the picture, you're like one of the family."

Evelyn realized that Stephanie had almost finished a bottle of champagne at dinner, so she couldn't be taken too seriously.

Stopping in mid air with the lipstick in her hand, Stephanie turned to Evelyn. "You know Kevin isn't exactly cash poor, he could help you get financing. You know how much he makes as partner now?"

"We're just friends. It's not my business how much he makes."

"Don't be immature. He's making deep into the six figures, and in this town that ain't bad."

The other women left the powder room without speaking to Evelyn or Stephanie, who also left and made their way to the bar.

Tossing her hair, Stephanie ordered a bottle of champagne.

"Well, now that I've been painted with the Stephanie Parker brush, I don't expect to win any popularity contests with this crowd." Evelyn said looking around the crowded room.

Throwing the flute of champagne back in one swallow, Stephanie drawled, "Honey, these women are so scared that their husbands might get a taste of me they can't see straight. But they don't have to worry. I do not screw the help." She poured another glass of Dom Perignon.

"I think the idea is to sip the champagne," Evelyn whispered.

"Who gives a damn? I don't. I need to get drunk. Every time I come to this high-class funeral parlor on a golf course, I get depressed. These hypocrites make me sick. They are probably calling the first Mrs. Parker right now giving that old wrinkled prune a play-by-play of the night. Now see, to me a real friend wouldn't do that. I mean it's only gonna make her sad that I still look so freaking good and Simon is just insanely in love with me. They think I'm beneath them! Every man at that table tonight and in this country club has a mistress. The only difference between them and me is Simon married me! I refused to be the kept woman. I deserved better. Hell, I was Miss Alabama, second runner up to Miss America."

So Stephanie wasn't as dumb as folks thought. In fact, she was quite shrewd. She had been married to Simon Parker for a little more than a year. When she insisted on a pre-nuptial agreement, that took him totally by surprise, but it gave him a strong argument to convince his children that Steffie, as he called her, truly loved him and wasn't after his money. Why else would she want a pre-nup?

As a one-year wedding anniversary gift, he gave her ownership of one of his shopping malls, because finding just the right "gift" was impossible, he told friends. This way, she had many gifts to select from.

Stephanie said she planned to get pregnant the second year of the marriage, to secure her financial insurance. As she put it, why worry about a prenuptial agreement when you've got a baby? That's like Christmas everyday. Her only dilemma was whether to adopt and spare her body the burden of nine months of gaining weight or to really place an emotional choke hold on Simon and get pregnant.

Evelyn didn't quite know what to make of this southern quasi-Beverly Hills, wanna- be club, but she could certainly do without becoming a member. She had a hard time understanding why Kevin thought it was so important to be a part of this social misfit club. He actually loved being with these people! He had kept a permanent grin on his face the entire evening.

So far this was the only thing she found troubling about this intelligent hunk: he was totally obsessed with being the FOB–the *F*irst or *O*nly *Black* .

Chapter 2

SONJA

Santa Baby

Santa Baby, a 54 convertible, too.
Light blue.
I'll wait up for you dear, Santa Baby,
So hurry down the chimney tonight.

Sonja had driven the ice blue Porsche 911 from Dallas to Birmingham in Daytona 500 record time. She couldn't wait on the next available flight. She knew her Mother was alone and needed her. So she drove all night without stopping until she got to Methodist Hospital.

After getting her stabilized, the doctor performed a battery of tests and concluded that her mother's recovery would be long and slow. Sonja and the doctor agreed having in-home medical assistance would be best. Sonja had to act fast.

She quickly bought a house that better fit her mother's recuperation needs and her own ego. She hired a nursing service and now she was faced with returning to a place she had vowed to never live again.

On that mild sunny morning, she silently cursed her fate while zooming down the Alabama state highway. Her sports car gave off a warning. The oil light was blinking and Sonja again cursed under her breath as she calculated how far Danny's Garage was from the mall. She knew it had to be at least ten miles. She remembered the light had come on briefly during her drive from Dallas, and now she prayed her negligence wouldn't cost her too much.

The thought of praying at all caused her to wince. It had been a long time since she had bent her knees to do anything, except to sit down and cross her legs. She adjusted the rear view mirror to get a full look at her face.

At thirty years old, she admitted to herself, she was still a striking woman. How many times had she heard that she looked like Lena Horne, except prettier?

It was true. She could be Lena's twin and she had used those Lena Horne looks ever since she realized how weak men were for a pretty face, shapely legs, long hair and light skin.

When she was eighteen and had just started dancing, she sat through every Lena Horne movie she could rent, borrow or buy. She wanted to know who this sexy screen legend was that folks always compared her to. If she was going to capitalize on it, she was going to do it the right way. She treated her looks as a business, as an investment that was going to pay off.

After high school Sonja had already decided that she (a) wouldn't go to college, (b) would not work at McDonald's, and (c) wouldn't get married to an everyday blue-collar worker.

She was determined to bank on the sex appeal and charm that Lena Horne used to become the first black, female sex symbol. Sonja used the best Hollywood had to offer in order to captivate and mesmerize men as one of Dallas's top billed, exotic dancers in an upscale men's club in Dallas.

The club's exclusive membership was the Who's Who in the Dallas money and power structure. The dancers were well trained and their elaborate performances, required special effects, costumes and choreography. Some were former Las Vegas showgirls. None of the typical strip club environment could be found at the Dallas Baron's Club.

There were no stripper's poles on the stage. No total nudity. Just brief topless performances, and no interaction with the clients unless they were a part of the business transactions.

The girls were featured in a brochure, which reminded Sonja of a fancy French restaurant menu with mouth-watering descriptions. The menu referred to the girls' stage names, measurements, ages and hobbies. When a Baron's Club member wanted to get to know the dancer, he would signal his table assistant during the performance and it would be noted on his account.

There was a gentlemen's understanding that they could be outbid for a date with the performer. This made for some interesting episodes when Sonja performed, often creating a bidding war.

The men never discussed a price directly with the performer, since that would be soliciting, according to the State Attorney General, also a member of the club. They simply signed their account as they would for dinner as a club member.

Sonja's paycheck would reflect her regular salary, plus a 50% share of her private dinners with the members. Her starting rate had been $700.00 a night as a rookie. Within a year, she was making ten times that each night. After three years, she was commanding $10,000 during the bid. That was when she knew it was time to make a more lucrative deal: make her a partner or she would leave. The owners knew that sharing a percentage of the top moneymaker's earnings was better than having her walk out the door.

As Texas oil business owners and executives got friendly with Middle Eastern billionaires, they frequently entertained them at the Baron's Club, which became one of the most heralded venues for the sheiks or members of a royal Arab family. Sonja's timing was perfect for making her ultimatum. And here she was, more than ten years later, returning to Birmingham financially independent.

When she left as an 18-year-old girl, she moved around in the Las Vegas and Los Angeles circuits. She discovered that Vegas was too transient and L.A. too perverted to count on a lasting career.

Dallas, on the other hand, had millionaires and billionaires who knew how to transact business. The oil industry was booming, money was good and plenty, and the men were rich and generous. Dallas was good to Sonja.

Sonja wisely decided to get a business degree and that shrewd move would allow her to move in an elite circle of men. One day, she thought, maybe she would use the business degree for a more traditional career, but for now no job could compete with the money she made as partner and performer at the Club.

Seduced by the money, Sonja kept dancing and lying to her mother, saying she was in pharmaceutical sales and had a hectic travel schedule. She never visited Birmingham, but in her mind she made up for being absent by buying the modest home for her mother and sending money each month. Her life was wrapped up in a neat little bow far away from Birmingham.

Now that fate had dealt her another hand, those days seemed far behind her. With her mother suffering a paralyzing stroke and needing around the clock private medical care, Sonja knew she would have to sacrifice her oil barons and lavish life style and move back to this boring, backward place. Being the only child, there was nothing else she could do.

It took only three or four months before her relocation created a stir in Birmingham, the first of course were her looks. Second, third and fourth, she was single, didn't work and drove a $100,000 dollar sports car. Added to that was the fact that she immediately placed her mother's small house on the market and bought a home in one of the most secluded and expensive subdivisions where there were very few African Americans.

She then hired a home health care nurse for her mother, who was confined to a wheelchair and was receiving speech therapy. Sonja had investments and a healthy savings account, but was still keeping in contact with some of her favorite Dallas men who in the past had financed cars, condos, diamonds and furs for her.

They were more than happy to pick up the phone and call Birmingham to wheel the real estate deal she wanted. They did this for themselves more than for Sonja. When scorned, Sonja Davenport could be treacherous to a marriage, business venture or political career. It also meant they could always find her when needed. For as much as she could be a pain in the ass, she also provided pleasure beyond imagination. As she pulled into Danny's Garage, Sonja couldn't help wondering how long before a new Lena would replace her in Dallas.

The garage owner, Danny Taylor, came outside wiping his hands on an already filthy rag. He realized it was Sonja and gave her a big grin. For as long as Sonja had known Danny, he had always been under the hood of someone's car.

He was the best mechanic in the state and made a rather decent living. Built like a professional football player with a thick, glossy black mustache and thick eyebrows, Danny was also rumored to be financially well off. He had always been a solid, no nonsense guy with little time for detouring from his goals.

He was proud of the fact that he had saved enough money to pay cash for his ranch style house just outside of town on over 10 acres of land. He was a loner and single, opting for his horses and farm animals for company.

Sonja and Danny used to play together as children and became best friends after he confided to her that her father wasn't dead. Her mother was Italian and worked as a maid with Danny's mother, so it wasn't unusual for the two women to confide in each other.

According to Danny, he overheard Sonja's mother telling the story of how she had met Steven Davenport when he was stationed in Italy with the Air Force. She got pregnant and they married, but her strict Italian family never accepted the marriage to an African American. When he was shipped back to the states, he left his young family behind, promising to send for them when Sonja was a little older. He never sent for them, wrote or made any contact. Sonja's mother told her he was dead after moving to the states. When Sonja was a little girl, she would ask daily about who her father was. Her mother tried to spare her the hurt by avoiding the truth.

It was after Danny's revelation that Sonja, at the young age of ten, decided she would never make the same mistake her mother had made by loving a man with all her heart and soul. In her youth, she hated the man she had never met, although she knew her mother was lying to her to create love and devotion that a daughter should feel for a father.

She resented her mother for protecting him, and obviously still loving a man who abandoned his wife and child. Her mother never remarried and still kept pictures of her father in her bureau drawer. He was a tall, dark, good-looking man. They had made a striking couple. She was sixteen, and he was a 22-year-old smooth talking New Yorker.

When Sonja was four years old, her mother moved to New York in hopes of finding Steve Davenport. Sonja and her mother lived with Italian relatives, a family of five, above the family run store in a cramped two-bedroom apartment.

Sonja hated New York. The winters were brutal and the summers suffocating. She could never dress warm enough or cool enough. When she was eight, they moved to Birmingham on the invitation of another cousin who got her mother a job as a maid.

If Sonja had been rich as a child, she would have been the perfect snob. She rarely spoke to or played with any of the kids in Birmingham. She considered New Yorkers classless and southerners ignorant. The blacks in her Birmingham school considered her stuck up and without a true identity: too dark to be white and too light to be black. The worse days of her life were during the popularity of *The Jefferson's* sitcom, as school bullies taunted her with George Jefferson's racist term of "zebra" for the bi-racial daughter-in-law's character portrayed on the show . There was rarely a day that she didn't hear whispers of "zebra" when walking down the school hall.

She really didn't spend much time thinking about being black or white. What worried Sonja Davenport more than anything else was being old, ugly and poor.

Licking her tangerine orange lips and taking a final look in the sports car rear mirror, she kept her eyes on Danny as he slowly walked up to her car.

"My, my, my. To what do I owe the honor of this visit? It must be life or death, since I haven't really seen you since you moved back. My Mama told me you were moving back. She's been asking about you for weeks." He leaned into the car window and gave Sonja a broad smile, showing off perfect white teeth.

"Danny, now you know I would come to visit more often, except Mama keeps me pretty busy. I'm not moving back really. I'm just here until Mama recovers. I didn't think I would need a mechanic, because the warranty on this car is still good and the dealership looks for any reason to complain when it comes to servicing a car behind another mechanic. But Danny, this is an emergency. My oil light keeps blinking."

"That means it needs oil. Didn't those fancy smart white boys service this thing just a few months ago?" He motioned for her to pop the hood switch.

"Well it's been about six months since I took it to be serviced, but that was just for a wheel balance or something. Remember, the week I drove up to Atlanta?" She opened the car door and walked around to the front of the car. Danny was checking the oil stick and had a serious frown on his face.

"You are completely low on oil, it's a wonder the engine didn't burn up. I hate to see a good car treated badly. You spent $100,000 on a car and can't remember to put $20 worth of oil in it?" He tried to keep his eyes from wandering from the oil stick to the low cut orange dress Sonja was wearing.

"Well, that's why they have oil lights right?" She gave him a pouty smile and pretended to be busy looking at the foreign wires and hoses. She knew the dress showed off the swell of her breasts and all she had to do was lean slightly towards Danny, to make the view even more daring. Of course, Sonja leaned.

If Danny noticed, he played it off rather well. Keeping his tone firm, he looked Sonja in the eyes.

"Sonja, you are not a dumb woman. Please cut the dumb blond act with me. I don't have time to play today. I'll have one of the guys to add some oil and you can be on your way in about 20 minutes."

He placed his towel back in his pocket and squinted to get a better look at her, " So, you're just passing through, huh? Must be nice to just plop down a lot of money on a mansion and not plan on staying." He turned and walked back towards the garage.

Sonja wasn't about to tell him she had a hair appointment in ten minutes and couldn't he rush this little oil change and make it less than 20 minutes? He was right. She wasn't dumb and she knew she had reached her limits with Danny.

"I didn't plop money down. I made an investment." She snapped.

She wanted to apologize for making him feel unappreciated or that his garage wasn't good enough for her business, but her stubbornness wouldn't allow it. Instead, she grabbed her purse from the car and walked into the waiting area. Business was good. Danny had several customers waiting and all of his service bays were full.

Sonja thought it was funny that all of the customers in the waiting area were women. She recognized a few of them but didn't bother to acknowledge their presence. Just as she sat down and started flipping through a magazine, one of the mechanics came in with a form and called her name. She filled out the basic customer information form and signed it.

Fifteen minutes later he returned and said she could leave. The other customers looked at each other and then at her. Obviously, she got special treatment, the kind of treatment Sonja Davenport liked, demanded and expected.

She looked for Danny as she walked to her car and spotted him on the office phone. She waved but he pretended not to see her. She turned to the mechanic and asked how much was her bill.

"Oh, Mr. Taylor said no charge. But you ought to come in for a oil change every 1,500 miles, especially if you drive long distances a lot … seeing you from Texas. We saw some other things to check, but Mr. Taylor said they could wait a while."

"Thank you. Tell Mr. Taylor thanks for the offer, but I insist on paying my bill, so how much do I owe?" She was pulling out her wallet and getting more steamed. The nerve of him! Chastising her, ignoring her and then treating her as if she was a charity case. His voice from behind her made her jump.

"You owe me dinner. At my house. I do the cooking. You do the eating and very little talking."

His mechanic smiled and walked away.

Tossing her hair out of her eyes she answered, "Fine. When and what time?" She couldn't believe she was going along with this.

Neither could Danny, as he stammered "Fr..Friday, eight o'clock. You do know where I live, right?"

"I remember. Big ranch, lots of land, horses and such. I'll let the smell of manure guide me." She was writing the dinner appointment in her Blackberry planner as she would any business appointment.

This appeared to annoy Danny. "Well I don't have oil wells pumping in my front yard and I don't make a practice of buying expensive sports cars for women, but I enjoy my ranch and the women who want to be with me buy their own cars."

Sonja's head snapped to attention in response to Danny's allegations. "What makes you think I didn't buy my car? And why is it your business if I didn't? You know what? Just forget it Danny. Cancel Friday. You obviously have some kind of problem with me, and frankly, my dear, I don't give a damn." Sonja jerked the car door open, jumped in and slammed the door shut.

Danny grabbed the steering wheel. "Okay, I'm sorry. I was wrong. Truce? You still fight like a cougar, huh? Please come to dinner Friday night. I'm a pretty good cook. I'll even do your favorite, lobster and champagne. Remember when we were little and you used to always say you were going to be rich and drink champagne everyday? How about it?"

That was more like it, thought Sonja. Beg. Little did he know, he didn't really have to beg that hard, she had already decided to go to bed with Danny Taylor, even if he hadn't apologized. And that worried her. He wasn't nearly as rich as she liked her men.

§§§§§§§§§§§§§§§§§§§§§§§

Sonja went shopping after her hair appointment and ate lunch alone. She had no choice, since all of her friends were back in Texas.

Well, friends might be an over statement. The women Sonja socialized with in Dallas were more like acquaintances. They shopped, did lunch and maybe a movie, but they never embraced each other as close friends. They were more like cordial competitors. But today was different for Sonja. She really was lonely.

Maybe it was being back in Alabama where everyone cherished close friends, and everyone knew everyone. She had been in Birmingham six months and not a day passed without someone asking how her mother was. Sonja was amazed at how many people liked her mother. Not only would they call to check on her, but they brought food, magazines and small gifts.

They always talked about people Sonja went to high school with, but she could never remember any names or faces. Now she regretted not keeping in touch with anyone. She was beginning to get bored, and spent every evening at home with her mother, who still had limited speech and could only communicate by gesturing or pointing and flashing those dark, expressive Italian eyes.

Sonja was leaving the downtown area when she thought about the date she made with Danny. She was going to cancel it. Seeing him was a bad idea and would only lead to trouble. Danny would never understand or accept her lifestyle and it was best for them to remain friendly on the surface. She would call him tonight. Her intuition told her it was best to avoid any problems.

As she was cruising the downtown area, a woman's dress shop caught her eye. Curiosity got the best of her and she parked her car and decided to browse the shop, *Exclusively Yours.* She immediately recognized some of her favorite designer collections and was glad she had stopped.

She was going through a rack of blouses, when a sales clerk walked up, "Hi, need some help?" She looked familiar, but Sonja couldn't remember how she knew her.

"Just browsing, this is my first time in here, and I can tell you, it won't be my last. You've got some very nice pieces. Are you the manager?" Sonja glanced at the shapely and tastefully dressed woman.

"Oh no. I'm the assistant manager and buyer. I'm Evelyn Williams. You look so familiar."

"I'm Sonja Davenport. I used to live here but I left immediately after high school. I'm back to take care of my mother." Sonja couldn't believe she was volunteering so much information. She must really be lonely.

"Is your mother Miss Sophia? On Capers Street? I heard my grandmother talking about her being sick. How is she?"

"She's much better. I think we're both a little stir crazy, being cooped up in the house so much." Sonja kept telling herself to stop talking so much, but Evelyn made her feel so comfortable and she seemed so genuine.

"I think you might know my sister. She's a year older than me, but I think you guys were in the same class. Helen Jones. She was a cheerleader."

"I do remember her maybe that's why I thought you looked familiar." Sonja remembered the Jones girls as they were called in school. All of them were smart and attractive and none ended up pregnant in high school, which was a real rarity in the early '90's.

"Listen Sonja, since you don't get out much, how about us grabbing lunch sometime? Are you married?" asked Evelyn.

"Well, I've had many husbands but none of my own." Sonja smirked as she inspected a very expensive suit. She couldn't believe she said that!

"Okay." Evelyn whispered.

Suddenly Sonja felt the need to explain and sort of apologize, yet she didn't know why.

"Evelyn, I'm not married and not dating anyone so please just ignore my weird sense of humor." She handed Evelyn the Donna Karan suit and her platinum card.

"Why don't you fill out this preferred customer card? It's for special trunk shows and gives me an idea of what your favorite designers are so I can keep you posted on new inventory." She knew this classy and bold woman was going to be an excellent customer and she hardly even blinked at the $1,500.00 price tag on the suit.

Sonja filled out the card and placed it on the counter, her 4-carat emerald and diamond ring dancing with magnificence. Evelyn admired the ring and then examined the customer card. Her eyes widened.

"We're neighbors! I live two streets down from you!"

"Oh really? Great, we'll have to visit each other." Sonja couldn't understand Evelyn's excitement until she told her how there only a few African Americans in the area.

"Wait until I tell my husband Kevin! He's been going crazy trying to figure out who the other family was. This is such a coincidence. Why don't you come to dinner Friday night? It's my day off and I haven't any plans this weekend, unless you can't make it?" Sonja shook her head as Evelyn was in the middle of her invitation. This was all going too fast.

"On Fridays I like to let Mama's nurse go home early and I really don't think …"

"Oh please, I'll bet they can send you another nurse for just a few hours. Kevin can invite one of his friends. It'll just be the four of us and you're just up the street. You'll be home early."

Sonja looked at the exuberance on Evelyn's face. She seemed almost desperate. Sonja smiled and realized she knew just the person to invite. She would tell Danny not to cook. Dinner with Evelyn and her husband would be a lot less intimate and get her off the hook.

"OK, but I want to bring an old friend, if that's okay. Danny Taylor." Sonja was walking towards the door and Evelyn grabbed her arm.

"Are you kidding? Danny's like family. My father works for him."

Sonja smiled weakly and thought to herself, *Birmingham is too small.*

§§§§§§§§§§§§§§§§§§§§§§

Friday came much too fast for Sonja and she decided to walk the short distance to Evelyn and Kevin's. Much to Danny's dismay, she insisted on meeting him at Evelyn's. It was a balmy, hot summer day and the sun was starting to go down, but the heat still made it sticky and the white gauzy pants and shirt had started to stick to her skin.

She casually strolled along the sidewalk, looking at the impressive large homes and ignoring some of the residents who were either driving into their yards or out observing their manicured lawns. Sonja exchanged pleasant nods and hellos with those within speaking distance and immediately noticed how they seemed to watch her saunter down the street.

She could imagine the traditional southern exchange of whispers about who she was and how she got here. How could a maid's daughter afford to live here? She walked to the first cul-de-sac, which was Evelyn's street, and turned towards the first house in the curve. It was a stark contrast to most of the houses in the area. Strictly California contemporary, without the southern white columns, red bricks and huge wrap around front porches. In fact, this house looked like it wanted to be viewed from the outside only, visitors not welcome.

The cedar exterior with the odd angled rooflines looked like a dangerous liaison of style compared to the neighborhood's mostly stucco and brick homes. Their open windows revealed the tastefully decorated, formal dining and living rooms. Sonja rang the bell and seconds later Evelyn was at the door. With a big smile, she waved Sonja inside and they touched cheeks.

"I brought a little something even though you said I didn't have to. It's a special blend of cognac that costs more money than it should. Plus I don't drink cognac, so here." She pushed the red velvet bag into Evelyn's hand.

"If you don't drink cognac then why did you buy it?" Evelyn peeked inside the bag.

"Why dahlin', to impress people of course." Sonja did a Hollywood movie star impression that made them both laugh.

"Girl, come on in. Danny's not here yet, and I was just about to set the table. You want some wine, or something else?"

"You got any vodka? On the rocks. I should have driven down here. It's hot as hell out there."

Evelyn handed her a glass of vodka on the rocks.

Looking around the spacious house, Sonja lied,"I like your home. It sure doesn't fit the old Southern Living style." Sonja looked around the open spaced kitchen and started examining the obviously expensive surroundings. Somehow, though, the style didn't match Evelyn's personality.

To Sonja, Evelyn was warmth and earth colors. The interior of this house was all light, cool colors, with lots of open spaces. Everything was sterile and perfectly placed. Evelyn was setting the dining table and shrugged her shoulders.

"Well, my husband Kevin lived in California most of his adult life and refused to let go of that architectural influence. Personally, I like lots of plants, pillows and richer colors. I tell my mother all the time that this house is so cold and open that I never feel I'm protected within a room. There are no rooms. Just big open spaces with furniture positioned in different ways. But you know how some men are."

Evelyn didn't see Kevin walk into the room, but Sonja did and quickly changed the topic.

"I was telling Evelyn how much I liked your home. It's a big difference from the usual southern architecture."

"It's California contemporary. I wanted to bring a different flavor to this sleepy little town. Not everyone understands the intricate rooflines and angles. It sets this house apart from every other one in this subdivision. Actually, in this whole town." Kevin re-filled his wine glass.

"The contractors understood. They charged the hell out of us for that intricate roof line," Evelyn muttered.

Not to be outdone, Kevin fired back, "Well, when money is no object, you get what you want my dear."

Dinner at Evelyn and Kevin Williams' would go down as one of the worst social experiences in Sonja's life. When Kevin wasn't talking about how much influence he had at his law firm, or how much money he brought into the firm, or about all of his wealthy and well-known contacts back in California, he was complaining about how backwards and unsophisticated Birmingham natives were. Evelyn barely talked at all and then she only addressed Sonja or Danny. It was as if she wanted to pretend Kevin wasn't there.

The only highlight for Sonja was Danny Taylor. He arrived with a bottle of champagne and something wrapped in aluminum foil. He was wearing cream-colored linen slacks with a matching shirt. The open collar revealed just a hint of thick silky chest hairs. The slacks gently caressed his muscular thighs and behind. Sonja was trying to remember was he this fine in high school?

Danny didn't miss how she had been staring at him and cleared his throat, "Evelyn wanted to know if you still wanted vodka. I know Cristal is your favorite."

"Oh, no actually, I'd rather have the champagne and what ever is in that aluminum foil."

"That's dessert from my Mama. Pound cake, from scratch of course." He gave Sonja a deep wide smile that made her heart skip a beat. He held her eyes with an unblinking caress as though he were challenging her. Who would blink or look away first?

Sonja couldn't believe he was actually flirting with her and she was flirting back.

Those were the most words Danny would speak during the evening, for Kevin monopolized the dinner conversation. He went on and on about traveling the world and making financial investments that would triple in value before he was retirement age. Sonja felt enough was enough.

"Well, Kevin, your investment options are rather conservative, at least that is my opinion. I invested in blue chip high technology stocks. The risk is greater but so is the return."

Sonja poured another glass of wine and tried to hide her amusement at Kevin's reaction, which was complete surprise mixed with a look of doubt that Sonja knew what she was talking about.

Danny picked up the conversation as if on cue in a stage play,

"That's a good point. I bought some IBM stock about ten years ago, then immediately bought AOL when it was only trading at $3.47 a share and everybody said it was science fiction stock. I don't have to tell you today, what that means to me."

Evelyn joined in, "Well, sounds like we have a couple of savvy investors and millionaires at this table Kevin. Honey, maybe you should get some investment tips from Sonja and Danny."

Kevin gave his wife a dry smile, "Maybe I should. How long have you been playing the market Sonja?"

"Fifteen years or so. I have friends in Dallas who are brokers and they were quite helpful. I think they call it insider trading, a nasty little label don't you think?" She smiled sweetly at Kevin.

Kevin was determined to embarrass Sonja and wouldn't give up. "Dallas is an interesting place I hear. What was it you did there? Evelyn couldn't seem to remember." He shot a glance at

Evelyn who was beginning to get up from the table and tried to change the topic of the conversation.

"Okay guys, let's go into the other room. I rented some vintage '70's movies. Shaft, Foxy Brown, and even The Mack," Evelyn said nervously.

Not easily intimidated, Sonja decided to shock Kevin into silence. "I was self-employed. You know the old saying, A Jack of All Trades, but a Master of Many? I was a Jill of All Trades, but a Mistress to Many. Didn't have many lawyers though. They don't make enough money."

Kevin's ears turned a deep shade of red.

Even that remark caught Danny off guard and he cleared his throat, "Well it's late, and even though I would love to spend the evening with Pam Grier, I should be getting home. Sonja, could I drop you off?" He stood up and reached for her hand.

Evelyn was disappointed, she really wanted Sonja and Danny to stay a while longer because she knew that the rest of the night Kevin would rant and rave about how Sonja had tossed out such a colorful remark and she was not in the mood for an argument. It seemed they argued more and more or she just suffered in silence.

Sonja welcomed the chance to leave the Williams' ugly ass house and she pitied Evelyn for marrying such an asshole. But later for them, for now, she had another agenda: Danny Taylor.

She said good night to Evelyn as Danny escorted her to his car. She was surprised to discover Danny owned a Mercedes 500. As she slid into the leather seat, she complimented his taste in automobiles. "Well it's one of the better built and designed cars." He responded.

"I would expect a mechanic to say that. You are full of surprises! IBM and AOL stocks, Mercedes Benz." Sonja leaned her head on Danny's shoulder. She could feel his muscular arm grow tighter.

He was quiet on the short drive to Sonja's house and it was obvious he was trying to decide how Sonja Davenport really felt about him. He didn't want to make a fool of himself.

He parked the car in her driveway and turned to face Sonja,

"I invested in IBM and AOL because I'm a pretty smart guy. Not just a grease monkey. I bought this car because I know quality and I enjoy quality things. I said some things tonight during dinner because I wanted Kevin to know I'm not a brother just standing on the corner waiting to change somebody's flat tire." He paused and looked at her, "I drove the Benz tonight instead of my truck, because I wanted to impress you. Woman I've been trying to impress you since I was ten years old."

His little confession excited Sonja, but she felt it was only fair to give him a warning, "Danny you have been the best friend I've ever had. Even when I didn't deserve it, you stood by me. I just don't want to mess things up with us by having a relationship. I'm always messing up relationships. I can't afford to lose you as a friend, but right now, at this moment, I got to be honest with you. I want to make love with you. All night long. Is that okay?" She was caressing his face and kissing his neck.

His breathing grew deeper and he responded to Sonja's question with a deep lingering kiss.

"Let's go inside. I've got to let Mama's nurse go home." Sonja couldn't stop kissing him, touching him. She didn't want the feeling to stop, not even for a short moment.

As soon as the nurse closed the front door, they fell into each other's arms with a fierce passion. Sonja quickly lit a dozen or so candles in her bedroom and Danny had found some romantic jazz cd's. Even though the mood was perfect, Sonja still had a nagging feeling that she was making a mistake.

She wanted to talk to Danny a little more, let him know that she had lived a different kind of life in Dallas and that she wasn't so sure she wanted to change. Every time she tried to speak, he would cover her mouth with his. Moaning in surrender, she felt helpless and she liked it.

Danny slowly undressed her, savoring each inch of her body along the way. Even though Sonja had been kissed over her entire body many, many times, this was the first time it felt right.

"I've wanted you for so long. I can't believe this is finally happening. I'm going to make you so happy. Happier than you've ever been in your life," he was straddling her and at that moment, she wanted him more than anything in the world. Sonja grabbed his shoulders and brought his head to her breasts as he guided himself into her. She heard a moan escape from her throat. He was powerful as he slowly moved inside her, both of them moaning uncontrollably.

Lifting her buttocks from the bed, Danny grabbed her, pulling her tightly against his abdomen. Her back and shoulders fell onto her canopy bed as she held onto the headboard for balance.

"Wait, look in my nightstand drawer. I've got something," she whispered.

He let go of her and rolled over to reach inside the drawer and retrieve a condom. Sonya was amazed at how fast he was able to put it on, all the while lifting her body to meet his.

Danny was sweating profusely as she tightened her legs around his upper thighs. Their eyes locked onto each other and she screamed for him not to stop. He didn't want to stop and told her so.

"I'm never letting you go, I've waited too long. Years and years of wanting you." He jerked Sonja up to face him and cradled her in his arms, slowing his pace and slowing her frantic motions against his body.

He had imagined her to be more vocal, but all she had done was moan while whispering his name.

"Baby? Is everything alright?" he finally asked while still holding her body in an upright position, her shapely legs encircling his waist.

She started slowly moving up and down, "It's better than alright. God, Danny, this is so good. How did you get to be so good?" Sonja's body was like a live wire, and everywhere Danny stroked it, a spark ignited. Danny could feel her muscles contracting around him, teasing him, releasing him and then pulling him in deeper.

"You're not half bad yourself, but I've got to finish this round or I'll explode and die from a heart attack." He started to kiss her neck, nibbling her ear lobes and she felt him getting even harder as he gently positioned her under his body onto her back.

Sonja thought, good ole fashioned missionary style, just like a country boy. She wrapped her legs around his waist and smiled at him, "What are you waiting for cowboy?" she teased.

"Don't talk that stage shit to me." He stopped moving.

"I wasn't doing that. Please, don't spoil tonight by picking a fight with me now," she begged.

"Ask me again and be nicer." He pumped her hard, once.

"Please Danny." Before she could finish her statement, he pumped into her a second time.

Danny growled, "Just relax Sonja. You can't be in control all the time. Tonight I take over."

She liked that he was taking control, yet she felt uncomfortable. Not having control was different for her, but she heard herself pleading with this gorgeous man to finish making love to her and she even heard herself promising to be nice.

"I'll be nice. Just don't stop. Don't stop, Danny."

Danny covered her mouth with his and kissed her long and deeply, slowly moving inside her with a sensuous circular movement. They both gasped for breath and moaned out loud before collapsing from exhaustion.

Sonja hugged his broad shoulders and he started to kiss her neck. For the first time, she was speechless after sex, and for the first time Danny Taylor knew he was in love.

§§§§§§§§§§§§§§§§§§§§§§

Sonja awoke to the smell of bacon frying in her kitchen and the best smelling coffee ever. Wrapping her naked body in a white satin robe, she half stumbled out of her room into the hall towards her mothers' room. The room was empty. Her mother's wheel chair was also missing. Sonja padded barefoot downstairs and the closer she got to the kitchen, the hungrier she got.

The scene in her kitchen made her stop in amazement. There was her mother in her wheelchair looking out of the window in the breakfast room and Danny was at the stove, draining bacon, "Morning sleeping beauty! Just in time. I hope you're good and hungry." He did a deep bow.

Sonja's mother wheeled around to face her and gave her a half-faced smile, the best she could do with the side of her face still weak. "Hey Mama. How are you?" Sonja bent to kiss her forehead.

She tasted a slight trace of perspiration, "Mama, you're sweating. Are you too warm? Let me pull you away from this window."

"We just came from outside. Had a nice morning walk. Well, I walked. She jogged." Danny winked at Sonja's mother.

With her good hand, she waved at Danny to hush.

"A walk? Are you crazy? Mama has to take it slow. Too much activity is not good, Danny. This is not funny." Sonja did not like Danny taking control of everything in her life all at once. Making love was one thing and spending the night was another. But now he was acting as if he was the man of the house.

"Here. Sit down and eat. Mama Sofia and I have a partnership. Before you came back, we used to visit all the time. She made me homemade pizza and I was teaching her to drive."

Danny was pouring a cup of coffee for Sonja and her mother. Her mother? Driving! Sonja couldn't believe her ears. Her mother was the most timid and shyest woman in the world and traffic intimidated her. Her mother was drinking her coffee and avoiding Sonja's eyes.

"Well, I guess I was going to be the last one to know. I still think too much for her isn't good right now." Sonja wanted to add that this was her mother after all.

"I told you she was a party pooper. Here have some more bacon and eggs," Danny said to Sofia's mother as he heaped more food onto her half-empty plate.

It was the most Sonja had seen her eat since her stroke. The nurse even said they would have to start giving her vitamin supplements if her appetite didn't improve. Her mother finished her breakfast and using her electric-operated controls, wheeled herself away from the table, but not before giving Danny a kiss on the cheek. Sonja watched her wheel into the great room and turn on the television.

"I didn't hear you get up or get Mama in her chair. I would have helped." Sonja was finishing off the last piece of bacon.

"It was no problem. Anyway, you were snoring so hard, I did-n't have the courage to wake you." He gave her a sly smile.

"I do not snore, Danny Taylor. Anyway, when did you get a change of clothes?" Sonja was looking at his jeans and t-shirt.

"I had them in the car last night, just in case." He got up from the table and started washing the dishes.

Just in case, huh? Sonja realized she had been played like a two-dollar fiddle, "I wonder does Mama think you just showed up this morning or what?"

"I think your Mama is much too smart and her hearing is too good to think that, my love. We did rock the world last night." He looked up from scanning the local newspaper, "I've got to get home and then go by the garage. You want to do something to-night?"

"How about renting some movies and just staying home? I'm a little tired, if you know what I mean." She walked up behind him and hugged him tightly.

He turned around, rubbed her hips, and to his surprise, discov-ered she was nude underneath her robe. His voice dropped to a whisper, "You know I can't take this, especially in the morning and your mother in the next room. What am I supposed to do?" he kissed her neck.

"Hurry back." Sonja grabbed his head and gave him a hard deep kiss. She couldn't believe she said something like that and really meant it. Danny couldn't believe she said exactly what he wanted to hear.

Chapter 3

Someone To Watch Over Me

He's the big affair I cannot forget.
Only man I ever think of with regret.
I'd like to add his initial to my monogram.
Tell me where is the shepherd for this lost lamb?

Gail parked her car in Laura and Ted Kennedy's driveway and even though she had taken the key out of the ignition, it kept making that choking, coughing ing sound that went on and on and on. By the time she was ringing Laura's doorbell, the car's coughing, choking noise was reduced to a sputter.

Ted opened the door, wearing a towel for an apron. He squinted at her sputtering car, "That comes from cheap gas. A few pennies more and your car wouldn't wake up the neighborhood." He joked.

"I'm used to it. It's our way of bonding." Gail walked past him into the kitchen.

"Well you and that car should bond a little quieter. The whole neighborhood is being disturbed." Ted was always in a good mood and ready for a friendly debate.

He was a dean at the University and had met Laura through Gail and her ex-husband Jonathan when they were all college students, in fact Ted and Jonathan had been roommates.

"What's for dinner? I'm starving!" Gail peeked into a large pot simmering on the stove.

"Spaghetti. You know Ted can only fix spaghetti on short notice. Well how did the meeting go?" Laura playfully shoved Ted away from the stove, ignoring his mumbling aloud about being the only one in the house who ever cooked.

"You know, I should take you guys out to dinner! I mean after all, *I am* the head of the trauma nursing unit now." Gail gave Laura a wink and pulled out a bottle of wine from her large purse. Laura screamed and gave her a big hug.

"Well hell, woman, I could have saved all this work." Ted threw a dishtowel at Gail and then gave her a peck on the cheek, "Congratulations! Now you can buy better gas!"

Dinner at the Kennedy's was always fun for Gail. Their two children were in Mississippi for the summer, but normally Gail's kids and the Kennedy's would keep the house noisy and filled with laughter.

Gail was sipping her third glass of wine, when suddenly she became very lonely. Here she was, on what was one of the best days she had in a long time and she was spending the evening with a married couple.

Laura noticed the change in her expression and gave Ted a quick kick under the table to say something funny.

"So Gail, Miss Supervisor, are you drunk with power yet, doing a little hiring or firing? Oh and my wife needs a raise." Ted joked.

"Actually, we'll be hiring staff. All it takes is one crisis or one overbearing patient to monopolize the entire floor and we are overwhelmed. First thing I've got to do is a staff analysis to make sure the best people are where they need to be for our most challenging patients."

"Yeah, like that Maceo Sloan. What a pain in the ass!" Laura refilled their wine glasses.

"Maceo Sloan was in the hospital? Why?" Ted asked.

"You know that jerk?" asked Gail.

"Everyone knows Mr. Maceo Sloan, owner and CEO of Sloan Construction." Ted looked at Gail in disbelief.

Gail and Laura looked at each other and shrugged their shoulders.

"He's very wealthy. Made his money on federal contracts and even did some work at the University. He is very connected." Ted got a second helping of spaghetti, shaking his head in disbelief that they were so socially uninformed.

"Well he ought to take that money and buy some manners. He is the rudest person I've ever seen. Even though he is fine!" Laura gave Gail a high five.

Close to 10:30 p. m. Gail started home. She was feeling mellow from the wine and wanted desperately to have sex and have it immediately. Larry came into her mind. Tonight she would see just how serious he was about getting married.

Realizing she needed gas, Gail pulled into an Exxon station only a few minutes from her house. This time she thought, she would splurge and buy the supreme gasoline. After all, she was moving up in the world.

She was pumping the gas, when a black Range Rover with tinted windows pulled up and stopped behind her. Gail was replacing the nozzle on the gas pump, when she heard a man's voice, "I can't believe Nurse Nightingale pumps gas!"

Gail turned around and looked into the face of Maceo Sloan, who was walking towards her.

"Some call me Nightingale. Some call me Nurse Nightmare. It depends on the patient. But I do pump my own gas, Mr. Sloan. What are you doing out of the hospital?" She was trying to remember if she needed to comb her hair and if her face was shiny. She knew it was. Wine always made her face shine.

"Well, it's a miracle cure. After you left my room never to return I might add, I made an immediate recovery. You must work 24 hours." He looked at his Rolex watch.

"Oh no, I've been over to some friends for dinner."

"And wine?" he smiled looking at her stained blouse.

Gail quickly followed his eyes to a big red wine stain on her blouse. She never felt so unattractive in her life. Normally people said she reminded them of the actress Angela Bassett, but tonight she felt like the Bride of Frankenstein.

Maceo Sloan was wearing a pair of faded crisp jeans and cowboy boots, and he smelled good enough to eat. Here she was, needing to comb her hair, powder her face, gargle and change her blouse.

"That was from dinner. We were celebrating. I got a promotion." She felt even worse, babbling on like a little girl excited about going to Disneyland.

"Oh, congratulations! I guess that call I made to Paul Monroe worked after all." he laughed.

"You called Dr. Monroe? *About me?* When?" Gail felt the blood rush to her head. All of a sudden, Maceo Sloan didn't look so attractive anymore.

He held up both hands as if defending himself and said, "Now hold on. Sure, I was pissed at the whole hospital staff, especially my doctor. I could have lost a lot of money on a pending deal and I did need a phone. But when I called Monroe to complain, I realized that most of the nurses on my floor were black and the one who I understood to be in charge, as I was told off the record, was you. And Mrs. Emerson, you did your job. A good job. I was proud of your professionalism and I told Monroe so."

Gail cleared her throat, "Well thank you." She finished pumping her gas and got into her car.

"It was good to see you again," she said, "take care of yourself."

She was about to start her car when Sloan leaned into her window. She could smell his cologne and he was so close that she could see some very fine clipped moustache hairs around his mouth.

"You obviously like wine, so maybe we could share a bottle soon, you know as friends. Here's my card. My pager number is on the back. I'm heading to D.C. tomorrow, so in a few days give me a call."

Gail tried to hide her initial excitement, but it was quickly replaced by suspicion. *Pager number?* What was this shit? He must be married or living with someone. *Later for you Maceo Sloan,* she thought.

She took the card and put it in her purse without looking at it, "You know how to find me. Take care." She pulled off without giving him a chance to respond.

At that moment, Maceo Sloan knew this woman could be more trouble than she was worth. However, he liked her, and like everything else in Maceo Sloan's life, what he liked, he obtained. Maybe Gail Emerson would be worth the trouble.

Maybe he should have asked her for her home number he thought.. He decided to send her flowers at the hospital tomorrow, sort of a congratulatory gift.

Gail pulled away fuming and decided at that moment that Maceo Sloan was used to women begging him, adoring him and obeying him. Well maybe the old Gail would have fallen right in line with the others, but no more. Today was the beginning of a new attitude for her, expensive gasoline and all.

Gail called Laura and told her she ran into Sloan at the gas station. They both decided he was still a jerk and bad news. Ted listened to the one sided conversation with amusement, for he knew the more Laura and Gail complained, the more effort would be put forth to hook Maceo Sloan. Ted felt sorry for the brother.

Laura hung up the phone and turned to her husband.

"Baby, is Maceo Sloan married?" she asked cuddling up to him and stroking his favorite spot.

Ted closed the book he was reading and looked at his wife with a sly grin, "He's divorced. Any more information is going to cost you."

Laura slid underneath the covers and mumbled out loud, "The things we do for love."

§§§§§§§§§§§§§§§§§§§§§§

The week passed without a lot of fanfare for Gail. She was warmly congratulated by some of her colleagues and ignored by the others, except when they wanted to bitch about the tiniest personnel situations. She was not quite used to dealing with that and felt she had acquired a set of new children overnight.

For the most part, Gail thought it was a bunch of childish bullshit, some of the stuff people actually regarded as official matters needing management intervention.

Every five minutes or so, she thought about Maceo Sloan. She had not called his office or paged him, even after she got his beautiful bouquet of flowers. She was beginning to feel like she was back in high school, playing a game of love chicken. Who would be the first to give in? Laura had confirmed he was divorced and heavily sought after by women from Florida to Boston.

He had a reputation as a generous lover, yet somewhat unpredictable and moody. He had left a string of broken hearts all along the eastern seaboard and Gail was determined not to be another casualty.

She called her kids everyday at their father's house and was beginning to feel as though she was intruding. Finally her exhusband got on the phone to ask if something was wrong. In other words, get a life and stop calling so much.

Just when Gail had every reason to be happy, she was suddenly restless and very lonely. She even thought about calling Larry for a late night snack. But even that thought was sour to her. Anyway, he seemed to be avoiding her and hadn't returned a few calls she made. What was his problem? Was he really getting married? Or was she losing her charm even to the womanizer?

Gail busied herself on Saturday morning by rearranging furniture in every room of her home. By the end of the day she was exhausted and still bored.

Walking from room to room with a glass of wine, she silently started to thank God for blessing her with two healthy kids, a nice enough home, her health, her recent promotion and a decent career. She was determined not to fall into another fit of depression and feeling sorry for herself.

She had prayed that if she got this promotion, she would write a new page in the book of her life, start going to church regularly again, do more things with the kids, take better care of herself and swear off men who offered nothing but sweaty sex.

She downed the last swallow of wine and was about to pour a second glass when the phone rang.

"Hello."

"Gail?" It was a deep male voice, with a little hesitancy. Gail couldn't quite figure out why the voice sounded slightly familiar.

"Yes, this is she."

"I'm disappointed. You didn't call. Did you get the flowers? Is this a bad time? It's Maceo."

"Oh, hi. Yes they were very nice. I've just been swamped at work. No, it's not a bad time. Are you back from D.C.?" She wanted to avoid why she hadn't called. After all, she couldn't tell him she had sworn off men who were destined to break her heart could she?

"I got back this morning. I was hoping we could have made arrangements for dinner tonight, but since you didn't call earlier in the week, I assumed that this weekend wasn't good. Is it?"

He assumed she would call? Assumed she would have dinner with him? Now he was assuming she'd just drop everything at the last minute and go to dinner? He was right.

"Well, actually Maceo, I was thinking I could cook dinner for us, if you don't mind a home cooked meal."

"Are you kidding? I'm a good ole country boy. I would love a home cooked meal. What time?" his voice was lighter and she could tell he was starting to relax more.

"Well ..." Gail mentally reviewed her refrigerator and cupboards. She remembered seeing peanut butter, cans of soup and some juice in the refrigerator. "I need to go to the grocery store."

"I'll go with you. What if I come over in about thirty minutes and pick you up?" This man was used to being in control. Gail liked it. As long as he was willing to pay the cost, he could be the boss.

Maceo Sloan was knocking at Gail's door in exactly thirty minutes as he said he would. She had slipped on a pair of jeans and t-shirt.

She opened the door and tried to sound natural, as though rich, good-looking men picked her up everyday for a drive to the grocery store.

"Hi! You are very prompt! Would you like to come in? We've a got a few minutes." she stood back to let him in.

He was still smelling good, wearing navy nylon jogging pants, a white cotton tee shirt and Nike's. He slowly walked into the foyer and looked around, his gaze resting at her photos of Jonathan and Jessica.

"Good looking kids. Where are they?" He seemed to relax as he walked towards the living room.

"They're with their father. Summer vacation." Gail put her hands in her back jeans pockets and leaned against the wall. Maceo was looking at the black art collection that was Gail's pride and joy.

"Yeah I remember those summers with the kids days. Thank God mine are grown now. They just call and ask for money."

"How grown are they?" Gail walked past him, went into the living room and sat down.

Maceo walked over to the sofa and sat down. His long legs stretched out and his arms draped over the back of the Queen Anne sofa.

"My daughter Tracey is 21, just finished Spellman and doesn't know what she wants to do with her life or her degree. So she's not doing anything. My son, Mack, is 22 and living in New York. Says he's going to be the next Spike Lee, except better. So in the mean time and in between time, they just keep on calling on Daddy to help make the ends meet."

Gail decided to change the subject, "So what are you hungry for? Pasta, chicken, steak?"

"All of the above. It's been a long time since I had a real home cooked meal. If you've got a grill, I could do a couple of steaks." He stood up and stretched and Gail followed his lead.

She wasn't about to tell him she didn't eat red meat. It had been at least a year since she had a steak. She thought it wouldn't be that bad and she could always take herbal laxatives to flush out her system.

After returning from the grocery store, they both claimed sections of the kitchen and started to cook. Maceo Sloan cooked like a typical man. He used every utensil, pot and pan in the kitchen. Gail was making a caesar salad and baked potatoes. They were both drinking beer, even though they had bought a good bottle of cabernet.

Gail's CD player was loaded with Motown oldies and on every record she and Maceo would sing out loud to a favorite Temptation or Smokey tune.

"This is the best date I've ever been on, Gail." Maceo was standing in the middle of the kitchen holding wine filled glasses. He looked surprised that he had spoken aloud what must have been private thoughts.

Gail was in the dining room setting the table. She hesitated while lighting the candles, "In what way is this the best date you've ever been on?" She walked up to him taking one of the glasses of wine and took a sip.

"It's not pretentious. It's relaxing and comfortable." He walked towards the table and pulled out her chair.

"Sounds like you're describing house shoes or an old robe." Gail smiled.

"In a way it's exactly like that. You know I'm usually pretty stressed out." He stopped short of finishing his statement remembering how they first met. "Well, I guess you found that out when we first met." They both laughed. "So anyway, house shoes and a comfortable bathrobe are very important to me. They say I'm home. Safe and comfortable," he nodded towards her plate,

" You're not eating your steak. Is it okay?"

Gail decided to play it straight; no lies to impress a man anymore. This was the new Gail.

"I don't usually eat red meat. Hope you don't mind." Gail was enjoying the food and the company, although she was still trying to put his last statements into perspective.

She felt she should say something to acknowledge his sensitive side, "I'm glad you feel safe and comfortable with me. It must be my bedside manner."

Gail was struggling with her logical voice, which was telling her not to start falling for this man too early. Even if he did seem vulnerable sitting here at her dining room table, eating on her best china and filling her house with his wonderful scent.

Maceo Sloan was thinking he could not start falling for this woman too soon. He did not have a good track record with women and she didn't seem like the kind you could write off as a bad investment. Tonight he had made a fundamental mistake, a mistake he hadn't made in years. He came across weak and vulnerable. Maceo Sloan was used to negotiating multi-million dollar contracts and he was never perceived weak and vulnerable.

An uncomfortable silence fell across the room as they both ate. Gail cleared her throat and glanced at her watch. It was still early, only 9:30. Maceo took her gesture as time to exit.

"Well, it's late. I should be going. I'll help with the dishes first. I made a big mess." He wanted any reason to stay a while longer. Maceo hadn't washed dishes in years.

Gail was thankful for any excuse to have him stay longer, "You don't look like a man who does dishes, but I will take you up on the offer." She started clearing the table. As they stood at the sink rinsing the dishes, Maceo spoke to break the silence.

"Gail, we didn't talk much about our private lives tonight, I mean, other than our children. I'm not seriously involved with anyone."

He stopped rinsing the dishes and turned to her, "I'm 54 years old. Too old for games. Plus, I'm too busy. I can be a real son-of-a bitch, but then I can be a really nice guy at times. I don't make promises I can't keep. Occasionally I like to be alone. Completely alone. Just part of my weird ways. I don't like a lot of parties, because people are usually full of shit, and parties usually enhance shit. I'm not looking to get married and I don't like to be given rules and regulations in private understandings."

The last line caught Gail by surprise. She was with him until that private understandings part. "What exactly is a private understanding?" She already felt she wasn't going to like the answer.

"My private life is just that. Private. I don't do relationships. I have understandings. Relationships are for people looking for some kind of happily ever after romance. I'm not that kind of guy."

"Did your mother beat you with wire hangers or what? You see, Maceo, I'm 38 years old and I've got three lives I'm responsible for. Nobody else. Sure, I've made some mistakes, but I'm not trying to land a man. Any man. Not even you." Gail felt insulted and more than that, insignificant. What was he expecting from her, a signed contract promising not to expect commitment and devotion?

She threw the drying towel on the kitchen counter and started walking to her front door. For some reason she felt like screaming and crying at the same time.

He was absolutely correct about one thing, she thought, he could be a son-of-a bitch. She turned to him with the front door open, "Sounds like you're a lot of trouble, Maceo Sloan. I don't do trouble or men who enjoy being sons of bitches. In case you hadn't noticed, I'm busy with my own life, too. Good night." She stood aside to allow him to leave..

"So are you saying I shouldn't count on seeing you again?" He looked at her with an innocent expression. He never moved towards the door.

"Why would you want to? I'm sure there are hundreds of women lined up waiting to be insulted by you and I don't want to stand in their way." Gail was starting to lose her nerve and her anger was fading. She was honestly beginning to believe he didn't mean to hurt her feelings.

"Gail, tonight was supposed to be fun. Once again I messed things up. I'm not really good at this sensitivity stuff. And, no my mother did not beat me with wire hangers."

"Maybe she should have." Gail couldn't resist one good upper cut.

Maceo smiled and avoided her eyes, looking down he softly said, "She would have agreed with you. She was a good woman, and she would have liked you a lot." He slowly closed the door and stepped closer to her.

Maceo Sloan had decided to take a gamble as he did with every successful business venture that brought him overwhelming returns.

Gail was trying to apologize about making a remark about his departed mother, but the words were getting stuck in her mouth. Her stammering allowed Maceo to pull her into his arms and they slowly rocked back and forth to a song that was playing, *Heaven Must Be Like This*, by the Ohio Players.

Gail's heart was beating so fast she was sure he could feel her trembling. Maceo whispered into her hair, "I want to see you again. I just wanted to say some things up front to avoid confusion. I didn't say them the right way. I don't want anyone getting hurt."

"I promise not to hurt you," Gail whispered into his chest.

He laughed deeply and squeezed her tighter.

"Seriously, Maceo. I'm a big girl. I don't look for Prince Charming anymore and I don't like kissing frogs either. I've got two young kids who are the center of my life and I can't afford to get involved in unhealthy relationships. I think we have a lot to learn about each other and we should take it slow and see what happens."

He nodded in agreement and bent his head to kiss her. It was a soft soulful kiss that made Gail swoon. She didn't want it to end. His body was tight and hard and Gail felt frail and small wrapped in his arms. Maceo was thinking her body felt as though it already belonged to him and he didn't want to release her, yet he didn't want to feel he needed her.

She had a sense of humor and strength, and she was no push over. He liked all of that, even though he didn't like her stubborn way of making him constantly apologize. She was what his mother would have called the right kind of woman to keep him straight. He had never had a woman who could keep him straight. They could be bought too easily, and he knew Gail Emerson had a price, too. He just had to find out what it was.

After what seemed like an eternity, Maceo pulled away from Gail's soft moist lips. He wanted to make love, but after that last feminist speech by her, he was afraid to create another Mexican stand off. Gail wanted this man to pick her up and carry her to bed, but after her feminist, "I Am Woman" speech, she felt she would look stupid and hypocritical by falling into bed with him so soon.

"I'll call you in the morning." He kissed her briefly and opened the door.

"Okay, drive safe." Gail was still holding his hand.

They kissed again in the door, this time Maceo's hand lightly brushed her breast. She moaned and gently pushed him away,

"Wow. This is going be interesting. I feel like I'm in high school again." She ran her fingers through her hair and fluffed it. A nervous habit she used whenever she was at a loss for words.

"I know the feeling. I should go before I embarrass myself." He gave her a big smile and walked to his truck.

Hours later Gail had taken a hot bubble bath and was in bed watching an old black and white classic movie when the phone rang. She grabbed it on the second ring.

"Hey girl. How was it?" Laura lowered her voice to a whisper. "Can you talk?"

Gail tried to hide her disappointment, "Unfortunately I can. He left hours ago. It was wonderful, unsettling and strange."

"Now you know men with money are strange. Does he like kinky stuff or what?" Laura was settling in for a long descriptive conversation.

"Not that kind of strange! He's just so intense, so insensitive. I mean he warned me that he doesn't do relationships, just personal understandings." Gail started channel surfing, her concentration was back to replaying the evening with Maceo.

"Gail, please! ALL men say that at first. Girl I bet he's at that big empty house right now wishing you were right beside him. I know what I'm talking about. Shut up, Ted!"

Gail could manage to hear Ted shouting in the background that Laura didn't know what she was talking about. She laughed and once again the lonely feeling started creeping into her heart as her two best friends joked around.

Chapter 4

Killing Me Softly

I felt all flushed with fever, embarrassed by the crowd.
I felt he found my letters and read each one out loud.
I prayed that he would finish, but he just kept right on.

Kevins' pride at being one of the first few African American families to buy a house in the new development came from how he got there. He made good money and had some strong influence through Simon Parker and the firm. What really irritated him was how other black families could afford to buy in this neighborhood. He was obsessing over who these people were and how much money they had.

Evelyn was glad other black families were there, whoever they were.

Her mother was tickled to death and had called every relative long distance to talk about Lynn's "fine home" and good husband. Evelyn thought Kevin was stupid to pay $700,000 for the house, even though she didn't have to use any of her own money. She had a migraine for a week after they closed the deal. She had never seen so much debt up close before.

Kevin kept saying the house would be worth more than a million dollars easily in California. She kept saying this was Alabama! The house cost too much! The developers were making a fool of him and of them. Couldn't he see that? They both knew they could have bought the same house in the affluent African American suburb for half the money.

All Kevin could see was that the area was exclusive. The house had 4,000 square feet, lots of open spaces, an office with a fireplace, plus four other fireplaces. The one story structure backed up to a lush forest and that was the only thing Evelyn liked about it. The floors were white marble and required daily dusting to keep the glass-like shine.

The master bedroom with its fireplace was the size of her entire little apartment. The bed sat on a raised platform and the master bath had a huge step-down Jacuzzi.

It was a nice house, but Evelyn hated that it would require so much cleaning, so Kevin hired a housekeeper. She knew that in the winter months those marble floors would feel like blocks of ice. It was not a house built with children in mind, either. Everything seemed cold and gray. Her family thought she was crazy when they saw the house she complained about, especially her mother. Even this past Sunday, Evelyn went to her parents' house, while Kevin played golf and she complained some more.

"Too cold? Child, light up one of them five fireplaces and enjoy! You need to go and put some babies in that house, give it some life. That's all it need."

Her mother, Patricia, was frosting a chocolate cake. Just like when Evelyn was a little girl, she handed her the bowl for her to lick.

Patricia was an attractive, tall dark woman, who rarely raised her voice and still managed to completely control the household, children and a husband.

Evelyn's father never made it beyond the 8th grade. He started working at 14 and had been working all of his life to support his mother and sisters and now his wife and daughters. He was a very good mechanic, but a little insecure that he never graduated from high school.

Patricia never forgave him for not getting a formal education. She quietly blamed him for keeping them on the "wrong side" of town. Blamed him for not being "somebody," for giving her girls and no boys.

"A mother needs boys. Boys will take care of their mama. Girls ain't good for nothing but trouble." She'd grit her teeth in anger at one of the girls.

Patricia worked for the county government community services program that provided job training to women being released from government assistance. The program was one of the many by-products of welfare reform.

The job was frustrating and had made her bitter and sometimes ashamed of being black when dealing with clients whom she felt were an embarrassment to her race. Evelyn's marrying Kevin was the proudest moment of her life. It meant she had not totally failed. Her daughter was on the other side of town, the right side of the tracks and that was like validation for the entire family.

"Mama, when you and Daddy first married, was everything good? I mean did he make you happy?" Evelyn was still shy about discussing sex with her mother. She felt more comfortable talking to her Daddy.

"Good? Evelyn, we were so poor, good was having a decent meal of black-eyed peas and cornbread. If I knew then what I know now, I never would have married at 18. No way. No how." Her mother was looking in the refrigerator, her back to Evelyn.

"Mama, I mean the sex. The lovemaking. Was it, right?" Evelyn's mother hesitated and slowly closed the refrigerator door. Her lips pursed into a tight line. It was the same expression she used to show displeasure for what she considered tacky conversation.

"Evelyn Marie, there is more to marriage than staying in the bed. Now I don't know what's wrong, right or good and bad. But I do know you got a good man, a smart man, who is taking good care of you. Staying in bed with a man never did that for me! See where I am today? See what I got? Bills! A 25-year-old house and a hard way to go!"

Suddenly Evelyn's grandmother walked out of her back bedroom and into the kitchen. Evelyn's middle name, Marie, was her grandmother's name. Her maternal grandmother had moved in with the family nearly two years ago after someone broke into her small house several blocks away.

"Aw hush, Patty! Sam is a good, hard working man, and you couldn't do no better in a million years. Hey, my baby. How you doing?" Mama Ree gave Evelyn a strong hug. She always smelled like her Jungle Gardenia perfume.

"Hey, Mama Ree. I didn't mean to start a family war. I was just making conversation."

"Well don't you listen to your Mama. I told her your daddy would be a good husband. A man who takes care of his mother will sho' take care of his wife. Lord knows Sam took care of Irene and those girls 'til the day she died, God rest her soul. And now look at him. Even taking care of me, just like he was my son. So don't you pay your Mama no never mind. Patty, these greens almost done. I'm gone turn them down a bit." Mama Ree not only irritated her daughter by contradicting her, but also by supervising her cooking.

Patricia Jones was fit to be tied! She took a deep breath, before she started to speak, "Mama, all I'm doing is telling her, what you told me 30 years ago about Sam. I'm telling her the same thing about Kevin. If you got a good man, keep him." She slammed down a spoon on the counter and left the kitchen.

"Well, your Mama is just as bullheaded as I was at one time. The only difference is I tried to make a bad man into a good one. Your granddaddy, God rest his soul, loved whiskey and women more than his family. I used to cry until I thought my brains would drop out of my nose. When I couldn't cry no more, I prayed. I prayed so much on my knees I wore a dent into the floor next to my bed. So you just put God first, He'll make it right." Mama Ree was stirring a pitcher of iced tea.

"God made Granddaddy stop drinking and chasing women?" Evelyn asked, biting her lower lip.

"Naw, child. God just sent the sorry bastard to hell and paid me his life insurance so I could take care of my children." Mama Ree smiled with a twinkle in her eye.

"Mama Ree! What a heathen thing to say!" Evelyn laughed and shook her head. Her grandmother's confidential talk gave her the nerve to reveal her problem with Kevin.

"Mama Ree, Kevin is very sweet to me and I love him. He gives me everything I could ever need or want, but we only stay in bed for a minute. You understand what I'm saying? Isn't something wrong with that?"

Mama Ree clucked her tongue, "Shucks child, get yourself a red candle and some Cleopatra oil. Rub that candle with the oil and burn it. Let it burn out on its own. Do not blow it out. That boy is just tired and probably working too hard. Y'all young folks don't know nothing about taking time to enjoy life. Just ripping and running all the time. He just a kid, you just a kid, neither of you know nothing about making real love yet, it can only happen with time. Just try that oil and candle and pray. You'll see a difference." Her voice had dropped to a whisper.

Evelyn felt very mature having a woman-to-woman talk with her grandmother. She leaned in close to Mama Ree and whispered, "Did you do that to Granddaddy?"

"Your granddaddy wasn't worth a candle. Just let me say, the Lord works in mysterious ways. And your Mama Ree wasn't no bad looking woman!" she chuckled.

"Mama Ree you still a fox today. I bet you got a red candle and some oil in your room right now," Evelyn tweaked her grandmother's cheek.

Pat walked into the kitchen at that moment, "Oil? What oil?"

"Hair oil, Patty. It's on my dresser, Lynn. Go on and make sure you buy me some. I think Harmon's Drugstore got it on sale," Mama Ree winked her eye.

Pat was already setting the table for Sunday dinner and didn't notice the wink, nor was she interested. She hated the fact her Mother still hot combed her hair in this day of chemical relaxers, weaves and even African braiding. If she was sending Lynn to Harmon's Drugstore, good! It meant she wouldn't have to go the "bottom" as they called the black section of downtown to the black-owned drugstore.

Evelyn carried some of her mother's Sunday dinner home for Kevin. She planned to go to Harmon's Drugstore the first thing Monday morning.

Evelyn didn't make it to Harmon's drugstore on Monday or the entire week. The dress shop was extremely busy and she was so happy to meet Sonja, another black person in the neighborhood, she put her complaints about Kevin in the back of her mind.

The fact that her mother was Miss Sofia, who was Italian, made it obvious her father must have been black. She had re-membered hearing about the beautiful half-white girl in high school who nobody liked. Of course, most Birmingham residents simply lumped all races into black and white or Asians. Being Italian meant nothing at all. If you weren't black, you must be white.

§§§§§§§§§§§§§§§§§§§§§

A week later, Evelyn was still catching hell from Kevin about inviting Sonja to dinner. Kevin did not like surprises and disliked mysterious strangers even more.

Evelyn was at the kitchen counter chopping onions and celery for her shrimp creole. Kevin had been pouting the entire evening and returned to the kitchen with a bottle of chardonnay and a corkscrew.

"So what does she do again?" he sipped the wine and handed the glass to Evelyn. She hated white wine. Wine period. It gave her an awful headache. She took the glass and raised it to her lips pretending to drink it. She didn't want to irritate him any more than he was.

"I didn't ask. Her mother's recovering from a stroke, so she spends a lot of time with her."

Kevin cleared his throat and continued in his best corporate lawyer tone, "So she doesn't work, lives in one of Birmingham's most prestigious areas, drives a Porsche, and shops in an exclu-sive women's boutique. This doesn't add up. Was she married to a rich guy or something?"

"I didn't ask Kevin." Evelyn let out a sigh of frustration.

"How could you invite someone into our home you know nothing about? I mean, you could have at least asked me first. I would never have guests here without asking you."

"It's no big deal Kevin. She's not a stranger. We all went to high school together. And Danny is like my big brother. Anyway, you're always complaining about not having people over to see the house." With that little jab, Evelyn took a healthy swig of the chardonnay. It was going to be a long night, so a headache wouldn't matter anyway.

Kevin Williams decided five minutes after meeting them that he did not like Sonja Davenport or Danny Taylor, and he told Evelyn he would not have either of them at his home again. Evelyn was stacking the dishwasher, trying to understand how he could be so insecure and uptight, but that didn't bother her. What really pissed her off was that last part about how neither of them could visit *his* house again. Surely he didn't think she was going to just take this without a fight.

Without turning around Evelyn said what was on her mind, "They are my friends. This is my house, too, and if we are about to start saying who can and cannot visit, then I'll get a damn sheet of paper and make a list of all the two faced, racist assholes who you call friends."

"Evelyn, I work hard, damn hard, to provide a lifestyle for you that I cannot afford to have ruined by some woman who obviously sleeps with men for money. She's bad news! You shouldn't lower yourself to even associate with that kind of person. I am not going to jeopardize my reputation, or be married to someone who jeopardizes what I stand for." Kevin's voice was rising.

"You're working to provide a lifestyle for me? That's a joke! I have never asked you for any of this shit! None of it! This is all about you Kevin. You're pissed because someone other than you had something to say at dinner. You weren't the center of attention or the only expert in the room. And you can't stand it. Well maybe you shouldn't be married to me, little old country bumpkin Evelyn!" She slammed the dishwasher door.

She was walking into the bedroom towards the closet. Kevin lowered his voice, "Don't over react. It's late and we're both tired. Let's just get some sleep and…"

Evelyn felt she was winning the fight and didn't want to quit now. She had a few other things to hit him with. "Get some sleep? That's all I've been getting lately. You haven't touched me in over a month and expect me to just take that too, huh? If I'm not what you had in mind when you were shopping for a wife, you can let me know. I cannot change who I am or how I am. Actually, I kinda like me. So let's decide right now. What's it going to be?"

Evelyn was standing in the closet, her chest was heaving and tears had started to roll down her cheeks. She had pulled off her dress: bra, panties, one hand on her hip—the universal black woman's' salute.

Kevin looked at her as he sat on the side of the bed. He had started to take off his shoes and stopped. He realized she was serious. He had never seen her cry before. He walked over to her and wiped the tears from her cheeks. Her breathing relaxed a little and the tears started to flow.

"Don't cry. Please don't. This is crazy. Look at us! Look at what we have here. A wonderful home, a new marriage…we both have some adjusting to do. Maybe I was little harsh. I love you. I need you." He pulled her gently towards him and Evelyn realized what made him such a successful attorney. He could convince an elephant to drink out of a thimble. Even though she was still mad, the feelings she had for him resurfaced.

For a moment she reflected on what he said. He had given her a wonderful home, money, prestige and even provided money for her family when they needed it. He could have had any woman, but he wanted her. Whatever the problems were, they would have to work them out.

She caressed his shoulders and started to cry louder. How many times had she wished for someone like Kevin Williams? She was a lucky woman. They made love right there on the floor of the large walk - in closet. It was more passionate than ever before and this time he didn't race to the shower afterwards. They cuddled and held each other tightly.

"Hey, let's just sleep here on the floor. I'll get our sleeping bags. Since you refused to go camping, we might as well use them tonight," Kevin whispered.

"You have to admit, using them tonight is a lot better than fighting mosquitoes and crawly things on the ground. Maybe I should fight with you more often." Evelyn kissed his chest, letting her tongue trace his nipples.

"You know make-up sex is kind of exciting. I like that tiger in you. I don't want to lose you, ever, even if it means fighting with you to keep you." He pulled her up to look at him. Evelyn sat straddle his stomach and reached for him again. He was ready. They never got the sleeping bags.

The next morning Kevin called his tennis buddy to cancel a match saying he wanted to spend this Saturday with Evelyn. They walked around the house in the nude until after noon.

It was better than their honeymoon and Evelyn laughed to herself when she thought about the advice her grandmother had given her about the red candle and the oil. If she didn't know better, she would have sworn her grandmother had sneaked into her house and put the magical items under the bed.

She could tell her this time there was no need for voodoo magic spells. Her marriage was going to be just fine. She wanted to call Sonja and at least see if they were still friends, but with Kevin under foot all day it was hard. She didn't want to create another fight just when things were going so well. In fact, to guarantee that nothing spoiled the second honeymoon, Evelyn turned on her answering machine.

Her mother called five times and finally Evelyn called her back, "Mama? Hey, what's up?"

"What's up? I believe you were supposed to take your grandmother shopping today. We've been sitting here for two hours waiting for you. I called the store and they said you were off. I called the house I don't know how many times. My whole Saturday is messed up. I could have been doing something else." Patricia Jones was on the kitchen phone with her hand on her hip.

"Ma, I'm so sorry. I forgot. Tell Mama Ree I'm on my way… no, I tell you what. Just bring her on over here and we can go to the mall from here."

"Where you been anyway? You can't even call people?" Patricia was reaching for her purse. She loved visiting her daughter's spacious home, looking at the new purchases and usually leaving with some item that Evelyn didn't actually like that Kevin bought.

"Okay Mama, I'll see you later." Evelyn was already thinking of what she could give her mother on this visit as a peace offering. Then she remembered she had ordered a moiré satin king sized bed ensemble from Spiegel that was still in the plastic bag. It had cost her close to $400. She bought it out of anger and frustration, so it didn't matter. It would be worth the price to keep her mother from ranting and raving.

82

Patricia and Mama Ree arrived in 45 minutes. Her grandmother was outside in the front yard with Kevin giving advice about planting flowers. She could tell from his expression he didn't quite appreciate Mama Ree's landscaping critique.

"But Grand Ma, this is how it's done. These are the finest shrubs in the nursery. You see how they compliment the architecture?" He was seriously trying to convince her about his landscaping knowledge.

Mama Ree was frowning and looking from him to the shrubbery. "Hon, you still need something with color. Some zinnias or azaleas would be nice. I could come over and set them out for you, cause I know Lynn don't know nothing about setting out flowers."

She was walking around the manicured lawn trying to decide a good spot for the addition to the landscaping. The mere idea of some elderly African American woman stooping and digging in his front yard wearing a large straw hat gave Kevin chills.

"No, no, Grand Mama. It's too hot for you to be out here. Let's wait until next year and I'll even let you tell the gardener what to plant, okay?" He was gently guiding her indoors.

Patricia was ecstatic over the bed linen ensemble. She kept saying how expensive it looked, much too expensive for Evelyn to be giving away, yet she never offered to pay for it or give it back.

Kevin walked over to Patricia and gave her a loud kiss on the cheek, "Nothing is too good for my mother-in-law or my Grand Mama." He gave Mama Ree a bear hug. She was giggling and slapping his arm.

Evelyn watched him expertly charming the pants off both of them. He could be charming when he wanted to be. He then walked over to Evelyn and gave her a passionate kiss, "I'm such a lucky man! Three beautiful women to take care of."

"Well yall actin like them couples on my daytime stories. All lovey dovey. I guess we'll be seeing some little ones real soon. You know I might not be around here much longer. I need to start spoiling some great grands." Mama Ree's eyes sparkled as she looked at Evelyn.

"Well I don't know about real soon, but soon. Right honey?" Kevin winked at Evelyn.

"Maybe after I open my business. Right now I really want to get that off the ground. I don't want to have to work for someone all of my life." Evelyn looked at her grandmother.

"You don't have to work at all. I wish your Daddy had offered me the chance to stay home," Patricia was looking at Kevin for support, "You should listen to Kevin, if he thinks it's okay to stay home and raise your children, I think it's a wonderful idea".

"What ever she wants makes me happy. One day I'm sure she's going to walk in the front door and say she's had enough of the rat race. Until then we'll see what happens." Kevin gave her another kiss on the cheek and left the room. This was the first time he had taken her side against her mother on anything.

Even her mother was shocked.

"Well, I see somebody been burning red candles," Mama Ree chuckled.

The shopping with her grandmother went much too fast for Evelyn. She hadn't been this happy in a while.

She felt that Kevin truly loved her and would not risk losing her. She made a silent vow to keep him happy. She really liked Sonja, but she would not allow this new found friendship to cause friction in her marriage. Even though Evelyn admired Sonja's brashness and take control attitude, she did seem to go a little too far.

She would keep in contact, but limited contact. Maybe visit her home, or have her over when Kevin wasn't home. That seemed safer. After all, Evelyn had perceived that Sonja wasn't too crazy about Kevin either.

After returning home from dropping her grandmother off, Evelyn drove down to Sonja's large Mediterranean style home. It was very different from the informal personality that Sonja presented. The house was very formal and traditionally furnished. Sonja seemed truly happy to see her and welcomed her in as though the two had been friends for years. Evelyn couldn't quite put her finger on it, but Sonja was different compared to the night before. She wasn't wearing any makeup, had on cut off Daisy Duke jeans and an over sized Dallas Cowboys muscle shirt. But even in her casual attire, her beauty was breathtaking and her body was toned and shapely.

Her great room was fabulous with arched doorways and one wall entirely of glass. It overlooked a deck and pool. The furniture was done in beige, pale blues and rich red fabrics. It almost felt as if you were in the Mediterranean with lots of cobalt and lapis blue colors accented by sculptures and artwork.

It was good to see Sonja's mother on the road to recovery, even though she still could not speak or walk. Obviously, having her only child home was making a big difference in her therapy. She was wheeling around the great room and using her good hand to look through magazines. She kept her Bible on her lap and would touch the book as though she was having a private conversation with God. Evelyn had the strongest feeling that Mrs. Davenport was praying, while everyone around her seemed oblivious to her actions.

Sonja was singing off key with Anita Baker's *"Giving You the Best That I've Got"* as she blended strawberry daiquiris in the kitchen.

"I had a really nice time last week. Next time we'll eat here, but I warn you … I'm a lousy cook." Sonja handed Evelyn a tall daiquiri.

"Maybe the men should cook. They love to bar-b-que, and with this great deck and pool we could have big fun. You might be a lousy cook, but home girl you can make some daiquiris. This is delicious!" Evelyn raised her glass in a toast.

"Thanks. Speaking of cooking and men, Danny is a very good chef. He served me in bed and made me breakfast." Sonja took a sip of her drink and laughed at Evelyn's expression of utter shock.

"You and Danny? This is unreal!" she squealed. "But I mean it's great. He's a good guy and every woman in this town is after him. We always heard that he had a hell of a crush on you that wouldn't stop. So, I guess it was true."

Sonja agreed, "He is a good guy. No, a great guy. You know he fed Mama, took her for a walk and then went into work. This is scary, but exciting. I have never felt this way before and it's not just sex, although, that helps."

"Yeah, I know what you mean. Kevin and I were having some problems, but it seems we're going to be all right. I was about to give up. I thought I wasn't doing something right, you know, to make him happy, to please him." Evelyn wished she had not said that last part judging from the expression on Sonja's face.

She quickly added, "But we're better now. Everything's going to be okay. Enough about me and Kevin, tell me about you and Danny."

Sonja could tell Evelyn had a lot more she wanted to talk about, but was beginning to feel uncomfortable. She wouldn't pressure her. When the time was right, they would discuss whatever it was. For now, Sonja was happy to report how Danny was becoming a part of her life.

"I've known Danny since I was eight years old. He has been my closest friend, but I never allowed myself to become interested in him. I mean, he represents Birmingham to the highest degree. Small town, quiet, settled. I knew the moment I finished high school I was taking the first thing smoking out of Alabama. Danny is here to stay."

"What about you? Are you here to stay now?"

"If my Mama recovers and agrees to move back to Dallas with me, I'm out of here. If I decide she's strong enough to move even without a full recovery, I'm still out of here."

Evelyn looked around Sonja's beautiful home, "But you just got here and look at this place! Why did you go to all this trouble if you plan on leaving?"

"Because, where ever I am I want to be in luxury. The doctors advised against putting Mama through too many changes too soon. So, when I sold her house, I felt one major change was enough at the time. But no, this town is not for me. Have you ever been to Dallas, Chicago, L.A. or Las Vegas?"

Evelyn shook her head.

"Well, I can't describe the feeling of freedom of being able to blend in with the masses if you want or to be in solitude … whatever your mood dictates. You can be anonymous. Danny would never understand." Sonja poured them another drink.

"Then what about Danny? You're just going to leave him here? I'm sure he thinks you guys have a chance for something serious. That's the kind of man Danny is, Sonja. You're going to break his heart." Evelyn took a sip of the drink and had a sinking feeling in the pit of her stomach.

Sonja's questions about moving away made Evelyn feel unsettled. Sometimes she feared Kevin might get that restless bug and want to return to California.

Evelyn felt more like she and Danny were in the same club. She liked Birmingham. She liked quiet and settled. She liked peace of mind, not the masses.

Sonja kept making her point, "I'm sure Danny knows me better than that. I'm not the settling down kind. Marriage and all that jazz are not for the kid. Can you believe it? A black woman in her 30's, never been married and not looking to walk down the aisle."

"Yeah, I can believe it. I also believe you're bluffing. Danny is going to make you change your mind. I hope he does. I don't want you to move away. I like having you just down the street." Evelyn raised her glass in a toast to Sonja. At that moment, the phone rang. Sonja answered and immediately broke into a wide grin. It was Danny.

"I'm leaving the garage in about an hour, you want to go out to dinner?"

"You know Mama's nurse has the weekend off. Why don't you grill something? I would volunteer to cook, but I like you too much."

Danny smiled and said that would be fine, "Oh, is it okay if I spend the night? I thought maybe waking up with you on a Sunday morning would be rather nice."

"It would be very nice. Thanks for asking, I would love the company. Evelyn and I were just having daiquiris, so I'll make a fresh blender for you."

"Tell her hi, and I'll see you in an hour or so." He wanted to end the conversation with something more personal, but other than saying he loved her, he couldn't think of a thing.

Sonja took note of his hesitation. "Okay, see ya soon. Kiss-kiss."

He liked that, *kiss-kiss*. Women were so smart he thought. At least this one was.

§§§§§§§§§§§§§§§§§§§§§§§§§§§§

Evelyn left minutes later and found that Kevin had left a note that he was at the Club playing racquetball. She thought about surprising him and showing up to watch his game, but his note said he would be back by eight o'clock. It was already seven and the Club was a good 30-minute drive. That would mean she would get there just in time for him to be leaving.

Instead, she drew herself a hot bath in the Jacuzzi and lit candles. She was planning to take advantage of their resurrected passion.

When Evelyn awoke, it was 11 p.m. and her bath water was cold. Those daiquiris must have been stronger than she thought. As she pulled the drain plug to empty the tub, she called Kevin's name, thinking he must have let her sleep.

The house was quiet; the CD player had stopped hours ago. She walked groggily towards the front of the house, and heard his BMW pulling into the garage.

Evelyn stood in the kitchen, trying to figure out what could have kept him so long. She could tell by the way he slammed the laundry room door connecting to the garage that he was in a bad mood. Whatever happened, she was determined not to argue about it.

Kevin walked into the kitchen carrying his racquet. His expression was one of surprise when he saw Evelyn standing there, "Hi. What are you doing up so late?"

"Waiting for you, since eight o'clock. What happened?" Evelyn was opening a bottle of Chablis.

"It's a long story. Frank and I played a couple of games, went to get something to eat, then when we were leaving the restaurant, he had a flat." Kevin stretched and continued, "Some guys are so smart in business and have no common sense. Here he is, a successful stockbroker, with no jack or spare! So we took the flat tire to be fixed, which took longer than I thought. Sorry, I should have called." He took a glass of wine from Evelyn and walked towards the bedroom.

Evelyn noticed he was in no hurry to stay in the kitchen with her. Minutes later she heard the shower. She knew Frank Miller, he was a successful white stockbroker and a pretty nice guy. He had a couple of kids and a very cute wife who didn't work and who in fact did very little without Franks' permission. The typical southern belle.

Kevin was usually so complimentary about the Miller's. This was the first time he had criticized his racquetball buddy.

When Evelyn walked into the bedroom, Kevin was already in bed, his back turned to the door. Even though it was summer, he had on a tee shirt, usually he slept bare chested.

Evelyn started pulling off her clothes, "I guess you saw the burned out candles. I thought we could have a romantic evening. That's why I waited up."

Kevin slowly turned over to face her, "And?" His eyes were as cold as his tone.

"What's wrong Kevin? When you left here today, I thought we were going to try."

"Please don't start with me tonight! Just because I don't want to fool around every night."

"Fool around? Is that what our lovemaking means to you? Fooling around?" Evelyn felt as if she was in a horror movie and the scene was being replayed from their last argument.

"I will sleep in the guest room before I have to justify to you why I don't want any sex tonight, and I don't want to argue or discuss it." Kevin sat up in the bed and she could see that the anger in his eyes was real.

"Sleep where ever in the hell you want Kevin." Evelyn walked into the bathroom and slammed the door.

She truly was at a lost for understanding what was wrong with this man. He was becoming harder to read every day. After her shower, Evelyn discovered Kevin had left their bedroom. She locked the door.

Chapter 5

Santa Baby

Santa Baby, I wanna yacht,
And really that's not a lot.
Been an angel all year, Santa Baby,
So hurry down the chimney tonight.

Waking up next to Danny Taylor was more than nice. Usually Sonja slept late, but this Sunday morning she found herself wide awake and restless at 6 a.m. She glanced over at Danny, who was still sleeping, his forearm under his head, his chest rising and falling steadily.

His dark skin looked like melted chocolate against her beige satin sheets. She couldn't help but lightly stroke his chest, tracing her finger down to his hard stomach. With feather like strokes, Sonja let her fingers move lower, gently caressing him until she could feel a throbbing sensation and suddenly her diminutive hand became too small to contain him.

Danny opened his eyes and blinked, turning to face her, "Woman do you ever sleep? You're going to kill me. What time is it anyway?" His eyes searched the room for a clock.

"It's a little after six. And a little before sex." She leaned over and kissed him, deeply thrusting her tongue into his mouth. She could taste the wine from the night before, mixed with her body.

"Hmm. Let me brush my teeth baby, in fact, let's both brush our teeth." He threw the covers away from his body, and Sonja felt her heart jerk in reaction. This man looked so good. Good enough to eat.

"Later for that. What I'm about to do to you, would only be a waste of toothpaste." She grabbed his muscular thighs and pulled him into the middle of the bed. Positioning herself between his legs, she repaid a wonderful favor from the night before.

An hour and a half later, Danny Taylor was begging Sonja Davenport to never leave him. He was telling her he would never leave her, that he loved her, had always loved her and always would.

Being in love made Sonja nervous, so she responded in the only way she could, with humor.

"You won't love me after you taste my cooking. I'm cooking breakfast this morning." With that announcement, she bounced from the bed and went into the bathroom, warning Danny not to come into the kitchen until she called him.

An hour later, Danny could smell something burning in the kitchen. Curiosity got the best of him and he sneaked down the stairs. The scene looked like a disaster movie. Sonja had three cookbooks open in front of her, a smoking empty skillet in one hand and an egg in the other. At least there was a fresh pot of coffee.

"Need some help?" Danny poured a cup of coffee and surveyed the damage. He assumed she was trying to fix an omelet.

"This is so frustrating! Omelets are supposed to be easy right? I mean it's just eggs, milk and whatever you want inside." Sonja fumed.

Danny noticed the mushrooms, onions, peppers, and cheese, which should have beaten with the eggs a long time ago.

"Honestly, I could be happy with just scrambled eggs, toast, and coffee. Let me help, before your poor mother starves to death." Danny started putting away the omelet fixings and took the skillet away from Sonja.

"And by the way, you are wrong. I do still love you." He kissed her on her nose.

It seemed like only minutes later that Sonja, her mother and Danny were eating deliciously scrambled eggs, buttered toast with jelly, bacon and coffee.

"So what's it going to be today ladies? How about a drive into the country? I've got a brand new colt I've got to check on."

"I think some of Mama's friends are coming over after church today, so we could drive out to your place while they're here. A brand new colt huh? How old?" Sonja asked.

"Three months and she is a beauty. Already got a buyer for her. Although, I would like to christen her, you know kind of claim her as one of the family first. All of my horses have names, something sentimental and family related."

"I can't wait to meet them. You have any idea what the new baby will be named?" Sonja started clearing the table, her back was to Danny.

"I don't know, something like Dancing Doll, after my baby sister, or maybe Lovely Lena."

She didn't know how to react. So she decided to play it dumb, "Interesting. Who is named Lena in your family?" Sonja kept wiping the spotlessly clean breakfast table.

"Someone I used to know. I don't think you've ever met her. She's long gone now. Probably won't ever come back." Danny had his arms folded across his chest, looking at Sonja for any sign of discomfort or maybe even acknowledgement. He saw neither, and she had the best poker face he had ever witnessed.

Sonja spent most of Monday trying not to think about the subtle clue that Danny had dropped using her stage name, Lovely Lena. So he had done some snooping. Now what? Was she supposed to confess? Confront him and ask for forgiveness? Tell him how little Sonja from Birmingham grew up to be Lovely Lena of Dallas?

In due time she would tell him the details. Experience had taught her that most men couldn't handle the complete truth about women and their pasts. She would spoon-feed him crumbs at a time, until he was ready to digest the full course.

She had called Evelyn, but all she got was the answering machine and the store employees said she was not at work. Sonja was thinking maybe it was time for a short trip, either to Dallas to see her girlfriends or even Los Angeles, just to have a little fun. She was becoming too much a part of the scenery here. She had never had a close friend who was married and although she really liked Evelyn, she knew they came from two different worlds and that eventually would mean disappointment and hurt feelings. Evelyn had a husband to make happy and that alone was enough to make Sonja keep her distance.

She was in the kitchen making sandwiches for her mother when the phone rang. The connection was static filled,

"Sonja Davenport?"

Sonja answered, "Speaking."

"This is Air Force One. Please hold for Senator Ramos."

Sonja smiled to herself. Raymond Ramos always did have style and loved to flaunt his power. She had met him when he was a freshman Texas Congressman, and four years ago, he shocked the Texas political scene by winning the U.S. Senate seat from a Republican incumbent.

He had been anointed the "new" Hispanic leader in American politics and the rising star of the Democratic Party, helping to usher in a Democratic Presidential victory two years earlier.

He was "the man." With movie star looks of a cross between Andy Garcia and Benjamin Bratt, the Senator was always in Newsweek, Time and even People magazine for his political savvy. He was one of the first men who taught Sonja that nothing in life is free, not even love.

Married with two children, he was never going to tolerate any threat that could detour his quest for the ultimate political brass ring: the white House.

He was aiming for the Presidential nomination in two years and his wife was just as committed to being the first Hispanic first lady. She allowed his taste in extracurricular activities as long as there were no blatant displays or embarrassments.

Raymond Ramos made sure of that. He taught Sonja not to be greedy, or too irrational when it came to being involved with a married man, but still she had fallen in love with him. It was to be expected, since she was barely 21 and he was nearly 40 when they first met. He called it her training wheels period on the bike of life. And trained her, he did.

"Ms. Davenport. I was just calling to reschedule our meeting for tomorrow. I'm enroute from Geneva and will need tomorrow to go over some committee issues with my staff. I'm sorry for the inconvenience."

That deep resonant voice still gave Sonja chills. He loved this James Bond 007 game playing. He always spoke in codes. So now she was supposed to see him on tomorrow in Washington.

"Senator, I fully understand. Thank you for taking the time to call me. I'll wait for your scheduler to call me and let me know when we can meet."

Sonja knew not to disappoint him. He had been very generous to her in the past ten years and truthfully, she had never gotten completely over him. He was the closest thing to her Prince Charming and she was looking forward to seeing him.

He was drop dead gorgeous enough to be named one of People magazines most beautiful people. He seemed to look even better the older he got. His medium yet muscular built frame was always clad in only the best Italian suits and custom-made shirts. Even his name had a ring to it that no voter could forget and the media reporters, especially the Hispanic ones, loved the way the r's rolled off their tongues when they said Raymond Ramos.

His hair was curly, which he hated and she loved, so he kept it cut extremely short which made it wavy more than curly. He could disarm you with a wicked smile. She had watched him for ten years use his uncommonly good looks to court the media and win votes of a largely female population. Just when the women voters thought he only had eyes for them, he would strategically grab his wife's hand and pull her into the view of the nearest camera, pacifying the potential male voters. He was crafty and could be ruthless.

Since the President was from Texas, there was always the unspoken belief that Raymond had some dirt on the Commander-in-Chief and was using it to garner white House support for his appointment as Chairman of the International Trade Committee, Member of the Senate Banking Committee and Member of the Senate Budget Committee. Unprecedented appointments for a newly elected member.

Sonja was walking toward her bedroom when she met the nurse coming out of her mother's room. "Oh, Miss Collins, I have to be out of town for a few days, starting tomorrow. Can you stay over?"

"Honey, I would love to! This house is like a vacation for me. All of the nursing assistants want this assignment, but I tell them that Miss Davenport expects only me and that's all there is to it. You don't ever have to worry about asking me to stay over." Clara Collins could talk a blue streak and there was never a one-word answer from her.

Even though Sonja's mother couldn't speak, Clara Collins would talk for the both of them, asking questions, answering them and laughing at her own funny stories. Sonja always paid her a little extra because she had become like a family member. She was a very fair-skinned, heavy built woman, with thick red hair that she wore in two thick braids wrapped around her head and bobby pinned together.

Sonja walked into her mother's room and realized it was times like these that she was almost relieved her mother couldn't speak. That way there could be no probing questions.

"Mama, I've got to go out of town for a day or two. I'm leaving tomorrow morning. Miss Collins is going to stay with you." Sonja kissed her mother's forehead. Clara Collins was still talking about what a good time she and her patient were going to have and for Sonja not to worry about anything.

As she was finishing her packing, the phone rang. This time it was Danny, testing the waters to see if it was safe to come by since his last visit.

"I'm in the middle of packing." Sonya was purposely evasive.

"Packing? Where you going?" He sounded genuinely concerned, also a little perturbed.

"Out of town."

He tried to sound uninterested, "I figured that much out. When are you coming back? Or am I being too nosy?"

"In a day or two. Something just came up. It wasn't planned," Sonja snapped her suitcase shut.

"We need to talk. I mean really talk. About us and where we're heading. My feelings and your feelings." Danny's words rushed out as though he wouldn't see her again.

Sonja exhaled loudly to show her level of impatience was growing, "I feel like I've always felt. That you are a nice person, but you need someone else in your life and I'm not the one, Danny. We want different things out of life."

"Like what? Being able to run off to God knows where with whoever?" He was finding it harder to hide his agitation.

"See there? That's what I mean. You always find a way to make things complicated. Maybe that is what I like, being able to run off whenever I want. You don't have to accept it, because I'm not asking you to accept it. I'm not asking anything of you. I really have to go run some errands." Sonja glanced at her watch.

"Let's have dinner tonight, we can finish talking then," he wouldn't give up.

Talking about a future with Danny was the last thing Sonja wanted. "You mean finish arguing or finish your lecture. Danny, I'm not a little girl anymore. I don't need you to teach me how to play t-ball or ride a bike or skip stones or rescue me from the playground bully. This is my life and I like it. I care about our friendship, but if you're getting ready to get stupid on me …"

Danny interrupted, "Who is he Sonja? Who can call you in a split second and you come running like a little puppy? Don't you want more from a relationship? You deserve more."

"A puppy? Oh, so now we have to go there. Yeah, I deserve more. That's why I'm saying no to you. I've got to go." Sonja hung up the phone and switched on the answering the machine. She knew Danny would call back apologizing, but she didn't want to hear it.

How could he judge her? Where was he when she was sleeping in her car with no food, money or friends? She had survived without him or his advice. She did what she had to, but she never hurt anyone in the process. She survived without him and his judgmental ways.

No matter how she tried to convince herself that Danny was being unfair, sleep didn't come easy for Sonja that night. She tossed, turned, and kept hearing Danny's words: "Running like a puppy."

She was more than that to Raymond. She knew he loved her in his own way, but he was driven by success and focused on his own agenda. She was a liability to him achieving that success. She was lucky to have him as a confidant, a lover and a friend.

Sure, he was selfish and demanding as most men were, but the truly successful ones had to be.

§§§§§§§§§§§§§§§§§§§§

It had been six months since she had seen him. She had flown to Houston and they had spent an entire weekend together. That was rare since usually he could only manage one night. Even though it was those one nighters that usually made Sonja feel empty, Raymond Ramos could always do something to erase the empty feeling. A diamond bracelet, a new fur coat or a weekend in Aruba. Most recently, when Sonja's mother became ill, Raymond gave her the money for the down payment on her new house in Birmingham, telling her not to touch her savings.

Raymond Ramos was the first and only man to tell Sonja to cut her waist length hair, because he felt it made her look too unprofessional. So she did.

He taught her how to dress, how to order the best wine in the best restaurants and how to let a man take the lead. He insisted that she start to invest her money. So she did.

He would often remind her that her dancers' body would only last so long; she needed to prepare herself for those years when she would be just another middle-aged woman who used to be a stunning young woman. At first, Sonja took his advice as criticism, but later as her investments started to pay off and she was able to partner with the private club's owners, she was grateful.

Raymond had taught her that discretion was everything. Being careless was costly. So she had played by the rules, pretending not to know him at political or social functions and crying herself to sleep afterwards.

He taught her that in order to attract money, you have look like you have money. He always had a car and driver pick her up at airports and made sure she was invited to highbrow events to meet influential people.

He said he had confidence in her, that all she needed was an opportunity, the kind he could give her. Sonja loved it when he talked to her like that. She felt like he was reading her a bedtime story; she was the Princess and he was Prince Charming coming to rescue her.

Deep inside, she knew it was only a fairy tale.

He would leave and go back to Houston with his politically correct family. He'd keep being the successful political leader, while she would keep their relationship a secret, always asking herself, *"What if?"*

The two-hour flight into Washington was uneventful. Sonja sat in first class with only three other passengers. A white rotund man from Atlanta named Walter kept making small talk, even though Sonja tried to ignore him.

By the time they had landed, he was offering her a ride to her hotel, dinner, maybe an after dinner drink. He was practically walking on her heels as they exited the aircraft. Sonja stopped walking and turned to him as they were entering in the jet way. She stepped up close to him, forcing his back to the wall.

"Walter? Listen carefully. Why in the hell do you think I would even consider riding in a car with you? Dining or drinking with you? Look at me, Walter. Look at how I'm dressed. I'm a knock out. Do I look like I'm in need of an ugly, boring, fat, sweaty white man?"

The man stammered and turned red. "No. I was just trying to be friendly. Sorry … Really I was just …"

Sonja had already turned and was walking into the baggage claim terminal when she saw a chauffeur holding a sign with her name on it. She thought, "Thank God for Raymond Ramos."

Even though Reagan National Airport was crowded, Sonja cut a sharp vision as she cat walked through the terminal. Her white, stiletto Manolo Blaniks sandals, the coordinating sunshine yellow and white horizontal striped fitted dress, which dangerously caressed her ample hips, and the white bucket style hat with her raven colored hair swinging with each step, created the drama and attention Sonja craved.

The Willard Hotel in Washington was where diplomats and foreign dignitaries stayed. The hotel was in walking distance to 1600 Pennsylvania Avenue and there was always a caravan of limousines parked in front of the beige French provincial brick structure.

After pulling the black town car to the curb, the Hispanic driver dashed from the driver's seat to open Sonja's door. The concierge who had checked her in , handed her the key and grabbed her luggage.

The suite was impeccable as always. A crystal vase of fresh cut flowers sat on the coffee table, with another vase holding a dozen red roses on the bedroom nightstand. As the bellhop went through his monologue of features in the suite and the hotel, Sonja tossed her hat on the bed and was opening a bottle of Perrier.

She knew the bellhop would be properly tipped on her check out, for Raymond always requested the same bellhop during his stay at any hotel. He said it guaranteed consistency in service and loyalty.

"Miss Davenport, is there something I can get for you?" He asked in broken English.

"No, thank you. How hot is it going to get today?" Sonja was looking out over Pennsylvania Avenue at the hazy sky.

The bellhop grinned. "Oh, very warm today. Mid 90's. It feels like Columbia. I don't miss South America during the summer here." He was stacking her bags on the luggage rack.

Waving her finely manicured hand in his direction, Sonja cut short his reminisces of his homeland. "That's fine. I can take it from here. I'll see you before I leave tomorrow." Sonja wanted to relax. Maybe take a bubble bath before Raymond showed up. The bellhop, Escovar would talk all day if she didn't dismiss him.

Sonja had barely submerged herself in the bubble bath, when she heard the hotel room door open. She could smell the faint scent of his designer cologne. Raymond walked into the bathroom and gave her a huge grin.

"I've never in my life wanted to drink anybody's bath water before now. Ay, ay my baby." His Hispanic accent flowed heavier than normal as he knelt down and gave her a passionate kiss.

Being careful not to wet his Armani suit, Sonja held his head a while longer and returned the kiss.

"You coming in?" She smiled.

"Of course. Let me make one phone call first," he stopped and turned to look at Sonja, knowing she was giving him a dirty disapproving glare.

"Damn Ray, you just left the office and you could have made that call in the car. Can't you give me five minutes of undivided attention?" she pouted.

Sonja was getting out of the tub, soapy water and bubbles were sliding down her breasts, to her stomach and thighs.

Raymond took in the sight and decided not to try to win this debate. He silently took off his jacket, tie and shirt, undid his belt and removed his pants and underwear. Standing stark naked he picked Sonja up and stepped back into the Jacuzzi.

As always, their lovemaking was wonderful and at 51 years of age, he was more energetic than men half his age and more accomplished than men who were older. He was as demanding in bed as he was in life. Sonja noticed his chest had a lot more gray hairs, which was deceptive compared to his head, which hardly showed any gray.

Lying naked in bed eating strawberries floating in champagne, Sonja and Raymond caught up on each other's lives since their last visit. Sonja didn't mention Danny even though Raymond talked in detail about his wife and kids.

He didn't appreciate any conversation about other men in Sonja's life and wanted to pretend she was sitting waiting on his next call.

"So how was Switzerland?" Sonja asked before popping a strawberry into her mouth.

"No matter how many times I visit, I'm always impressed at how beautiful that place is. I'm in South Africa next month. I finally convinced the White House to hold an international development conference there instead of Europe. You ought to come." He reached over and stroked Sonja's exposed thigh.

"That's too long to leave Mama. I wish I could though."

"How are things in Birmingham? Are you okay? I mean how's your money?" He was tracing a champagne soaked strawberry on Sonja's thigh.

"I'm okay. I'm not on welfare yet, but I am getting bored with Alabama. I can't wait to get back to Dallas."

"Well if you're so bored, why don't you accept some of my invitations? There is a state dinner at the White House next week for the President of Mexico. I can get you invited."

"Won't you be married then?" Sonja was starting to get annoyed.

"Yeah, she'll be there. She doesn't miss any White House events. You can be my brother's guest. I would love to look across the room at you in the White House," he reached over and smacked her loudly on the lips.

Sonja sat up in bed and crossed her arms over her chest, "Why? We can't be together. We can't even sit together. It would be a waste of my time."

"It wouldn't be a waste. It would be sexy and exciting. Because I get hard just looking at you. I've never been hard at the White House before. In fact, we could try to do a JFK or a Bill Clinton and sneak into a closet or something. I'd really like that." He was nuzzling her breast.

Usually that act excited Sonja into complete submission, but today was different. She needed more than sexual validation.

"Do you think I would enjoy watching you and your wife hold court at the White House while I pretend to be a date for your brother? All that matters is how you feel. You would get a kick out of having me in the same room, no matter how bad I felt. You are so selfish." Sonja threw the sheet over her nakedness and turned her back to Raymond.

"I don't have time for this. I have to argue enough with racist, idiotic Republicans and some Democrats who aren't much better, everyday. I don't expect to come here with someone special and fight my way through every conversation." Raymond looked at his watch as if to judge how much time he was going to give Sonja to get over her anger.

With her back still turned to him she responded, "If I'm special, then why do I have to be hidden away, used as a decoy? How long do you think I want to be treated like some puppy?"

"Puppy? Come on Sonja! Once a year we have this conversation and each time it is unnecessary. When did you become so insecure? Do not let that hot Italian blood make you start acting stupid. I taught you better than that." He was getting out of bed and heading for the bathroom.

"Taught me? Or trained me? I am not a pet, Ray! Yeah, you taught me well. You taught me to expect the best. Not to settle for less. So why am I supposed to settle now? And what you refer to as stupid is the other half of my blood line, the African half that doesn't like being used like the masters slave."

Sonja followed him into the bathroom where he was examining his face in the mirror.

"Look at this skin. Do I look like a white slave master to you? Spare me the race card bullshit, okay? I am the master of that game. I got an infected hair follicle. Look at this bump. Can you pop it for me?" Raymond changed the subject just like that.

It was this innocent child-like personality that Sonja loved and yet hated about this man.

Obediently she popped the small pimple on his shoulder, making it a lot more painful than necessary. Raymond locked eyes with her as though to acknowledge her intent. His speech was reverting to broken English, a sign that he was getting upset,

"You want to break up with me? Is that it? You're starting a fight over nothing so we can stop seeing each other. It won't work. You know I love you. I wish things could be different, but they're not. They can't be. It's a part of life that comes with happiness. Thirty minutes ago, I was the happiest man in the world, only you can do that for me. Now you're driving me crazy, only you can do that, too."

He took her silence as an opportunity to continue, "I try to make you happy, I just can't be there like a normal guy and you know this. I am begging you not to take the one pleasure in my private life away. I couldn't take it right now. I need you more than ever." By now he was holding Sonja around the waist, pulling her closer to him.

"Ray, I need more. I need you, too. I'm getting older now and I need normal." Sonja rested her head on his chest.

"Is there someone normal in Birmingham?" he quietly asked.

"He might be." She whispered.

"Is he good to you? Gives you the world? Treats you like a queen?" He was stroking her hair.

"Yes." Sonja didn't want to hear what Raymond was going to say next.

"Sounds like I taught you too well. I wouldn't want any man not giving you the world. Unfortunately, that means competition with me. Sounds like this is one race I might lose." He held her tighter.

"You'll never lose me Ray. You'll just be releasing me, letting me go on my own." Sonja whispered.

"What am I supposed to do without you? It's been ten years, baby. Ten years of growing, loving and laughing. Letting you go is going to be hard. Right now it's tough just thinking that after tonight I can't hold you, kiss you."

"It's been tough for me for ten years Ray. Wondering why I can't have you the way I want. Seeing you in magazines, on television. Knowing your speeches before anyone else. Laughing at how you manipulate other politicians you don't like, just the way you say will. I've been your silent partner, keeping your secrets, your wishes and your fears hidden just between us." Sonja was softly crying into his chest.

"Let's not talk about saying goodbye. It will never be goodbye. Maybe we should just take a little break," he quickly glanced at his watch again, as his cell phone started to ring, "duty calls."

Tonight would be different for the both of them. Though neither wanted to admit it, they knew it was the end of the road as secret lovers. They had fought many times in the last ten years, with each of them vowing to leave the other one, but tonight it was real.

Tonight was the beginning of the end of her fairy tale. As much as she loved Raymond Ramos, she knew in her heart he would replace her and do so immediately. He had to have that kind of outlet, no matter how much he denied it.

They went to dinner at one of Washington's best restaurants, went dancing and came back to the suite to make love, as they always did. Neither said goodbye nor brought up the subject of the affair ending. For 24 more hours, Raymond got to live out his fantasy and Sonja lived out her fairy tale.

Tomorrow reality would set in on her flight back to Birmingham and she would have to decide if Danny Taylor was going to be the man to take Raymond's place.

Chapter 6

Someone To Watch Over Me

Although he may not be the man some girls think of as handsome,
To my heart he carries the key.
Won't you tell him please to put on some speed,
Follow my lead.
Oh, how I need someone to watch over me.

G ail and Laura attacked the mall with a frenzy to celebrate Gail's promotion and raise. They had the entire Saturday planned.

Shopping, lunch, shopping, dinner, shopping and then maybe a movie. They had finished the first round of shopping and were having lunch to refuel their energy.

"I don't want a salad today, even though I need to lose at least 20 pounds." Laura was examining the menu. Gail raised her eyebrows on that comment and cleared her throat.

"Okay, 30 pounds, but damn that's hard to do Gail. Soon as I start seeing some progress, I have to bake something for the kids or Ted wants to go out to dinner and my will power evaporates."

"You have to be strong Laura. Sometimes the people who love us the most hurt us without even knowing it. Just say no."

"Oh, I'm supposed to be Nancy Reagan? What do you mean people who love us hurt us? Girl, please. Ted could care less how fat I am. Waiter, I'll have the shrimp alfredo, another glass of Chablis and a large salad with extra thousand island dressing." She handed the menu defiantly to the waiter. The teenage waiter innocently asked. "Is that low fat dressing Ma'am?"

"No. The regular kind. Why did you ask me that? Do I look like I need low fat dressing?" Laura snapped.

"No, Ma'am. It's just sometimes people forget to tell me," he stammered.

Gail interrupted, rescuing the young waiter while giving Laura a reprimanding look. "Baby, never mind her. I'll have the same and we'll have dessert later."

"We'll just be fat together." She added.

"You are not fat heifer. Don't try to make me feel better now. Later on this summer when we go to the beach, I will still hate your guts. Speaking of the beach, is Mr. Sloan going to join us this summer for our Florida getaway?" Laura bit ferociously into a bread stick.

"I doubt it. He is not the kind of man who takes vacations. He is not the kind of man who does a lot of things that are normal. This man is bad news. I've got to stop myself before it gets too late."

"Maceo Sloan is just like any other Negro man. Talks a tough game to avoid commitment. This man is yours if you want him. I know what I'm talking about. Even if I'm fat." Laura took a sip of her wine.

"I don't think I'm willing to go through any changes to get him though. I might be out of my league on this one."

Laura would not be detoured from her mission. She leaned her elbows on the table and moved closer towards Gail. This usually meant some juicy gossip.

"Ted says Maceo is a millionaire. Liquid money, honey. Not just in holdings or assets. I mean hard cold cash. He built a fabulous home ... excuse me—estate—about 30 miles from here. I thought maybe we could drive by there. What you think?"

Even though Gail was curious, she would not behave like a tack head. "I think you're crazy. I am not going out there snooping around some man's home. Anyway, you don't really know where the house is. Do you?"

"Yep. I know where it is. Never seen it, but I know how to get there. Ted's seen it and described it to a tee. You know how he is for detail. C'mon, Gail. I'm dying to see it. We'll just drive by and keep on going."

Gail thought, what was the worse that could happen? He could see them, "What if he sees us? I would be so embarrassed." She shook her head.

Laura had a ready answer, "The house has some kind of fence and a security gate and sits off the main road so he'd have to be in the middle of the road to see us. Girl, go look at your investment. This is your future."

Laura was chomping on her salad and french bread. Gail loved her best friend, but sometimes she wished she would take her weight problem more seriously. The idea of driving out to Maceo's house had taken her appetite. She was picking at her salad and giving Laura's suggestion some thought. After all, he knew where she lived and he had been to her house.

However, she had invited him. There was a big difference. "I don't know Laura. It seems kind of childish."

"I'm driving and I want to go and since you're riding with me, you have no choice. I need some more wine. Waiter! Hurry up, girl. I want to get out there before it gets dark. We can order dessert to go."

During the entire drive, Gail kept trying to convince Laura to turn around, but her dearest friend was not having it. She was determined to peek at the private world of Maceo Sloan, even if it meant doing so through a security fence. It was in the rural section of the county and the landscape was dotted with sprawling homes each on several acres. It was peaceful and beautiful. Gail felt as though she was intruding and that at any moment, they were going to be stopped for trespassing.

"Ted said it was on this main road and was the only one with a brick and wrought iron fence. I think that's it up ahead. Damn! Girl this is bad!" Laura was slowing down and looking to the passenger's side of the road. The house seemed to sneak up on them, and then devour them.

The two-story Tudor was at least 10,000 square feet and before Gail could say she doubted if this was the house, she saw the black Range Rover parked near the back of the house. It was then she noticed a Lexus parked at the front door, right behind a convertible BMW.

"Looks like he's got company." Laura was still creeping past the house. Then it happened. The garage door opened and two large German shepherds ran towards the front of the house, heading straight to the fence barking at Laura's car. Then Gail saw her.

A woman wearing white shorts came out of the house, yelling to the dogs. She was tall and thin with a ponytail.

Gail's heart was beating a mile a minute. "That must be his daughter," she whispered and she hoped, "Drive faster Laura, go! This is crazy!"

Laura speeded up a little, but not before Maceo came out with another woman. This one was shorter, with short hair and she had her arms wrapped around his waist.

"How many daughters does he have?" Laura whispered, and then she accelerated. She realized this might have been a mistake.

Gail answered, "He has one. At least that's what he said. Well like my Mama always said, you go looking for trouble, you're sure to find it. Let's get out of here." They drove back to Gail's in total silence.

Laura was trying to think of something positive to say and Gail was trying to sort out how she really felt about Maceo.

Gail spoke first, "It was just a date anyway. I mean we are both adults and have other lives. It's not like we made a commitment to each other. Well at least now I know this man is full of shit."

They were pulling into Gail's driveway and Laura tried to ease her best friend's mind, "It was my fault. I shouldn't have gone out there. But you know she could be a friend of his daughters, or even a relative." Laura put the car in park.

"When was the last time you hugged a relative like that? I'm okay. Better to find out now than later. I wonder which car was hers. I bet he bought it, too. When will I learn to just look for a plain and simple man?"

"Because you are not a plain and simple woman and you deserve more. What are you going to do now?" Laura asked.

"Well, I'm going inside and take a long hot bath and then watch a movie." Gail lied. She was going to call Larry Coleman and throw herself at him. Tonight she needed to be held, made love to and even lied to.

Larry was a master at all three.

§§§§§§§§§§§§§§§§§§§§§§§§§§§

Larry's tongue was circling Gail's navel and two weeks ago, that simple little feat would have brought her to an indescribable level of ecstasy. Tonight, her mind was wandering to the woman holding on to Maceo Sloan's waist.

Larry was a good looking man and he knew it. He stood up, towering over her in her bed. He was stark naked, fully aroused and wanted some attention. He positioned his torso to the side of her face and was about to move over her into the bed, when Gail turned her head.

"What's wrong with you? Need something special tonight?" he smiled.

Larry bent down, went back to her navel, and then lower. This time Gail crossed her thighs and sighed.

"This is a mistake Larry. I can't do this."

"You can't do this? Baby you love this. You called me. So now you've made a mistake? Well, don't let me waste my time. I got other things I could be doing." He got up and switched on the bedside lamp.

"You mean other women you could be doing," Gail sat up and searched the room for her clothes while Larry looked for his. They kept picking up each other's articles of clothing by mistake, adding to the frustration.

"What is with you tonight? You know the deal on me, Gail. You always have. I treat you good, help you out financially when you need it and don't hassle you."

"I thought you were getting married. What's going on with that?" Gail didn't really want to know, but she could guess he was getting cold feet.

"Some technical difficulties. We have a few matters to sort through first, and then it's on." He was pulling on his jeans.

Gail enjoyed looking at Larry clothed just as much as when he was naked. Narrow waist, six pack abs, just a wisp of chest hair and large muscular thighs that filled every inch of his jeans.

"Hey, let's go get something to eat and just talk. I really need to talk to someone tonight." She tugged at his arm.

"You could have said that two hours ago." He gave her nose a playful tug.

"If I had, you wouldn't have come over." She smiled.

"Yeah, you right there. You want to talk? Call Laura. She's the talkingest woman I know." He was pulling on his shirt.

"I need a man's perspective. And I need honesty. Come on. I'll even treat. I know you're hungry. You're always hungry. There's a pancake house around the corner." She knew he loved pancakes.

Tucking his shirt into his jeans, Larry paused, looked at his watch and shrugged his shoulder. "Am I supposed to be advising you on how to get some other man?" He gave her a suspicious glance.

"Kind of. What I really need is some friendly advice. I need some truth in the way only you can give it." She gave him a peck on the cheek.

Gail and Larry were enjoying the pancakes, sausage, bacon, eggs and the small talk, when finally Larry got to the point.

"So who is he?" He asked between bites.

"I don't know if I should call names. That's not really important anyway. I have to make a decision on whether to actually compete for a man. I usually give up without a fight." Gail took a large swallow of orange juice.

Larry was giving her every word deep thought. He liked being thought of as an expert on love.

"Well, first of all, does he really want you or some other woman? Has he committed or is he confused?" he stabbed his fork into a stack of the pancakes.

"He doesn't believe in commitments. At least that's what he says. He believes in personal understandings." She answered.

"He must be an old guy, huh? Sounds like one." Larry stopped chewing and waited for Gail to answer.

"Not too old. Larry, what makes a successful man want a woman? A man who could have any woman he wants. What makes him select one woman over another?"

"So he's old and got money? Hmm, let's see. If I were rich, not too old and could have any woman I wanted, I would go for a very pretty, smart, independent woman. Why? Because, if she's smart, then I don't have to worry about what kind of mother or wife she'd make. I mean, do I want our kids to be able to read and write. Plus, in public she won't embarrass me. If she's independent, then I know she'll want to make her own money. So if things go sour, she can survive. And pretty. Well that speaks for itself."

Larry looked at his watch and was growing impatient in his newfound counseling duties. It was close to eleven o'clock and this evening had not panned out as he thought it would.

"Do I fit that description? Any of them? We can go in a few minutes."

"Yeah, you do. You're smart, very independent and good looking in a different kind of way. Shouldn't have cut your hair though." Larry ducked the napkin Gail threw at him just as his cell phone started to ring.

With a devilish grin, he put his finger to his lips to shush Gail as he started to talk, "Hey, baby girl, what's up? You sound sad."

Glancing at his watch, he motioned for the waitress to bring their check as he continued making plans for an obvious rendezvous, "I can be there in about 20 minutes. You know I can't say no to you. You my baby. I'll always be there for my Hersey Kiss, okay?"

Gail suddenly felt embarrassed by listening in on a conversation that sounded familiar. She wondered had she sounded so desperate when she called Larry and if any other women were allowed to witness his whore time dialog with her.

"Listen, forget about him. He's an ass hole and that's all there is to that. Just meet me at our place in 20 minutes. Bye." He clicked off the call and smiled at Gail, "What can I say? I'm in demand tonight. Thanks for the pancakes, for the company and the conversation, but I gotta bust a move." He tossed the money for the food on the table for the waitress.

"Just how many women are you seeing?" Gail asked.

"You really don't want to know the answer to that." Larry stood up and stretched. Even the waitress coming back to give him his change paused to admire how his jeans hugged his rear end.

Gail defiantly answered, "Yeah, I do. I can handle it, cause I am not going to be one of them anymore."

"Now you about to make me late, but I'll take a few minutes to drop some knowledge on ya. Look, I never promise any woman anything I can't deliver. You are one of my favorites, cause you real grown, you know? I mean, you been through some things and not looking for some perfect man to sweep you away. Now the honey on the phone just now? She's looking for a perfect situation. Ain't gonna happen. At least with me it ain't. So she gets married and is going through hell. I'm Doctor Feelgood. That's all. I stroke, pet, kiss, lick, hug, whatever it takes to make her feel good again. Then she's off to be abused again until she can't take it anymore, and then ring-a-ding-ding and I save the day." With a swift kiss to Gail's cheek and a wink, he swaggered out the restaurant.

§§§§§§§§§§§§§§§§§§§§

Gail forced herself to get up in time for church and she was glad she did. The service was uplifting and the choir was better than ever. She even allowed herself to shed a few tears during the minister's plea to unsaved sinners who were searching for a church home. Gail had been a member of the church since her wedding. She actually joined the church in order to get the sanctuary for a minimal wedding fee, something she became ashamed of later on, after her marriage broke up. God does work in mysterious ways.

It was a small congregation by modern standards. While many of the black churches were spending millions of dollars on huge buildings, Mt. Pleasant Baptist Church was still frugal, opting for more community focused projects instead of striving to be the biggest church in the city. It had held its own and remained one of the most respected churches, with the best-run summer enrichment jobs program for teenagers.

Gail said her hellos and gave her Sunday best hugs before buying a church dinner and heading for home. There was another good thing about the service. She discovered she had not thought about Maceo Sloan at all in the past two hours.

Walking into her bedroom, she tossed her purse and hat on the bed. She noticed the phone's red message light blinking. Two messages.

"Gail, it's Laura. I guess you went to church. Well call me when you get in. I feel like a movie … maybe that new Eddie Murphy film. I could use a good laugh. See ya." Laura sounded different. No jokes? No punch lines? Not the usual Laura.

"Hi Gail, it's Maceo. Happy Sunday. If you're free later on this evening, I'd love to come by and maybe do an early dinner … or whatever sounds good to you. Oh I know. There's a new jazz club out at the lake. I hear it's pretty good. Call me when you get in. Bye."

Gail was unzipping her skirt and stopped in her tracks. She wasn't sure if she could see Maceo after what she and Laura had witnessed only 24 hours earlier. She picked up the phone and called Laura.

"Hey, why are you sounding so sad on the machine?" Gail asked.

"Oh, it's a long story. What you doing? How was church?" Laura was definitely in a funk.

"Church was great. You should have come. I'm just getting in and I have two invitations for this evening. One is from you and the other is from Maceo." Gail cradled the phone on her shoulder as she struggled to peel her pantyhose off.

"You are lying! What did he say about yesterday?" Laura's disposition improved immediately.

Gail could hear her smacking on something, "What are you eating? That is the rudest thing to do, smack in someone's ear!"

"Sorry. You know your life is like a movie to me. I always need a snack for the play-by-play. Anyway, who was that woman?"

Laura resealed the large bag of potato chips and reluctantly put them in the kitchen pantry. Out of sight, out of mind. *Yeah right*, she thought.

"I haven't called him back yet and when I do I will not ask about any woman. Who am I kidding? I don't think I'm ready for this yet. I know I can't see this man without asking who she was. And then he'll know that me and my goofy girlfriend drove out to his house like a couple of 15 year olds." Gail was looking in her closet for something to wear to a jazz club. Just in case.

"Well, I would call him back and see him. Just play it cool. Let him do all the talking and keep baiting him. You know men are so predictable. I'll bet in less than an hour you'll know the whole story." Laura picked up an apple, smelled it and put it back in the fruit bowl.

"Are you sure you don't mind not going to the movie?" Gail started feeling guilty. She could tell Laura was really different today.

"Naw. Go on. I just bought a new Terry McMillan book I haven't started on yet, so I'll just relax and do a little reading."

"Where's Ted?"

"Where he is every Sunday. Curled up on the couch with the sports pages, waiting for the first baseball, football, basketball, hockey or whatever in the hell season it is, game to come on."

Laura loved Gail like a sister, but she still couldn't tell her the truth. Ted had not come home last night and it wasn't the first time. She had to decide if it she would continue to live a lie and risk losing the best thing that had ever happened to her, or if she was going to finally meet his demands.

She hung up the phone and opened the refrigerator, searching for the last half of a lemon meringue pie that she had started on the night before.

§§§§§§§§§§§§§§§§§§§§§

Gail called Maceo and agreed to go to the jazz club with him. She was as nervous as a teenager on prom night. Gail tried on seven outfits, drank half a bottle of merlot and tried on another three dresses.

She finally settled on one that made her look thin and not too preoccupied with trying to dress up. The simple black spaghetti strap sundress had tiny pearl buttons all the way from the v-neckline to the hem, which hit her ankles. She unbuttoned the bottom of the dress to open just above her knees. The thin fabric moved like a willowy dandelion on a windy day and was just transparent enough for a hint of a silhouette of her figure.

Slipping on a pair of black high heel sandals, Gail gave herself one final look over before the doorbell rang. Gail walked towards the front door and made herself slow down and count to 10. Maceo rang the bell again at the count of five. Wiping her sweaty palms on the skirt of her dress, Gail opened the door on 10.

"Hey, sorry, I was just finishing getting dressed. Come in."

He slowly pulled off his sunglasses as though he was seeing her for the first time and liked what he saw. He stepped into the house and gently bent down and kissed her on the cheek. His wonderful aroma surrounded the both of them. Wearing brown casual slacks and a matching knit cotton, short sleeved shirt, Maceo looked older and a little heavier compared to when he wore jeans. Gail liked the look.

"You look incredible. Pardon me if I stare, but I really can't help myself." He touched the side of Gail's cheek with his finger, drawing an imaginary line from her cheekbone to her chin.

Gail tipped her face so that it filled the palm of his hand. Taking the hint, Maceo pulled her closer and never taking his eyes off her, kissed her mouth. "I've missed you," he whispered.

Even though her legs were weak as water, Gail couldn't fight the demon inside her head screaming for her to ask him about that woman. Gail was telling the demon to shut up, not to make her lose another man because of jealousy and immaturity. The demon was yelling back for her not to be a fool. Again. Stand her ground, get some things straight out in the open. The demon won.

Pulling free from Maceo, Gail gave him a serious glare. "When did you find the time to miss me?"

"What do you mean?" He frowned, examining her expression, searching for a clue.

"I think you know what I mean. I take it your other personal understanding left town and now you have a little free time." Gail felt a momentary victory.

"I'm assuming you've got something to say, which is really confusing to me, 'cause you're obviously pissed off, yet you got dressed up to go out with me. So are we going out or are you going to stay here and fight?" He almost seemed amused, which only upset Gail more. Now she knew she was about to make a fool of herself and he knew the same thing.

Gail decided to cut bait and get the hell out of the boat, "I can't do this. I cannot be one of your women. I deserve more and I expect more. I am too old to have to play a chess game with any man. Me today, some other woman the next day. But you were honest. You told me the rules. I just can't play the game. Sorry, I guess we're not going out."

"You are not one of my women. In case you are wondering, when I decide to take a woman as my lover, or confidant, we discuss it. It is a mutual understanding. I don't believe you and I have slept together, nor have we discussed it. I thought we were friends. Was I mistaken?"

Gail felt the floor slipping from under her feet. Was he saying he didn't even want her? Stammering, she found her voice. "No, that was no mistake. I was wrong ... but ..."

"So what do you want to know? Am I seeing someone? Yes. Is it serious? No. In fact, I haven't seen her for three weeks. About the same time I was admitted to the hospital."

"Ha! Three weeks, huh? I guess I lapsed into a coma and three weeks was this weekend," Gail started walking towards the kitchen. All of sudden she was unbearably thirsty.

"This is not funny anymore, Gail. What in the hell are you talking about?" Suddenly, Maceo's face relaxed into a complete grin, "Okay, wait a minute, this weekend?" He was stroking his chin as if in deep thought.

Gail was pouring herself a glass of Coke. She never responded.

"That was my daughter and my ex-wife. We went to dinner and they left Saturday evening going back to Atlanta. My daughter had convinced her mother to buy her a new car, which was a joke since I paid for it. They drove up here for me see it. A little BMW. So I don't know who saw us and felt the need to report back to you, or why they felt the need to tell you who I'm seen with at all, but when you rely on hearsay, you only get half of the story. Look, I'm starving, so are we going or not?" He sounded like the matter was resolved.

Gail wanted to ask him which one was his daughter, but she couldn't without giving away the fact she had been spying on him.

"You know, you remind me a lot of my daughter. She just cut her hair short like yours and she looks more mature than her mother, who insists on wearing clothes that are too tight and too short, but keeps her hair long. Contrary to popular belief about black men, long hair does not turn me on." His eyes twinkled.

For a brief moment, Gail had a sinking feeling that Maceo knew. He knew she was spying on him. She was going to kill Laura. It was time to end this conversation before she lost her advantage.

"Sure, let's go to the club. I 'm curious to see what it's like." Gail grabbed her purse and keys.

"What? No more questions? No more accusations? I'm disappointed. Come on, this is your last chance, because after tonight, the only conversation you and I will be having will be on a much more intimate basis."

Gail spun around to look at him. "Intimate? What does that mean?"

"You really didn't hear a word I said did you?" he laughed. "You are not my woman, Gail, but I want you to be. We'll talk on our way to dinner. Let's go." He grabbed her hand and walked her to his car. It was the Lexus she had seen in the driveway.

"Just like that? You make it sound like a business deal. There isn't a romantic bone in your body is there?" Gail put on her seat belt as Maceo started the car.

"I know more about business than romance. That's why we would make such a good couple. You'd help me and I'd help you."

She was getting ready to tell him that she didn't own a business and really didn't plan on doing any business with him when he leaned over and kissed her.

"Did I do that right? Was it romantic enough?" His voice was deep and sent shivers through Gail's body.

"You could stand some work and I don't mean at the office," she whispered back.

"I work at home, too, you know." He gave her a sly smile as he put the car in reverse.

Gail didn't know what she was in for. All she knew was at this moment, she was in.

The jazz club was a real treat from the usual clubs in Birmingham. The club located on a recreational lake was surrounded by palatial homes and the early beginnings of commercial development.

The trio on the small stage filled the air with a wide range of jazz classics, like Billie Holliday, Duke Ellington and some more contemporary numbers by Al Jarreau. The audience was middle aged and older. The atmosphere was hypnotic with the club bathed in a deep orange glow from the sun setting over the lake. The service was excellent and the food impeccable.

Gail and Maceo ate and appreciated the band. Maceo would occasionally reach over to squeeze Gail's hand. By the time their strawberry sorbet arrived, Gail and Maceo had finished two bottles of wine and she was leaning onto his shoulder, his arm wrapped around her waist.

Gail realized that she was nearly drunk and tried desperately not to seem too anxious. Gail was quiet as they started back to her house.

Maceo broke the silence. "When I'm with you, I feel like I'm on my first date. I want to do everything right. I'm nervous and excited."

"I kind of feel the same way. You are so different from any man I've known. I don't know why you want …" Gail stopped herself from revealing a deep insecurity about Maceo wanting to be with her.

"Why I want to be with you? I hope you weren't going to ask me that. I don't know what kind of men you are used to, but they were damn fools to let you get away, and lady, I'm no fool."

Gail and Maceo drove the rest of the way in silence, letting the soft jazz music on the radio do all the talking. For the first time, Gail wasn't preoccupied with worrying about setting the mood at her home, or if she was wearing sexy underwear. In fact, she was wearing a pair of plain black cotton hi-cut briefs and no bra.

She was not going to set any romantic traps or play any games. Tonight she decided to try being a real woman with a real man.

As she unlocked her front door, Maceo kissed her on the back of her neck.

"I wish I could pick you up and carry you inside, but to tell you the truth, I overdid the wine tonight," he whispered.

"Save your strength," Gail whispered back and wrapped her arms around his neck, gave him a sensuous kiss and locked the door behind him.

Maceo and Gail did a blind walk towards her bedroom, kissing and stumbling all the way along the hall. Undressing as they took several steps, they only paused long enough for him to slip off his shoes and socks. Gail simply kicked her high heels across the room.

Slipping her dress from her shoulders, Gail let the material fall to the floor. The dimly lit room cast a romantic shadow on her body and Maceo inhaled deeply as he touched her bare breasts.

"Oh, God. You are so gorgeous." Caressing her buttocks and pulling her close to him, he gently kissed her shoulders, her arms, her breasts and her stomach.

Gail slowly massaged his shoulders as he kneeled before her, kissing her thighs, her knees and calves. "Come down here with me, I want you on the floor first." Maceo murmured.

Gail quietly obeyed, hugging him tightly, as she pulled him on top of her and wrapped her legs around his waist.

He took his time, touching her and kissing her until she thought she would explode. Inserting his fingers to test her readiness, he played with her until she begged him for something more.

Gail hadn't noticed him putting on a condom. When did he manage that?

"I know, it's not the best feeling in the world, but it's a habit I can't break right now. If you want me to stop, I will." Maceo had stopped moving inside of her and was looking intently at her face, trying to read her signals.

"No, it's okay. You're right, I just wasn't expecting it. I know I should. After all, I am a nurse." She lifted herself up, to meet him and signal that she wanted to continue.

"It won't always be like this. I do want to feel all of you." He kept moving slowly, then faster.

Gail started to relax, as she met his tempo. His body was harder than she had imagined. His shoulders wider that his tailored shirts revealed and his chest had lots of gray hair. She liked what she saw and what she felt.

Managing to catch her breath between their rhythmic lovemaking, Gail said, "I hope you brought more than one … a whole lot more."

"Don't worry about that … Come with me … Come with me now." He begged. She did.

At some point during the night, Maceo had managed to pick Gail up from the floor and place her across the bed. She woke up with her head lying on his chest, his arm draped around her shoulders. She was extremely thirsty and the room seemed to be slowly rocking back and forth.

Clearing her throat, she gently tapped Maceo on the arm, "Hey, you want some water?"

"Nope, you got a Sprite or Coke?" he pulled her closer.

"I finished the last Coke. I've got Kool-Aid."

"Strawberry?" he smiled with his eyes still closed.

"I've got kids. Of course, I've got strawberry. I'll be right back." Gail untangled her legs and arms from his body and started into the kitchen stark naked.

"I want a large glass. In fact, bring the whole pitcher." He shouted after her.

Maceo thought to himself, he couldn't remember the last time he had Kool-Aid. He had been a caffeine man for a long time. Maybe it was time for him to go back to all the simple things he really liked. The basic things, real things. He got up and turned on Gail's nightstand lamp. Looking around her bedroom, he could tell she was unpretentious. The room was neat, but not obsessively clean. He walked to her dresser and picked up some of her jewelry. She obviously loved silver and he would store that in his memory for future use.

He could hear Gail wrestling with ice cubes in the kitchen.

"Maceo! Are you hungry? I've got some cheese, crackers, grapes and pate." She yelled from the kitchen.

"Do I look like I'm on a diet to you? I need some meat. You got any bologna? Ham? Wieners?" He flopped back on the bed and covered his naked body with the sheet.

Gail walked into the bedroom carrying a tray with a pitcher of strawberry Kool-Aid, two champagne flutes, a plate of bologna, crackers, grapes and a large plastic cup.

"I thought we could toast with the champagne flutes and then you can gulp your Kool-Aid in this cup." She carefully positioned the tray on the bed and Maceo moved over to make room.

"Sorry, I have no class. Great! Bologna." He bit into a slice of the meat and lifted his large plastic cup to toast with Gail's champagne flute.

"You know, most times when you grow up on a certain type of food, you start to hate it as an adult, but I still love bologna. My Mama used to buy that large tube of bologna and have it sliced. We had bologna everyday. Morning, noon and night and in between. I still love it today."

"You're a smart man, Mr. Sloan. You never forgot your roots," Gail started to giggle after imagining herself sitting in bed naked, with a naked handsome man, eating bologna and drinking Kool-Aid.

"This whole scene is almost unbelievable. I mean you eat at some of the best restaurants in the world and here you are in bed with me, eating bologna and drinking Kool-Aid. No one would believe this."

"You're right. No one would ... except for my Mama." He laughed and then pulled her head closer so that he could kiss her. The simple kiss reignited a fire in both of them and Maceo moved the snack tray to the nightstand.

Chapter 7

Evelyn

E velyn stayed in the master bedroom all day Sunday. She could hear Kevin moving around the house, making more noise than necessary. She didn't even leave her room to eat, substituting drinking water from the bathroom basin instead. She was surprised that hunger pains didn't force her to raid the kitchen, but apparently, anger is more powerful than hunger.

On Monday morning, she heard Kevin leave the guest room, slamming the door as he left. She considered calling in sick, then remembered she had to help take inventory for a major sales event scheduled for the next weekend. Pulling her hair into a ponytail and slipping on a casual pair of navy cotton slacks with a ruffled white blouse, Evelyn headed to the boutique, sans make-up.

Two of the part-time clerks, along with the store's manager, were already re-tagging and separating the merchandise.

"Good morning," Evelyn mumbled. She put her purse in the storage room and picked up a clipboard with merchandise assignments on it. The two sales clerks cast a quick glance at her from head to toe.

They had never seen her looking so plain. In fact, she had been the example they followed for looking chic. The store manager, Grace, eased to Evelyn's side and whispered.

"Are you feeling okay?"

"I'm just a little tired. That's all." Evelyn avoided her eyes.

"We can handle this if you need to go back home. But, on second thought, today wouldn't be a good day to be absent. I'm expecting a call from Houston today," Grace said as she walked away.

Houston was where the store's owner lived and he was looking to sell off a few of his stores. The Birmingham location was not doing the quota he expected.

Evelyn had already been thinking about making the owner an offer of buying the store. It would mean that she could possibly get a better deal since he was trying to cut his losses. She never told anyone except her father that she was considering such a move.

Everytime she tried to ask Kevin about it, he would change the subject. This time she would make the decision on her own, whether he approved or not. The inventory work went swiftly and the staff was just finishing rearranging the last sales rack when the phone rang.

Grace took the call and as she always did when she was nervous, she placed her hand on her stomach as though she was trying to ease a pain. Evelyn walked towards the counter and could hear Grace's side of the conversation.

"Well, I can certainly understand that Mr. Hooks and I appreciate you offering to take care of us. I don't know what my immediate plans are. So if we've got 60 days, I'll let you know something ahead of time … Sure, she's right here." Grace handed Evelyn the phone.

"Mr. Hooks, hello. Well I guess this means, you are selling the shop, huh?"

She could visualize Tank Hooks, pulling on one of his famous cigars, shuffling papers behind his massive desk, before he answered in a raspy voice.

"Evelyn, my dear, that's just how business goes sometimes. I wanted to let you know how much I appreciated your loyalty and dedication while you worked as my assistant manager and that I will make sure you and the others are taken care of. I'll make some calls and make sure you get good offers at some other locations."

"Well actually, Mr. Hooks, I do have some plans of my own. I would like to discuss with you the chances of buying this store. I've been wanting to own a shop like this since I was a teenager."

Hooks hesitated, coughed, cleared his throat and then spoke, "Well that's a mighty serious thought to have Evelyn.

"Going into business takes a lot of money and hard work. I'd hate to see you and your husband taking such a risk without looking at all the options. I know you've been working for me since you were in college, but I've got to be honest with you, working it and owning it are totally different. It ain't easy."

"Mr. Hooks, I imagine it is different. I imagine that owning it is a whole lot better. That's why you are where you are today. Oh and it's just me, not my husband who wants to buy this place."

Evelyn turned her body to guard from Grace's prying ears. Grace was pretending to fold articles that were already folded as she tilted her head towards Evelyn.

Hooks cleared his throat again. "Now dear, you have been the best assistant manager and buyer I've ever had. Hell, you were the one who warned me that the new mall with Macy's in it was going to create some serious competition for us. I want everyone to get in life what they want. If you want to talk serious, I'm a businessman, and hell, I need to unload the place. So let's talk on tomorrow. I can tell you now that I'm looking at nothing less than $800,000.00 and that's pretty good for just the building itself."

Hooks puffed on his cigar waiting for Evelyn's reaction.

She knew right away that she was out of her league, and ill prepared to haggle with such an old horse over a business deal.

Damn! She wished Kevin were with her on this. He would know just what to do. Grace was looking right in her mouth and Evelyn developed a sudden blinding headache.

"Well, I sort of thought that since I had worked for you for so long, that we could make arrangements that could help both of us." Evelyn said as she massaged her temples.

"Well, honey, this ain't like borrowing a cup of sugar from the neighbor. This is high finance. You think about what you want to do, and get back with me. I don't foresee making a decision before the next 30 days anyway. I gotta go now. Take care."

Hooks hung up the phone, crushed his cigar, and spoke to his empty office. "Damn women. And especially these young black ones. Trying to take over every damn thing. Well that should cool her little heels for a while."

Evelyn hung up the phone and looked at Grace. She thought to herself, D*amn white folks.* They think you good enough to work for them, but not good enough to supervise them or control your own destiny.

Grace flipped her blonde bangs out of her eyes, "Did I hear you right? You thinking about buying this place? Where did you get that kind of money?"

"Don't worry, Grace. I'll give you a job." Evelyn pushed past her and went to get her purse. Being rude was never in Evelyn's DNA, but she was so confused, scared and frustrated, the meanness came with very little effort. Right now she wanted to go home, her real home, her Mamas' and Daddys' house.

Half and hour later, Evelyn pulled her red Miata into her parents driveway and saw one of the curtains in the front of the house flutter open. Minutes later Mama Ree came to the front door.

"Hi Suga. I thought you were at work." Mama Ree had an apron full of red ripe garden fresh tomatoes. She was into her summer ritual of canning tomatoes, getting ready for the winter, when she would make the best homemade soup and sauces.

"I got off early. Mama and Daddy home yet?" Evelyn didn't want to let her Grandmother know something was troubling her and she would have to work real hard to disguise her troubles from her namesake.

Mama Ree was looking at Evelyn. Actually, she was looking through Evelyn, right through her designer sunglasses, straight into the large emotional eyes of her granddaughter that she knew so well.

"Something wrong? Why you looking so down?" Mama Ree touched Evelyn's cheek.

"I just need to talk to Mama and Daddy that's all." Evelyn kissed her grandmother's hand and brushed past her into the house.

"Well, your Daddy in the den, taking a nap. Patty called and was stopping by the new mall. So God knows what time she'll be back. I guess I'll just go and finish my canning." Mama Ree mumbled, obviously offended at being kept out of Evelyn's business.

Walking into the den, passing the dozens of high school, prom and graduation pictures on the wall, Evelyn started missing her family.

Missing the way the house smelled like biscuits, cornbread, spices and life. Her father was sprawled in his favorite recliner, the television remote on his stomach, his mouth slightly open, enjoying a deep sleep. She hated to wake him, but maybe it was best to talk to him before her mother got home.

Whispering and gently shaking his arm, Evelyn leaned towards her father, "Daddy, you asleep? Daddy?"

Her father jumped and focused his eyes. Then he smiled. Evelyn had his dark brown complexion, and she had his eyes; large and soulful. Eyes that showed emotion, compassion and love.

"Daddy why aren't you wearing your glasses? We spent two hours in the mall last month to get those glasses." Evelyn looked around the room for his glasses.

"Oh, those thangs just give me a headache. Once I squint a little, I can see pretty good. What you doing over here? Looking for your Mama?" He started flicking the television remote.

"Daddy, I need some help and some advice."

"Is this about Kevin?" He said his name as though it left a bitter taste in his mouth. He had never liked his son-in-law.

"No, Daddy. Remember I told you that Mr. Hooks is selling the store? We spoke today, and I told him I want to buy it. I think I can make it work. I've been studying and working real hard on this business plan and I know I can do this." She sat on the ottoman at his feet.

"Well. What you want me to do?" He shut off the television and turned to look at his daughter with overwhelming pride.

"I might need to borrow some money. A lot of money. I might have to get you and Mama to co-sign. Kevin will never agree to help me on this."

"I ain't surprised at that. That selfish bastard ain't for helping no one but self. You can forget about Pat helping, too. She 'bout as crazy as he is. How much help do you need? You think I would let you take on that kind of debt by yourself?"

"But Daddy, Mr. Hooks is talking about at least $800,000. I figure I can offer him $250,000 and let him finance the rest …"

"Hold it right there baby. First thing you got to learn in business, is never expect no favors, especially if white folks involved. I can let you have about $75,000.00 and then we'll just go to the bank and start seeing what we can do."

Evelyn couldn't believe her ears. Where did her father get $75,000.00?

"I've got $20,000 in my mutual fund account, but Daddy, even with close to $100,000. We've still got a long way to go. And where did you get $75,000?"

Her father sat up straight and spoke to her without hesitation, "Baby girl, I been working since I was nine years old and saving since I was 15. I was going to surprise Pat for our anniversary and look at buying another house, but you know, I kinda like this house. I'd rather see my daughter with her own business. I wish I was smart enough to own a business instead of working like a slave for almost 40 years. I won't complain. Danny Taylor has been good to me these past years, and he pays me good money as the shop manager. Nobody else would have done that for someone who didn't even finish high school. He set up the whole crew with one of those 401K plans."

"A 401K Daddy? That's great. Don't you ever let me hear you say you aren't smart. You're the smartest man I know. You know

Mama will have a stroke if she finds out you're giving me her house money. She might even leave you." Evelyn warned.

Her Daddy's eyes twinkled with mischief, and he leaned in real close to Evelyn, "Let's call her at the mall and tell her now."

Then in the fashion Evelyn was used to, he slapped his thigh and let out a loud laugh. They both laughed uncontrollably for nearly five minutes. Evelyn thought how ironic, that she and her father were making such an important decision without the blessing or knowledge of either of their spouses.

Evelyn refused to break the silence with Kevin. As usual when they had a fight, he would try to start a conversation about some unimportant issue: the weather, sports, where was his blue shirt. Anything to get a reaction from Evelyn. This time she didn't co-operate, in fact, she avoided him totally. She was tired of being his whipping post for whatever was bothering him.

She was eating all of her meals in her bedroom and was locking the bedroom door to prevent him from dropping in. Whenever he needed something from the closet, she would simply place it outside the door.

This had been going on for three days and finally Kevin broke. He was standing outside the master bedroom door pleading with Evelyn to talk to him.

"I've apologized over and over. What do I have to do? Just name it. Anything." He kept turning the doorknob as though if he jiggled it enough it would unlock.

Taking the cue, Evelyn jumped from the bed and opened the door, "I need $100,000 dollars." She gave him a defiant look.

"What? For what?" He was too shocked at the request to be happy to finally have her open the door.

"I want to buy the store. I want to make an offer of $200,000 in cash and get financing for the rest. I've got $100,000 already."

"Where did you get one hundred thousand dollars? And how am I supposed to get $100,000 just like that?" He snapped his finger and gave her his "you must be crazy" expression.

"My Daddy and my savings. You help other people get millions of dollars everyday, so I know you can get a loan for this deal. I'll even accept limited partnerships. Stephanie said Simon would love to do something like ..." Before she could finish, Kevin cut her off.

"Oh, so now you're taking financial advice from Stephanie? The biggest airhead in the south? Great! I am not going to Simon Parker with some half-baked idea. That is not the way we do business at the firm!" He gave her a look of disbelief with a condescending tone.

"Fine. Sorry I bothered you." Evelyn was about to close the door, but Kevin put his foot between the door and the wall blocking her attempt to shut the door in his face.

"Wait a minute. How do you even know the place is worth $800,000? Have you done any due diligence, or homework on this deal? I might be able to get some investors who will buy it out right, and then you can manage it."

"I know what due diligence means Kevin. Yes, I have and no, I don't want to work for someone else. Why can't I own it Kevin? Why do you think that I am so inferior?" Her bottom lip was trembling as she tried to hold back the tears.

"So is this what it takes for us to make up? That's not fair." He gently pushed his way into the bedroom.

"It's not fair the way you treat me. Hot and cold. Up and down. I never know what kind of mood you're going to be in. I don't deserve that." She still held onto the door.

"Wait. I'm sorry. Let's go to dinner and talk about it."

"Are you going to help me with the store or not?" She wouldn't back down.

Realizing she was not going to give in on this one, Kevin agreed to at least examine the deal. He would have agreed to just about anything. Kevin missed his Jacuzzi and having his belongings in his room. He missed not having someone to pay attention to him at home. It was becoming too inconvenient to keep this fight going.

Evelyn reluctantly allowed him to move back into the master bedroom. She was still cautious of his promise and for the first time she realized she didn't trust him. She couldn't trust him to look out for her best interests and they weren't a team. He was only concerned with taking care of his high paying clients and Evelyn felt she was more of a liability than an asset.

She had already made up her mind to visit Stephanie and approach the idea of Simon investing in her idea. Nothing was going to make her change her mind.

As she was mentally going through her business strategy, she kept her back turned to Kevin in bed. He was doing his best to arouse her, but her mind was stuck on how to convince Simon Parker to help her. The trick would be in not allowing the conversation to center around Kevin. She didn't want to make Simon feel uncomfortable, so she would have to rely heavily on Stephanie to soothe any misgivings he might have.

Her train of strategic thinking was slightly broken as Kevin tried to slip her nightgown from her shoulders. She wasn't giving him any assistance and he was starting to get agitated.

"I thought you wanted to make love." He stopped tugging at her nightgown.

"No, I don't and neither do you. You want me to want you. You want to convince me to change my mind. It's not going to happen." She answered without emotion.

"I've missed you, and I do want to make love." He said kissing her shoulder.

"I wish I could believe that. But if you want to, go ahead," Evelyn pushed him away and sat up in bed. With one swift movement, she pulled her gown over her head and tossed it to the floor.

Completely naked, she lay back in bed with her hands behind her head.

Kevin's initial reaction was anger, then disbelief and finally revenge. He quickly mounted her as he would a carnival ride. Without exchanging words or kisses, he started to have sex with her.

Evelyn was surprised he lasted longer than his usual two or three minutes, maybe anger caused a reserve of stamina. She never changed her position, her hands remained tucked behind her head and for the first time, she wished he would hurry and finish.

When he finally exhaled and collapsed on top of her, this time she was the one who rolled out of bed first, and dashed to the shower. It was then that her tears started. She knew it was over. This marriage had no trust, no love and no respect.

After her shower, Evelyn put on a clean nightgown and went into the guest room. Locking the door, her mind returned to talking to Stephanie. She felt good about the decision and she knew it was the right thing to do.

Stephanie was thrilled to have Evelyn call and say she was stopping by for a visit. She and Simon usually entertained for business purposes, but rarely did she have someone drop by just to visit her.

When Evelyn drove up to the massive colonial style house, she was reminded how her mother used to take them for Sunday drives in this neighborhood to look at the huge magnificent homes.

It was where the old money of Birmingham lived. The historical mansions were featured on architectural design television shows, and created an intimidating image to first time visitors. The neighborhood always looked deserted to Evelyn, and now with the heat of the Alabama summer stifling most activity, this afternoon took on that same isolated appearance Evelyn remembered as a child.

Simon's first wife had kept the couples' house a few blocks away, and Stephanie selected this museum style structure immediately after their marriage.

It was by far the largest house in the neighborhood, previously owned by an international investment banker who went under during a federal investigation into junk bonds.

Stephanie wanted to prove to the Birmingham elite that Simon Parker could still afford anything in town, no matter how much it cost, or what his divorce settlement demanded.

The circular drive way seemed to swallow Evelyn's tiny sports car. She walked up the concrete steps and rang the doorbell. A black maid opened the door and showed her in through the receiving hall. Even though the temperature was threatening 98 degrees, the Italian marble entry hall with its huge white columns created a cool comfortable environment.

Walking through the gathering room towards the double French doors, which opened to the patio and pool area, Evelyn couldn't understand what two people could do in a house that had

15,000 square feet. She recalled how her mother had reacted the first time Evelyn had brought her over. Evelyn was slightly embarrassed at how Pat wooed and aahed over every table, chair and piece of artwork she passed.

"Evelyn! Come on out here. I'm in the pool." Stephanie yelled as she floated in the pool on an inflatable chaise, "You bring your suit? I've got Bloody Marys. Pour up and suit up." She said.

Evelyn didn't waste time with pleasantries, "No, I came on business today, not pleasure. I need a favor. More like a partner. I want to buy the store and I need some investors to go in with me. I thought maybe you and Simon would be interested." Evelyn poured herself a tall glass of the Bloody Mary mix.

"Uhmm, I don't know. Simons' been pretty stressed out lately. He might not want to do anything independent right now. I mean, we're not having any money trouble or anything, it's just we own half of Alabama now. What can one more little store do for us?" Stephanie took off her sunglasses and waited for Evelyn to answer.

"Then how about financing me? You know I'll work hard to make it a success, plus my father is in with me. If Simon can get me $100,000 then I'm in."

"What does Kevin say about all of this?"

"This is about me. Kevin is not involved. "

"You know Simon is going to talk to him don't you?" Stephanie warned.

"I have to take care of myself." Evelyn snapped.

"You don't have to get so snippy! What are you talking about? Take care of yourself? You have a husband who is supposed to do that! Stop being so independent! It's not attractive."

"I have no choice Stephanie. Kevin and I are over. We have no marriage. It's just a big lie. He doesn't love me and I don't love him." Evelyn sat back in a reclining patio chair and took a long sip of her drink. She had finally said it out loud.

"I don't believe this! You are letting this gorgeous, successful man get away? You are way too smart for something so small to make you give up on a gold mine. Honey, re-think your options." She floated to the edge of the pool closer to Evelyn.

"I have. My mind is made up." Evelyn fought back tears.

"So what? You had a fight! Get over it. Go buy yourself something expensive and make him pay for it. Some situations are worth living through. I got a secret for you. I love Simon. I love what he can do for me, just like he loves what I do for him. He takes care of me, I don't have to worry about anything, and I make him feel good. I make him look good. Let's face it, Simon is 30 years older than I am. There are some things that he cannot do, but do you think I'm going to throw away the baby with the bath water? I have someone else who satisfies me in bed and I plan on keeping it that way."

Evelyn couldn't believe her ears. Here was a woman who had a rich man who simply adored her and gives her the world, and she was sleeping around on him?

"Stephanie, how could you do that to Simon? Especially when he divorced his wife for you. This man loves you to death. If I had someone like that …" Evelyn's voice trailed off.

"Well if I had someone like Kevin, someone young, virile and strong and who could please me, it would be different. Honey, you know what I'm talking about. You can't tell me Kevin isn't a good lover." She was searching Evelyn's face for a reaction as she climbed out of the pool.

"What do you mean, I know what you're talking about?"

Adjusting her thong bikini, Stephanie leaned in to whisper to Evelyn, "You know what it's like to have a black man and so do

I." She smiled sweetly and stood up to jump into the pool, leaving Evelyn with a glimpse of her naked behind.

Stephanie was giggling in the pool and splashing water on Evelyn. Still in a mild state of shock, Evelyn regained her composure.

"Stef, look, I know you're used to getting what you want, but this is Alabama, and I know no black man in his right mind is fooling around with the wife of the richest white man in this state! So he's got to be crazier than you are. Somebody is going to get killed."

"I'm very careful and you are the only person I've told. And I know he isn't talking. He's smarter than that ... God, Evelyn, I never knew sex could be this good!" She squealed and ducked under the water.

"Stephanie! This is serious. You have to stop this. This town is too small for you to be seeing anyone and if Simon ever heard anything about you and another man, he would go crazy! He would destroy the both of you." Evelyn tossed her a towel as she resurfaced.

"I can't stop it right now. I don't want to. I will when the time is right. It hasn't been going on that long, maybe a month or two. I am so sick of feeling like a Viagra nurse! Simon has to take damn near ten pills to get it up," she was drying her hair with her back to Evelyn.

At that moment, the phone rang and the maid came to the door to announce Stephanie had a phone call. Her expression said it all. It was her lover.

Keeping her back to Evelyn, she picked up the cordless phone. Evelyn overheard her say something about the new Marriott Suites Hotel on Highway 65.

Hanging up the phone, she turned to face her new confidant with a mischievous smile. Evelyn shook her head in disbelief.

"Evelyn, you don't understand. Have you ever tried on a mink coat, no, make that a chinchilla, top of the line, and didn't want to take it off? It felt so good, soft, and rich, you just hugged yourself tighter, determined to take it home? That's how I feel when I'm with him, all good and soft and warm. It's a feeling I'm not ready to give up. Not right now."

"Stephanie, I could understand if you loved this man, but he is not a fur coat or a little puppy. He is a man who has emotions, anger and fears. He can't be put on a shelf. And he's black. Why couldn't you pick a white man to make you feel all warm and fuzzy?" Evelyn had her purse on her shoulder and was getting ready to leave. She could tell a rendezvous was about to take place, and her hostess would be departing soon.

"I didn't plan on this. He was just there. He could be white for all I care. I'm not into that southern belle with a black man thing and you know it. He is just so good looking and sophisticated. And in bed, he makes me feel like a queen, but he also demands that I treat him like a king. I have done things I never thought possible and I like it. I gotta get dressed."

"Stephanie, does he have money? Or is this just lust?"

In her heart, she knew it was a black man/woman fantasy role for Stephanie. Love was not a part of the equation. It was hard to imagine what black man in the Birmingham could compete with Simon Parker's millions. Money equaled love for Stephanie.

Walking over to Evelyn, Stephanie flashed a brilliant sapphire and diamond ring on her right hand, "See this? Simon bought it for me. He can do that. My lover cannot, but it doesn't matter. That's what husbands are for. Lovers take care of the inside, husbands of the outside. Simon knew what he was paying for when he got me. Men with money pay for things they want. I'll talk to him about your store. I guess I have to now, especially since you can blackmail me."

"Don't believe your own p.r. I don't have to blackmail anyone for anything. Forget it. I'll find the money," Evelyn started to walk away.

"Oh, and let me give you some advice Stephanie. You might be used to dealing with men with lots of money, but a broke bastard can be a lot more treacherous than a rich one. A broke man has nothing to lose. Remember that."

§§§§§§§§§§§§§§§§§§§§

Sonja had returned to Birmingham from D.C. and resumed her normal schedule of sleeping late, spending time with her mother and reading. It had been three days, and Danny had not called.

Several times she had picked up the phone to call him, but couldn't go through with it. He owed her an apology and she wouldn't forgive him without it. She had decided that she wouldn't even speak to him without it.

Later in the week, Sonja had a visit from Evelyn, who was looking totally out of character. Her hair was in a ponytail, she had on faded jeans, a tee shirt and no make up. She even looked like she had lost weight.

Sitting in Sonja's breakfast room and staring out of the glass patio doors, Evelyn's obvious depression was enough to force Sonja to say something.

"What in the hell is going on with you?" Sonja took her magazine and slammed it on the table to get her attention.

Evelyn looked at her with expressionless eyes,"I'm a failure. I married the wrong man, I'm at a dead end career, and I don't know how to get myself out of it. If my father helps me with this store and I lose it, that's his entire savings. My mother is totally pissed that he's even considering helping me, Kevin is pissed because I went to his bosses wife, I have made a mess of everything." She quickly wiped a tear from her cheek.

"Don't start that. You are not a failure. If this is something you really want, you have to go for it. There's nothing wrong with that. Although I am a little hurt you asked everybody to invest but me." Sonja handed her a tissue for her face, which was streaked with tears.

"I...I didn't think you'd want to...you just met me and I know you don't like Kevin, and I was trying to keep our friendship..." Evelyn blew her nose.

"I've got an idea. What if we put together a team of investors? Me, Danny, your father, and maybe someone Danny knows. Forget that white man at the law firm. We can do this."

Sonja was getting excited about the idea, plus it gave her a valid excuse to call Danny. She started dialing his garage as Evelyn just sat there looking defeated.

Danny answered the phone in the middle of a conversation that had him laughing. He certainly was in a good mood for someone who had lost the love of his life.

"Hi. It's Sonja. You busy?"

He hesitated as though it was a trick question, "Not really, I was talking to a buddy who had stopped by. Why?"

"Well, Evelyn and I want to talk to you about an investment opportunity. Tonight if possible," she allowed her tone to match his, cold and unfeeling.

"Can you come over now?" he asked, "I'll be busy later on, plus there's someone here now who might want to hear what you've got to say."

Sonja looked at Evelyn from her sandaled feet to her un-combed hair, "Sure, but we need about an hour. We'll see you there."

They both hung up the phone without saying good-bye.

"Go get changed, comb your hair and be ready in 45 minutes, I'll pick you up." Sonja pulled Evelyn from her chair and pushed her towards the door.

Forty- five minutes later they were zooming in Sonja's Porche on the freeway to Danny's garage. Sonja wanted to look like she hadn't missed Danny at all. She wore a tomato red linen dress, with red raw silk pumps and pulled her hair into a french roll.

Even Evelyn had managed to transform to her usually profes-sional style in a baby blue St. John knit dress. Sonja thought Eve-lyn was such a pretty dark skinned woman, it was a shame she married such an asshole. They made a traffic stopping pair as they marched into Danny's office. He was at his desk talking to a man whose back was to the door.

Both men stood up when the ladies entered. Danny seemed caught off guard at the site of Sonja. Regaining his composure, he introduced his guest to them.

"Sonja Davenport, Evelyn Williams, this is a friend and busi-ness associate, Maceo Sloan."

Everyone exchanged handshakes and hellos and took a seat. Maceo Sloan gave Sonja a look loaded with questions. She po-litely ignored him but wondered what had she done to deserve such a reaction.

Sonja looked at Evelyn, who looked at Danny who was look-ing at the both of them with curiosity.

Evelyn cleared her throat and started her sales spill. Danny stopped her after about twenty minutes of rambling chatter. She was obviously nervous and was only confusing her potential investors.

Maceo Sloan kept looking at his watch and patting his foot on the floor. Now even Sonja was nervous.

Getting up from behind his desk and walking to the door, Danny asked his secretary to bring in four cold soft drinks.

He then turned to face Evelyn and shot her a warm smile, "Look, we're all friends here. You and I have known each other since we were kids, Maceo and I have been friends for years, he was one of the first people to help me get this garage financed, and Sonja is like family. Just tell us what you need, and how we can make some money from this dress shop."

Sonja took over from there, "I have been to this place, it's the best women's' boutique in Birmingham and with some marketing, we could easily start pulling business away from the new mall. It's small, but personable and there are a lot of possibilities for growth."

Maceo fired a question, "Yeah, but the clientele was mostly white, right? Now if you're expecting them to remain loyal to a black woman owner, you might be wrong, so we're talking about losing a large percent of your customer base. And let's face it, black folks traditionally do not patronize each other, especially when a mall is the competition. How do you recover from that?" He took a long swig from his Coca Cola.

Evelyn didn't hesitate, "Mail order and online merchandising. I've been trying to get Mr. Hooks to provide mail order catalogs and a dynamic website online shop for over a year. We could even expand nationally and internationally with that. It's very profitable and I know it could work, also we need to establish our very own customer account system, with a credit account system."

Maceo took notice of Evelyn's business savvy and enthusiasm, "So you are the assistant manager? What is the profit margin like?" Maceo was taking notes on a tiny notepad.

"Monthly net averages $250,000. But on those special occasion shopping months, December, May for Mother's Day, and February for Valentines we easily double that." Evelyn was getting excited and scooted her chair closer to Maceo.

"Let's do the basic math. Danny and I can go in equal partners with you at twenty-five percent each...that means we each, all four of us have shared stocks, major management decisions. But you Evelyn, will run the day to operations, including hiring staff, merchandise buying and marketing. I feel certain we can get the bank to finance whatever we need, with Danny and me as partners. You rework the numbers, bring me the final plan tomorrow and we'll take it from there."

Evelyn had the biggest grin on her face that made her look like a little girl on Christmas morning, "Deal! Let's celebrate! Come on, dinner is on me." Evelyn grabbed Sonja's hand.

Maceo was smiling and then begged off, "I wish I could, but I'm just getting in from D.C. the past couple of days, and I need to get home." He looked at Sonja.

"Oh yeah, how was the Prez?" Danny teased.

"His usual. Full of bullshit. I made a few good contacts. I got back yesterday. The best part of the trip was staying at the Willard Hotel, it's my favorite place in that grimy city." He never took his eyes away from Sonja.

Danny was oblivious to Maceo's attention to Sonja. Being the smooth operator she was, Sonja decided to stop the I-Spy games,

"Yes, it's a really nice place. I normally stay there too. Why were you in D. C. Mr. Sloan?" Sonja asked.

"Please, call me Maceo. It was an economic summit. They do this dog and pony show twice a year and invite a cross section of business owners, political leadership and corporate CEO's for a dialog session. Well, it's been nice folks, but I gotta run. Evelyn, we'll meet at my office 8:30 tomorrow morning, sharp. Danny, we'll talk tomorrow too. Wish I could join you tonight, but we'll have plenty of other times to celebrate." Maceo left the room.

Evelyn was jubilant, "I can't believe he said he would finance the balance of the shop. I just can't believe this. Danny I owe you my life!"

"Well when your husband finds out, all of our lives might be in jeopardy. Are you going to be okay with that?" Danny asked.

"I am going to be fine. I've got my two best friends, and my Daddy. What more does a girl need?" Evelyn put her arms around Sonja and Danny and gave them a group hug.

The three went to dinner at the towns' new restaurant and jazz club on the lakefront. Sonja was glad when Evelyn excused herself to go to the ladies room. Looking at Danny, she realized he was ignoring her because she had truly hurt him. He wouldn't look her in the eyes.

"How long are you going to be mad at me?" She leaned in closer to him.

His voice was barely above a whisper, "I am not mad at you. I just realize that we want different things, and I am not what you want. Never have been, now that I look back at how I used to always try to impress you. Always buying the biggest Valentines card in the drug store, always asking you to wear my class ring, my football jacket. And always getting turned down. I got to admit one thing, you were always consistent. You never tried to play me. I wasn't even worth the trouble. So now at nearly 40 years old, I finally get it. We're still friends, but that's all we'll ever be. I gave it my best shot. Sometimes things just aren't meant to be." He finally looked at her and gave her a halfhearted smile.

"What if I told you that this unexpected trip I took is the last one? That it was a good bye visit to a part of my past. What if I told you that I want a different future?" Sonja gently touched Danny's hand.

"Sonja, how long will this good-bye last? Until a new diamond ring or a new fur coat, or another invitation to some island? I can't go around wondering how long it will be until some guy with deep pockets comes along and makes you a better offer. I can't function in a relationship like that."

"It's not like that Danny. There is so much you don't know about me. I went through a lot to get where I am today. I didn't steal, kill, cheat or hurt anybody and that's saying a lot by today's standards. I was lucky that a few people looked out for me. Is that wrong?"

"These few people who looked out for you, were they all men? Never mind. It's your life." He motioned for the waiter to bring another bottle of wine.

"I am not a saint. I never said I was. I made mistakes, but I learned from them. When I first left Birmingham, all I had was the package God gave me. I didn't want to be hungry and poor, so I let my looks get me in the doors I needed to get in."

"Sonja, we all make choices. No one wants to be hungry or poor, but most of us work to avoid that. It's not normal to...." Danny's voice trailed off.

"Not normal to do what? Are you calling me a whore? Is that what you think I am?" Sonja's voice started to tremble with emotion. Not allowing Danny to answer, she quickly leaned in closer to him.

"I am not a whore! I used to dance and men liked what they saw. I danced at the best establishment that probably outranks the Playboy clubs in this country. I made more money in a week than you make in a month. It was up to me if I wanted to form any kind of relationship with any man. I was not forced into doing anything.

"Let me tell you, it beats the hell out of sleeping in a car, and eating french fries for a week from McDonalds because that's all you can afford. I know. I did it. I tried to work like you good Christian folks, and you know what? Every job I got, I had some redneck or low life Negro man trying to put his hand under my dress. So much for working 9 to 5! So I made a decision. If I was going to get propositioned, it had better be for more than minimum wage. That was the decision I made.

"You know what? A real whore gives it away and gets nothing in return. I made a business decision and it paid off and I'm sorry if I disappoint you with that. Could we please leave now? I don't want to damage your reputation by being seen with me." Sonja was choking back angry tears, but it was useless. Finally she snatched a napkin from the table and held it to her face. She no longer cared if anyone saw her crying.

Evelyn came back to the table and gave her two friends a puzzled look.

Danny held up his hand for Evelyn not to say anything. He then signaled for the waiter, who brought the check.

"Evelyn, take my truck keys, and you guys go on while I take care of the bill." Danny's voice was low and he avoided looking at Sonja.

Evelyn sat in the front of Danny's Jeep Cherokee and Sonja silently got into the back seat. The celebration dinner had suddenly changed into a funeral. No one spoke the entire twenty-five minute drive back to town.

Danny dropped Evelyn off at her home and then went back to his garage for Sonja's car. He needed another chance alone with her. He wanted her to know that he cared for her. He was going to swallow his pride and tell her he loved her and he didn't care about her past. All he wanted was to start a future with her and he wanted her to want the same thing.

He had made up his mind. He had loved her since he was ten years old, and he was too stubborn then to give up, he might as well keep trying. He had made up his mind; he was going to ask Sonja Davenport to marry him.

Danny Taylor had practiced and rehearsed this moment a million times. Of course, during those rehearsals, Sonja wasn't furious with him like she was tonight.

He drove to his garage and was unlocking the gate to let Sonja get her car, and kept hoping he wasn't about to make a fool of himself. Again. She had refused to ride up front with him, and that meant there had been no conversation at all.

Before he could even return to his truck, Sonja had jumped out and was walking to her car, the truck headlights silhouetting her shapely frame. Danny met her at the car and blocked the driver's side door.

"Look, I want to say I'm sorry, again. I was wrong, again. I love you, again. Please, marry me." His voice dropped to barely a whisper on the last few words.

It was hard for Sonja to see his face in the dark, but the truck lights were casting a faint glow on his face, she could tell his eyes were misty.

"If this is some kind of sick joke, then you must think I'm either a fool or desperate." Sonja snapped.

"I don't think you are either of those. I know you love me; I know you need me even though you don't want to. I know you better than any man...I will love you for the rest of my life, even if we never get married. Doesn't that count for something?" He grabbed her hand.

"Danny, we just had one of the worst fights we've ever had! Doesn't that scare you? Because it scares the hell out of me. I don't want to go into a marriage that is doomed."

"Then stop dooming it. Start loving me back, with all my faults. Accept me for having the <u>one </u>weakness I can't shake. You. Is that so bad? To have a man who would give you the moon and stars if he could? All I ask in return is for you to be faithful, love me and give me a few beautiful little babies that look just like the two of us. That's all I ask. Say you will."

Sonja didn't know what he said that made her start to cry. It could have been the part about being weak for her, the moon and the stars or the babies. By the time he had finished, she was crying uncontrollably. Between the tears she managed to whisper "yes."

Danny grabbed her in a bear hug and was spinning her around, and making her dizzy as her shoes flew off her feet. He stopped spinning around and looked at her laughing.

"You know what? I'm going to make love to you right now."

"Here? At the garage?" Sonja asked looking around.

"Right here, at OUR garage, all night long. Call your Mama's nurse and tell her you're going to be late," he was covering her face with wet kisses.

Refusing to put her down, he carried her to his office and made good on his promise. They set a date that night, for the Labor Day weekend, only 30 days away. Danny said he had waited since he was ten years old, he wasn't waiting any longer to make her his wife.

Sonja kept complaining that they had so much to decide. Where would they live, her house or his? When could they move furniture and get settled? Danny said they could either build a new house or buy another one, he didn't care. Those were just minor things. They had more important things to discuss, like how soon could they have a baby? Sonja heard herself saying, nine months.

They made love as though they were creating a baby that very night, and Sonja was already beginning to fantasize about how the little angel would look, and how lucky he or she would be to have two parents who would provide everything under the sun he or she wanted. There would be no shame, abandonment or missing father.

§§§§§§§§§§§§§§§§§§§§

Evelyn was surprised to find Kevin at home. He was still pouting because she had asked her father and Stephanie for help.

"Where were you today?" Kevin asked.

"I had a meeting. Why?" Evelyn kicked off her heels in the kitchen and looked at him.

"I called the store and they said you were off. You've been off for a few days. What's going on?"

"Nothing is going on. I had things to take care of." She opened the refrigerator and pretended to be very interested in the contents.

Groaning and throwing his hands in the air, Kevin became dramatic in his questioning, "Please don't tell me you're out here embarrassing me again, asking God knows who for money for this store?"

Evelyn slammed the refrigerator door and walked past Kevin, taking a seat and turning on the television. She stared at the movie on HBO.

"Okay, I won't tell you," she answered. The movie was Kill Bill Vol. 1. How appropriate, she thought.

"Evelyn, I'm serious. This has gone far enough. I told you I would check around, let me handle this."

"I didn't say you couldn't handle it. For some reason I don't believe you really want to handle it. So I don't want to waste your time. I know how busy you are and all," Evelyn turned the volume up higher on the television. Uma Thurman was deadly with a knife and so was Vivica Fox.

"Your mother and I talked today. How could you convince your father to give up his entire savings for this hair-brained idea? How could you be so selfish?" He walked in front of the television to block Evelyn's view.

"That is between me and my father. I don't have to explain a damn thing to you about what he wants to do for me. Get out of the way Kevin." Evelyn craned her neck to watch the set. Damn! Vivica got whacked. A sister just can't win in this world not even in the movies.

"What about your mother? Your sisters? They have needs. He is not married to you, he is no longer responsible for you. You are a married woman now and I forbid you to take that money from him. If you do, this marriage is over!" He turned and pushed the power button off on the television.

Evelyn looked up at him from the sofa, "This marriage is over? It was never a marriage! What I want to know is why me? Why did you choose me to torture? What did I ever do to you? Do I remind you of someone you hate?"

Laughing and rubbing his chin, Kevin sat in the chair facing her, "No, my dear. You were someone I wanted to help. I wanted to teach about the finer things of life. You had potential. You just don't realize what an opportunity you have thrown away. I took you from nowhere, gave you things you could only dream about, took you places you have only heard about, but this, this little country town is all that you can aspire to. I'm going to the American Bar Association convention in Los Angeles next week, I assume you no longer will be making the trip, so when I get back, have your things packed and out of here. Take only what you brought. I'll have someone at the firm draw up the divorce papers." He paused and waited for Evelyn's reaction.

She sat on the sofa in stone silence. A huge lump was in her throat, preventing her from saying anything. So was this how it was going to end?

"Kevin, I have to ask you something. Is there someone else?"

"If there were, I would never admit it. I am an attorney, you sell dresses. You can't win. I'll be in the guest room." He left the great room and she heard the guest bedroom door slam.

Evelyn's stomach was doing cartwheels. She wanted to cry, scream, kill him and pretend this night had never happened. She couldn't talk to her mother, she was on Kevin's side.

She didn't want to worry her father, he was going through enough dealing with her mother.

She thought about her grandmother. But she wouldn't understand and would probably suggest burning another candle. Evelyn felt so alone.

Kevin's words were still stinging her ears. Especially the part about her fathers savings, her sisters, and the fact her father was sacrificing this for her.

Self-doubt started to take over and plague her mind that this business could ruin her father and now her friends if it didn't work. She wanted to call Danny and Sonja and tell them to back out, it wasn't going to work. Then she remembered how something was going on with those two at dinner.

She sat in front of the blank television screen feeling totally numb and empty. What had started as the best day of her life was now one of the worse. Evelyn sat for hours until she dozed off to sleep. She didn't hear Kevin leave the next morning and would have slept longer, had it not been for the phone ringing. Glancing at her watch, she stumbled to the cordless phone.

"Evelyn! What are you still doing home? Maceo is waiting for you." It was Danny and he was fuming.

"I don't...what time...oh my God, it's almost nine o'clock! I'm on my way." she stammered, then she remembered she had slept in her clothes.

"Evelyn look, Maceo is doing this deal because of me. Don't make me look bad. Is anything wrong?" Danny asked.

"I can't talk right now. Please call him and tell him I'm on my way, I'm so sorry Danny. It was a long night and some things went down last night."

Danny exhaled loudly, "Look Evelyn, don't make me look bad on this. Maceo is a serious businessman and if you're not ready for this, tell me now."

"I'm ready Danny, I just overslept because this week has been so long and I've been really stressed out. I won't let you down. I've got too much riding on this. This is the last time I'll disappoint you. I promise."

Danny said he would call Maceo to give Evelyn enough time to make it to his office.

Just as Danny expected, Maceo started warning him about the ills of doing business with women. They were too emotional, too unpredictable and normally too soft. And always crying about something.

In this case, he said he would make an exception. What he didn't tell Danny was that it was apparent Evelyn's friend, Sonja had quite a lot of influence on him, and Maceo surmised that she used that influence quite well on others. Especially men with power, which made him curious as to what she wanted with Danny.

He didn't tell Danny that he had spotted her in Washington last week, the obvious guest of a well- known politician. Maceo Sloan had learned long ago, not only to avoid doing business with women, but also to avoid meddling in personal affairs, especially when it could affect business.

Chapter 8

Gail was having one of the best weeks of her career. The hospital staff seemed to have adjusted to her management style, there were no major catastrophes and her kids were due home in another week.

The only fly in the ointment was Laura. She had been distant and preoccupied. Everyone at work had noticed the change and Gail couldn't understand what was wrong with her best friend. In fact, Gail felt Laura was actually avoiding her. She was prepared to give her space, until Laura started making too many mistakes at work. Misplacing patient's charts, leaving calls on hold and basically being irresponsible.

Gail knew she would have to speak to her about her behavior, all of the other nurses knew they were close friends, and would measure Gail's ability to reprimand her friend and demand the same level of performance as she did from them.

Laura was at the nurse's station, making notes on a chart when Gail walked up to her, "Hey Soul Sister...what's up? You seem a little down lately."

"Well, there are days like that. Can't be happy all the time." Laura didn't stop writing.

"We need to talk." Gail lowered her voice.

"What about?" Laura snapped her folder shut and turned to face Gail.

"Are you mad at me about something?"

"Nope. I do have other things on my mind. I have a life too and it doesn't evolve just around you."

"What does that mean? I'm trying to talk to you as a friend, not as your supervisor Laura, you've been making some critical mistakes and I just want to know what's wrong?"

"Oh, I see. I'm a good enough nurse to cover for your butt, but I make one little mistake and I need counseling. What next, suspension?" Laura turned her back to Gail.

"We're not talking about little mistakes Laura. You assisted Dr. Gallager on that tonsillectomy patient who was allergic to penicillin and you put penicillin on her chart for antibiotic prescriptions? If Doris hadn't caught that, you would be in real trouble. You know Gallager doesn't except any excuses and covering for me being late isn't the same as endangering a patient. I cannot let you get away with this. What is the matter with you? You've been rude to patients, or in some cases just ignored the call buttons," Gail touched her on the arm.

"Just because your life is filled with Daddy Warbucks now, I don't count. I'm just a fat friend who is in the way, making you look bad at your big job. I guess you and everybody else have a real good time discussing poor Laura and her incompetence. I don't need this wishy-washy friendship." She jerked away from Gail.

Other nurses were starting to notice as Laura's voice rose. She was near tears and so was Gail.

"Take some days off. If you don't want to tell me what's wrong, then fine, I'm still your friend whether you want me to be or not. Take a few days and get some rest." Gail turned and started to walk away.

Surely, Laura wasn't jealous of her relationship with Maceo. It had to be more than that. Laura had been with her through many romances and this had never happened before. Gail thought about calling Ted to see if he knew what was going on.

Then she decided to just wait until later that evening. She would drag Laura out of the house and take her shopping and then to eat, including a really sinful chocolate dessert binge.

Gail wanted to pretend that whatever was troubling Laura was simple and could be solved in an evening at the mall. However, she kept replaying the words Laura had thrown at her.

Calling Maceo Daddy Warbucks and calling herself fat, was pointing to a serious level of disrespect that neither of them had crossed before.

Gail spent the rest of the day trying not to dwell on what was wrong with Laura, but she found herself replaying the uncomfortable scene repeatedly in her mind. She and Laura had never had a fight like that before. Sure, they disagreed and argued about things like how to discipline each other's kids; how much money to spend shopping and how to keep a man. Nothing had ever threatened the friendship like this.

Gail thought it was ironic, that for the first time in a long time, she had found a man who filled a void in her life, and now she was about to lose her only and best friend.

She called Laura the moment she got home and told her she was going to pick her up for dinner. Sounding distant and distracted, Laura declined.

Several hours later, Gail's phone rang and it was Ted. Gail could hear screaming and shouting in the background, and glass breaking.

"Gail, could you come over here? I don't want to have to call the police and maybe you can talk to Laura." Ted's voice was mono-toned and matter of fact.

"Ted, what in the world is going on? Is Laura okay?" Gail was searching the room for her purse.

"We'll talk when you get here...right now she's trying to destroy the house. Laura! Stop this! This is crazy!" He hung up the phone before Gail could ask any more questions.

Gail ran to her car, all the while trying to sort out the cause of such behavior. Maybe Laura was having a nervous breakdown.

Minutes later, Gail was pulling into Laura's driveway. The front window curtains were partially torn down, the front door was open and so was the garage. Ted's car trunk was up and items were stacked inside.

Before Gail could open her car door, Ted came outside with a bundle of clothes. Laura was behind him, hitting him with her fists and screaming.

"I hate you! You think you can do this to me and get away with it? Why Ted, why now?" Laura didn't even notice Gail in the driveway. She was like a woman possessed. She was still in her nurses' uniform, which was filthy, her stockings were ripped at the knees, and her face was streaked with tears and makeup.

Ted kept walking to his car, ignoring the outburst from Laura.

"Laura, what's wrong? Laura, please talk to me," Gail was holding onto Laura's shoulders, as she started to sink to the ground. Both of them sat on the ground and Gail knew the neighbors were starting to take notice of this spectacle. She held her friend in her arms, and Laura started to cry, rocking back and forth.

"He's leaving me. He's leaving me and the kids. Tell him not to go, please Gail, he'll listen to you."

Looking bewildered at Ted, Gail was speechless. Ted walked over to where they were sitting and looked down at the both of them.

"The neighbors are staring. Could we go inside please?" he sounded more like he was in faculty meeting instead of a family crisis.

Helping Laura up from the ground, Gail walked inside the house and sucked in her breath. The house was wrecked. Chairs were tossed over, papers were everywhere, and broken glass covered the floor.

Seeing Gail's expression, Ted said, "She did all this. Look at this mess. I can't take this anymore. I have tried to be patient with Laura. Gail I have tried. I can't take it anymore, it's not working."

"It's not working because of that whore! Tell Gail about your whore Ted. Tell her! That's the real problem. That's where he's going. Tell her the truth!" Laura was screaming, and her face was contorted.

Ted raised his voice, "That's not true! This is about you and me. We've been in trouble for a long time and you know it. How many years have you been losing the weight? How many years have you been promising to keep the house cleaner? I can't do this anymore. We didn't start like this! I don't like my life anymore and I'm going to do something about it. Whether you like it or not!" He kept looking from Gail to Laura. Gail felt she should say something.

"But Ted, Laura loves you and your kids need you. I know marriage is tough, but you can make it. Don't devastate your family like this, please don't." Before she realized it, Gail felt the tears streaming down her cheeks.

Gail's plea to Ted gave Laura a renewed burst of energy. This time she grabbed Ted by the neck in a headlock.

"I won't let you leave me like this! I'll kill you first! You hear me?" She was much stronger than Gail had thought as she tried to wrestle Ted free from his wife's death grip.

Ted kept his calm and was trying to loosen her hold on his neck, by now he was bent over with his head under her arm.

He managed to choke out a few words, "See how she acts? Everytime we try to discuss our problems, she does this crap and I always back down, but no more. I'm leaving Laura. Don't make me hurt you, stop it!" he finally shoved her away from him and she hit the wall. This time Laura went into a crying fit of hysteria.

"Ted, pleasse... this time I'll do better...I lost 3 pounds last week... didn't I Gail?" She was sitting on the floor, her legs sprawled apart.

Gail thought she looked even bigger than ever, but she was afraid to disagree with her, "Yeah...she did...Ted, she is really try-ing...I'll help her, just give her a little time." Gail was holding Ted's arm as he started towards the door.

"Life is too short Gail. I'm out of time. I love my kids and you know I'm a good father. I deserve to be happy too, I'm sorry if I've disappointed you, but as a friend, I hope you understand my side of this. This separation is needed for both of us. I gotta go." Pick-ing up his duffle bag, he walked out of the door.

The silence in the house, seemed to last forever, as Gail sat on the floor with Laura. "Why didn't you tell me Laura? I thought we were close enough friends to share everything."

"I couldn't tell you. I thought I could fix it all and make him stay. I was ashamed to tell you I was losing my husband. I'm al-ways telling you how to keep a man, and look at me. I begged him to stay. On my knees begging," Laura closed her eyes and laid her head against the wall.

"Is there someone else?" Gail asked.

"Yeah, I think he's got someone, but he keeps denying it. I guess he was ashamed to tell you that. It's been going on for a while. I guess I thought as long as I didn't try to make him choose, I would at least still be the wife. I was willing to take that role. You know the old saying, a piece of man is better than no man at all." Laura was struggling trying to lift her size 18 frame from the floor.

Gail was reminded of the twenty or so years Laura and Ted had been married. He looked the same, except for a little gray hair in the top of his head. Laura though, had gone from a size 8 to 18.

She had been such a knockout during her college years, with lots of spunk and a laugh that could be heard clear across the college campus. She and Ted had seemed like such an odd couple then.

He was always the serious one, smart as a whip and very timid around women. Laura simply captivated his heart, and he had started to depend on her brashness and bluntness to make up for his lack of directness. It often worked well. Now, it apparently had caused an end to the marriage. Laura was never serious about anything, including losing weight, or cleaning the house until it was a crisis.

"Boy, did I make a mess. Well, I guess I ought to clean it up...what the hell? Screw it." Laura had picked up a flowerpot, and on second thought, threw it back on the floor.

Gail had an idea, "Why don't we hire a maid service to clean this up? My treat."

"Naw, I can't do that. They would charge too much. This is a hell of lot more than just vacuuming." Laura stood in the middle of the living room with her hands on her hips surveying the damage.

"So what? I insist. Anyway, we have a date to go shopping, so get cleaned up and let's go."

"Gail, I'm sorry about today at work. I was crazy. Please forgive me. You know I didn't mean what I said." Laura was starting to get weepy again.

"I know. It's okay. You had a lot on your mind and you still have some major decisions to make. I've been there." Gail hugged her friend.

"Oh, I've already decided. I'm going to get Ted back, I'm going to lose 30 pounds, and make him fall in love with me all over again. No woman is going to take my man without a fight. I know Ted still loves me, this is just his way of making me get off my butt and take action. I'm going to take a quick shower and I'll be ready in 15 minutes." Laura gave Gail a quick squeeze and rushed down the hall towards her bedroom.

Gail had mixed emotions. This denial of Laura's did not feel good, but as her friend, she had to support her. She decided that she would be her cheerleader and her conscience. She started by going into the kitchen and trashing all of the Oreo Double Stuff cookies, Lay's potato chips, and Reese's peanut butter cups.

Gail had convinced Laura to clean the house, and remove the remnants of the wrestling match that had practically broken Ted's neck.

They ended up throwing away a lot of junk that no longer served a purpose and discussing the upcoming school year for their kids. Both boys played junior high football and that would mean hours of driving to and from practice and games.

Laura seemed to be regaining her composure and would even crack a joke or two. Then she would remember that her life was on the verge of major change and she would lapse into silence.

Gail tried to persuade her to pack an overnight bag and come to her place.

"I'll be fine. I need some time to myself and since my house is the cleanest it has ever been, I really want to enjoy it. You probably have a date anyway, right?" Laura was looking around her recently cleaned house with pride.

"Probably, but Maceo would understand. He was in Washington for some kind of White House business summit. He's supposed to be flying in tonight, so he might be tired."

"White House like the President, the one in the White House?" Laura asked obviously impressed.

"Don't be impressed so easily. It's all based on politics. According to Maceo, political donors get invited to these brainstorm sessions to talk about what's wrong and right with business in America. Then you lobby your Congressman to push the President's agenda. Sounds really boring if you ask me." Gail was stacking dishes in the cupboards.

"Yeah, but the White House! You get to visit the White House! You didn't want to go?" Laura asked.

"Well, I wasn't exactly invited. I get the impression when Maceo works, he's really focused. No distractions. Real tunnel vision. Anyway, if I was in Washington, I couldn't have been here to rescue Ted from your Hulk Hogan headlock. Girl, you were crazed! Do you really fight like that with him?"

Laura laughed and wiped a stream of perspiration from her top lip, "It's just a scare tactic. I could really whip Ted if I wanted to. He is such a whoose. He likes to discuss, analyze and draw a consensus. You know that phd junk. So I just grab him and then he gives in. The fight is over and I'm still the greatest of all time!" She did a poor imitation of Muhammad Ali.

"This time is different Laura. You have to do better. Ted is a good man. I know he's screwing up now with some other woman, but he's only human. Girl you don't have to pay any bills, cook or clean the place and it's been that way since you got married. I don't know too many marriages like that anymore. I never had one." Gail was making a fruit salad and saw Laura searching the pantry for her junk food stash.

"I know that. I was raised to expect that, so I can't help if I expect certain things. Have you seen my Reese's peanut butter cups?" Laura was becoming frantic in her search. Gail debated whether to confess that she had trashed them.

"Naw. Come on now, we're supposed to be losing weight. Forget that junk. Look at this fruit salad. All you can eat. No fat, no sugar, no cholesterol." Gail was making herself busy in the kitchen to avoid Laura's glaring eyes.

"Did you throw my candy out?" Laura folded her arms across her chest and waited for Gail to answer.

"It was best. If this stuff is around, you're going to eat it. I'm going to help you to save your marriage, even if you don't want the help. Now let's eat our salads." Gail quickly started placing the fruit salads on the table.

When she didn't get a response from Laura, she turned around to find her friend silently crying into her hands, her shoulders shaking from raw emotion.

"I can't do it Gail! I can't get him to come back, it's over."

"It's not over. Ted still loves you, and that means a lot. It's tough out here trying to make it alone. Take it from me, it's not easy with kids, and trying to date. If you've got something worth working on, work on it. It's too hard trying to love somebody new, take some vacation days, get yourself together and go and get your husband back."

171

Laura wiped her face and blew her nose on the tail of her shirt, "Should I forgive him for having an affair?"

"You're asking me, a woman who had a husband who had many affairs, and then turned to dating the dog of the town? I might not be the best person to ask, but I do know a good man when I see one, and I don't think Ted is like Jonathan or Larry. I still can't believe Ted cheated on you. But if he did, that is something you guys have to work out, to make sure it doesn't happen again. Nobody's perfect. Listen, come spend the night at my place tonight, we can talk, watch movies and drink too much wine."

"But what about Maceo? I thought you had plans." Laura's voice was meek with a lot of desperation. Gail knew her best friend wanted company more than anything in the world.

"He'll keep. Come on, throw some things in a bag and let's go." Gail slung her purse on her shoulder and Laura walked into her bedroom to start packing.

Glancing at her watch, Gail knew Maceo had arrived from Washington and had probably called. She checked her messages from Laura's kitchen phone.

The recorder listed three messages. One was from Jonathan Jr. complaining that his sister had worn his Sean Jean shirt and his father didn't make her take it off. Some things never change thought Gail. The second message was from, who else, Jessica, whining that her brother had shoved her because she was wearing his shirt. Gail was still considered the disciplinarian even at her ex-husbands house. Well he would just have to deal with it.

The third message was from Maceo.

"Hey little lady. I just got back, I'm leaving the airport and could sure use some Kool Aid and bologna. How about it? I'll be home in an hour, give me a call. Bye." Gail smiled. There was nothing like having a man hungry for you. She dialed his home number and he answered on the second ring.

"Hi. It's me. How are you?" She asked.

"Lonely, and missing you. I even decided I would make the Kool Aid. Can you come over?"

Gail's heart dropped. She couldn't leave Laura, especially tonight. Besides, Gail remembered she had a half-gallon of butter pecan ice cream in the freezer, and she knew Laura would devour it without supervision.

"I can't tonight. I'm sort of in a crisis with a friend." She whispered.

Maceo hesitated. Then he cleared his throat. "Where are you now?" Was that a tone of suspicion in his voice?

"At my friends, she's spending the night at my place, and I can't leave her."

"Sure, I understand. That's what friends are for. Is there something I can do to help?" His voice relaxed.

Gail liked this man more and more. "How sweet, no I wish there was something, but it's going to take a little time."

"How long is she staying with you?" Now he was sounding impatient.

"Just for tonight. We can get together tomorrow...I promise. I'll call you later tonight." Gail saw Laura waddling towards her with the largest overnight bag she had ever seen.

"Okay. Later." Maceo hung up.

Laura's face was damp with perspiration, "Whew! I tell you trying to find things in a clean house is hell! At least I always used to know where everything was, when shit was all over the place! I'm ready."

Gail hoped Laura didn't plan on more than one night, but by the looks of her bulging overnight bag, Laura had prepared for several nights.

§§§§§§§§§§§§§§§§§§§§§

Laura was pushing every button Gail had. It had been three days and two nights, and Laura didn't seem to miss her house, kids or husband. Gail kept trying to get her to call Ted for a heart to heart, but Laura would always avoid making the call by pretending to be too tired, not feeling well or getting ready to run an errand.

The only good thing about her homesteading at Gail's was that she was starting to lose weight. With the kids away for the summer, Gail rarely bought food, and Laura never cooked. The weight loss was more from laziness than motivation. Gail began to understand why Ted was always at the stove when she visited.

Maceo had been patient. They had gone to the movies and she went to his house once. The buildup from lack of lovemaking was making them both crazy. Neither could remember the name of the movie, the plot or the stars and ended up leaving after 45 minutes of trying to watch the film.

Gail had been wary of the days winding down until Laura's and her kids returned for the summer. She hoped Laura didn't plan on moving them in too, her house was beginning to lose its identity and starting to look more like Laura's, before the clean up effort.

It was Gail's day off and she slept late. Laura was still at the hospital, so it would have been a good time to give the house a good cleaning. Maybe the not so subtle hint would catch her attention. Gail had finished the living room, kitchen and den and stood staring from the hallway into Jessica's room that Laura was using. It was amazing how one woman could totally junk up a room in three days.

Gail had decided to let Laura clean up this mess, when she suddenly spotted a pharmacy bag under the bed. Kicking aside the shoes, underwear, magazines, and diet soda cans, Gail retrieved the crumpled up bag, and looked inside.

She discovered at least fifty assorted pills, and a blank prescription pad. Gail didn't want to believe what her mind was telling her, that Laura was forging diet prescription pills. She was going to have to confront her with what appeared to be the damaging evidence. Gail neatly folded the bag and took it to her room.

Her concern for Laura was quickly replaced with anger. If this caught the attention of someone at the hospital, it could even implicate her. Everyone knew how close the two were.

She finished cleaning the rest of the house and poured herself a glass of wine to calm her nerves while she waited for her new roommate.

An hour later, Laura came dashing into the house with several shopping bags under both arms. Breathing hard, she plopped down on the sofa.

"Girrl! Did you know that *Exclusively Yours* is going out of business? They're having a sale you wouldn't believe! Look at what I got! Everything was 40% off." Laura was flinging items out of the large bags like a woman possessed.

Gail guessed that she must have spent several hundred dollars and had bought everything from lingerie to bubble bath. Gail was silently examining the outfits and started noticing the sizes. They were all size 6!

"Laura? Who is this stuff for? These are all size six."

Laura grabbed a skirt and looked at the tag, "Damn! I thought this said 16." She started going from article to article, and keep muttering "damn" at each one.

"Even if it was a 16, you couldn't wear it Laura. You know you wear at least a size 20." The wine had made Gail less sensitive to her friend's weight problem, and the fact that she was popping illegally prescribed pills, plus had made a pigsty out of Jessica's room added fuel to the fire.

Laura didn't notice the sarcasm, "I can't believe that dumb salesgirl sold me all these size 6's! No exchange, no refund. What in the hell am I going to do with a size 6? I could have sworn these were 16." Laura kept talking faster and faster, seeming to not even to realize she had bought the wrong sizes. Laura threw the dresses back into the bag with disgust.

"Well, hell. Never mind, I'll give them to someone else, I'm tired. Going to take a nap."

"Need some diet pills to help you get your energy up?" Gail held up the bag of pills.

Laura stood frozen.

"Laura, how long have you been doing this?" asked Gail.

"At least three or four times a day. Some for breakfast, lunch and dinner and before I go to bed. I started two days ago. Why? And how did you find out?" Laura started pacing the floor.

"Never mind how I found out. You do realize that you're committing a crime? Forging prescriptions drugs? Are you crazy?" Gail screamed.

"I had to do something. I couldn't make it on my own. I needed help, and these are the only way I can lose the weight this summer." A bead of perspiration was starting to form on Laura's lip.

"You have got to stop it. Now. I don't want to turn you in, but I will. Not only are you jeopardizing both of our jobs, but you could go to jail!"

"Oh that's the real problem ain't it? Your little ten cents job! That damn job has made you think you shit on a stick and that asshole you sleeping with got you thinking you all that. Well we both know he won't last long don't we? I'm outta here. I'll just take my pill-popping ass home. Friend." Laura snatched the pills from Gail and walked into the bedroom.

Gail thought about stopping her, but she was not in the mood to play psychologist or beg forgiveness for being right. Plus, she really wanted her house back.

Gail had started preparing to drive into Mississippi to pick up Jessica and Jonathan Jr. without Laura. Every summer they had made the trip together to retrieve their children and start getting ready for the fall school year. Her ex-husband always shared the summer with their grandparents.

Laura hadn't called since she left and Gail refused to keep trying to reach her. She did call Ted, who was very nonchalant about the entire thing, and it was evident he was going on with his life, for he was staying with a woman.

Gail felt sorry for Laura and Ted's kids, who would have to come back to a broken home. She knew how tough it was on her own kids. Finally they seemed to have adjusted and were normal as most other kids.

She arrived at her parents and packed up Jessica and Jonathan who kept asking where was Laura. Then the conversation turned to what they had been doing all summer. Gail was half listening to the chatter when her cellular phone rang.

"Hi. Where are you?" It was Maceo.

"Heading back to Birmingham. I've got my offspring and we're a family again." She smiled and glanced over at Jessica who was sitting next to her.

"Good. How about a barbeque and the kids can come over and swim? I'd like to meet them."

"Today? I don't know. Hold on...hey guys, you want to go a friend's house for a barbeque and swim?"

Jessica's eyes lit up, "Yeah! Can I bring a friend?"

Jonathan mumbled, "Whose house is it?"

Ignoring Jonathan's surly attitude, Gail answered, "No, you cannot bring a friend. So what you want to do?"

"Okay, I want to swim." Jessica looked at her brother, who was on the back seat, staring out of the window.

Gail decided to ignore him and put the phone back to her ear, "Okay, you got a deal. What time should we be there, we're a good 45 minutes away."

"Oh, in couple of hours would be fine. I got hot dogs, ice cream, burgers and the universal meat, chicken. I don't do potato salad and that other stuff, so could you take care of that?" Maceo asked.

"Sure, no problem, thanks Maceo. This is really sweet. Oh and speaking of sweet, Mama sent a sweet potato pie home, so I'll bring it."

Jessica was grinning up at her mother and starting singing. "Mama's got a boyfriend...Mama's got a boyfriend..."

Clearly irritated by the idea and his sister's singing, Jonathan swiftly thumped her head. "Shut up! She does not! Why you got to always start lying!" He yelled.

Gail jerked her head around to look at him. "Boy, have you lost your mind?" By now, Jessica was howling with huge crocodile tears streaming down her face.

"Don't you ever let me see you do that again! And she is not lying. I don't know what kind of crap your father puts up with, but I am not having this behavior from you. Do you understand?"

Jonathan never met her glare, and mumbled. "Yes Mam'm."

Jessica quickly recovered and started asking questions. "Who is he Mama? What does he do?"

"His name is Maceo Sloan and he owns his own business."

She could hear Jonathan Jr. sucking in his breath.

"Is he rich? Cause he has a pool right? Does he have any kids?" Jessica was smiling.

"His children are grown, and I don't know if he's rich, and don't you ask him either." Gail glanced in her rear mirror to look at her son, who looked like he was holding his breath under water he was so mad.

She knew she had to say something to help him to deal with yet another man in her life. "He's a very nice man. I like him a lot."

"You gonna marry him too?" Jonathan looked at his mother.

"I don't know Jonathan, we're not that serious yet, but I would like to think that if I decide to marry him, you will support me and not act like you're acting right now."

"Why you got."

"And stop saying 'you got'. Every time you leave for the summer you come home speaking like a slave!" Gail snapped.

"Why do you have to marry him? Why do you even need him? I'm not going to like him and he's not going to like me."

"Yes he will Jonathan. Just be nice," Jessica chimed in. "Right Mama? Everybody always likes me, cause I'm nice," she looked at her mother for affirmation.

"I don't need him Jonathan, and right now I'm not even sure if we'll get married. I do like him. When you get older, you'll understand. Just be yourself and everything will be fine," she nodded at Jessica and smiled.

She glanced at her son through the rear view mirror filled with unconditional love. He cast her a sly look and returned to staring out of the window. She realized he was afraid of losing her, and having to share her again, with someone else. The divorce from his father had been hardest on him, and Gail knew he had never really given up on his parents getting back together.

The rest of the ride home was in silence and Gail was having serious second thoughts about going out to Maceo's. Maybe this was too soon. She called Maceo to tell him they would have to take a rain check, but he insisted.

"Hey look, I have two spoiled children and I don't think there's anything a child can do that I haven't already experienced. Plus, I can't eat all of this food by myself."

"Okay, but I can't make any promises. Jonathan is feeling pretty insecure right now. Of course, Jessica can't wait to get in your pool."

"You just leave Jonathan to me. I haven't lost a project yet." He smiled.

By the time Gail turned on the isolated road leading to Maceo's house, Jessica was chatting away about all the trees and flowers, and the pretty houses along the way. Jonathan was still stone silent. Until he saw the two German Shepherds.

He suddenly sat up to get a better look at the two dogs, running towards the car, his eyes betraying his attempt to pout.

"Whose dogs Mom?" He asked.

"Maceo's. Pretty aren't they?"

"Will they bite? I'm scared." Jessica interrupted, her eyes darting around to follow the dogs, which were barking by now.

"No they won't bite. They just bark to let Maceo know someone's out here." She pulled into the driveway to the English Tudor style house and started honking the horn.

Jonathan was already out of the car. The two shepherds, Solomon and Sheba were taking cautious sniffs at him.

"Mom, why can't we get a dog? I love dogs." Jonathan was softly petting the ears of the animals that had decided by now that the guests were harmless.

"Yeah Mom, why don't you get the kids a dog?" Maceo was wearing a man's barbeque apron that had Kiss The Cook on it.

"No encouragement from you. Dogs take time, money and space and I don't have any of the above." Gail said as she greeted him with a peck on the cheek.

Jessica was still in the car, not convinced the dogs were safe.

"Hi, I'm Maceo Sloan," he extended his hand to Jonathan, who shook it and returned the greeting.

"I'm Jonathan, good to meet you. Is it okay if I play with them?" He motioned to the dogs that were sitting obediently, looking up at their master's face.

"Sure, they would love it. What about the little princess here, she's not getting out of the car?" He peered into the car at Jessica.

"Oh she's afraid of everything. Come on Jessica, they won't bite...see watch!" Jonathan grabbed the dogs around the neck and let them lick his face. Jessica was still not convinced.

"I'll get her." Maceo opened the car door and Jessica jumped into his arms. Gail knew it was love at first sight for both of them. Maceo carried Jessica to the patio and pool area, while talking to her in soft tones.

"Maceo, she is too old to be carried. You're spoiling her." Gail complained.

"That's what little girls and big girls are supposed to be. Spoiled. And I love doing it, can't you tell by now?" He winked at Gail.

The afternoon was picture perfect. The kids were splashing in the pool, even the dogs jumped in, and without protestations from Jessica.

Gail was having a wonderful time. She quietly observed how Maceo interacted with the children and loved what she saw. During a private moment when the kids were running around with the dogs, Maceo came over and sat next to Gail.

"You've got great kids. You've done a good job with them."

"Thanks. It's not easy. The pay is lousy and the hours are long, but it's the best job in the world." She turned to look at him.

"My kids, never appreciated any of this, it was always never enough. I guess they took that from their mother. But then, I should have been tougher. On all three of them."

Gail took his hand, "I thought you were a tough guy."

"Well everyone has a weakness. Kids are mine. And you," he leaned over and softly kissed her lips.

"Is this a dream? Are you for real? Tell me now so I can prepare myself," she whispered.

Giving her a perfect smile, Maceo said, "Get prepared to be totally swept off your feet, because baby, I'm for real."

Chapter 9

The next day was extremely busy for Sonja. She immediately called a wedding planner to help with selecting invitations, florists, and a reception facility. She called a few of her Dallas girlfriends and each refused to believe she was getting married, but said they would be there just to witness a miracle. Her mother was ecstatic. Her face was pulled into as much of a smile as she could with the stroke impairing her facial muscles.

Danny was on the phone calling friends and relatives and trying to explain the rush. Many relatives were planning on visiting for the Labor Day holiday, so the wedding was going to be even more of a reason to make the trip.

Sonja decided she only wanted Evelyn in her wedding party, which presented a problem for Danny, who had two brothers and two close friends he wanted. Sonja said it was no problem, they could all be in the wedding, and they just wouldn't have any bridesmaids to escort.

She had bought a stack of bride's magazines for them to start selecting tuxedos. She already knew she would have to fly back to Dallas to choose a wedding gown, but Danny persuaded her to go to Atlanta instead. She didn't want to cause him any discomfort, and she agreed, Atlanta would do fine.

So far that had been Danny's only contribution to the wedding plans, everything else he left up to Sonja. He didn't want to concentrate on a lot of details, and perhaps create a fight. He had heard that lots of couples fought over how many guests to be invited, the color and styles of the tuxedo and even the music. He really didn't care about those things, plus he trusted Sonja's taste and he knew she would have the wedding of the year for Birmingham.

Because most of the guests were Danny's friends and family, Sonja decided to have the ceremony at his family's church. Evelyn was happy with that news, because she attended the same church, but it also brought back memories of her own wedding. She hoped she wouldn't breakdown the day of Danny's and Sonja's wedding.

Chapter 10

Sonja had decided to go with a Vera Wang gown. Evelyn was jumping up and down because her shop would place the order.

"This is going to be great publicity!" She screamed.

"Great publicity? For who?" Sonja lifted the veil to make eye contact with Evelyn.

"For all of us. The store, you, Danny. I mean this wedding will bring a touch of class to this town that is needed. You're wearing a gown by Vera Wang! Pearls and diamonds from Harry Winston's! It's like a fairy tale and you're Cinderella. I know I can get the style editor of the newspaper to do a complete section on this wedding, would it be okay if I called her?" Evelyn was assisting Sonja undo the back of the gown.

"I'll have to ask Danny." Sonja stepped out of the gown.

"Wooow! Asking permission already huh? You're going to be such a good little wife!" Evelyn joked.

"Shut up. I'm starving. Let's go to my house. I thought people only brought food when someone died, but since the news of the wedding got out, these friends of Mama's have been bringing stuff over for days. Chicken salad, cakes, pies, fried chicken."

"Well, I guess folks think you're going to have a lot of out of town guests so they want to help out. That's how your mother used to do things. She used to tell us about the Italian tradition of celebrating weddings weeks before the actual ceremony for the family. She brought food to my parents' house for my wedding." Evelyn got suddenly quiet. The reality had sunk in.

"Still no word from Kevin?" asked Sonja.

"Nope. He took an extra week out of town to give me more time to pack my things. So I guess he's still in Los Angeles." Evelyn was re-hanging the exquisite gowns.

"Listen, I hope you take anything you want from that house. It's your right. Do not leave there empty handed."

"It's worth it just to be away from him. He is truly evil, the things he said to me, and I could swear that man hates me. But why?" Evelyn turned with tears in her eyes to look at Sonja.

"Because, women remind some men of their faults, fears and insecurities. We are supposed to cure their ills or at least hide them, but strong women like you and me, cannot be used as bandages. That's when the problems start. You deserve better anyway. He's an asshole. Let's go." Sonja grabbed Evelyn by the arm and escorted her to the front of the store.

Evelyn had hired new sales clerks and a new assistant manager. The inventory clear out sale was winding down and there were only a few customers browsing the racks. In a month, an entire new winter and fall shipment was scheduled to arrive.

She had plenty to keep her occupied, but her broken marriage kept sneaking its way to the forefront of her thoughts. She also knew she would have to tell her family and find somewhere to stay. The house with Kevin never appealed to her and didn't reflect her sense of style. All it held were bad memories.

Sonja's house had taken on the air of a gala activity. The usually spotless rooms had opened and unopened boxes and gift papers strewn about. Bride's magazines, catering menus and swatches of fabric covered chairs and tables.

The most remarkable difference was in Sonja's mother, who had gained a lot more use in her arms, and her speech was less muffled. The wedding had given her a new lease on life and her eyes were beginning to return that Italian sparkle when she looked at you. Evelyn also noticed a change in Sonja. For one thing, she was a bundle of nerves, instead of the cool collected diva she always portrayed, which was normal for a new bride, but Sonja also demonstrated a kind of sadness. There would be times when she would become quiet and moody, shutting everyone out, even Danny.

The last few weeks had seemed like a dream to Sonja. She was jumpy and nervous and at times down right evil. She knew she was sending Danny through emotional changes, but he never complained. He simply kept his distance until she calmed down. She knew it was fear.

Fear that her past would be on the other end of the telephone, asking her not to get married. It worried her that she wasn't sure how she was going to react if that happened, while at the same time, it made her angry that so far, such a call had not come in.

She recognized that she rarely said *"I love you"* to Danny, and that bothered her. In her heart she felt she really did love him, but fear was stronger than love in this case. Fear that she wouldn't be a good wife, couldn't readjust to sharing her space, her time and decision making with someone else. The biggest fear of all was that she would become bored with the mere idea of marriage, of staying in Birmingham and of being boxed in.

The only silver lining in the cloud was how her mother was responding to the wedding activity. She had more life than Sonja had ever seen since her stroke. The nurse said she was cooperating better with her physical therapy and was even attempting to write notes.

When Sonja would throw a tantrum or start complaining, her mother would vigorously shake her head and squint her eyes at her daughter to let her know how much she disapproved. Sonja had been complaining about everything and everyone. She hated her bridal gown, the bride's maid dresses and she hated the church, the caterer, the music and the flowers.

With the wedding less than a month away, gifts were arriving by UPS and FedEx daily, from people she didn't really know, but who obviously loved and respected Danny. Maybe that bothered her as well. Birmingham had become a strange town to her, she didn't have any friends here and the few friends who were coming from Dallas would be expecting her to marry the richest man in the state. For the first time since accepting Danny's proposal, Sonja realized that she would have to defend her choice. A choice six months ago she would have never made.

Evelyn was chattering on and on about the store while preparing sandwiches for the two of them in Sonja's kitchen. Sonja was quietly sitting and watching television, while sipping on a glass of merlot.

She flicked the television remote to find something more entertaining. *Oprah*: How much in love Barbara Streisand was. This month, thought Sonja.

The View: how to take a married man from his wife, an expert's advice. Spare me, moaned Sonja.

CNN: terrorist groups invade California. Good place to start Sonja mumbled.

Meanwhile, a weather bulletin came on announcing a severe thunderstorm moving into the state from the Midwest. Heavy rains and winds were already detected in Mississippi.

Sonja clicked over to HBO, and glanced at her watch. Nearly five o'clock, maybe a decent movie would be on. No such luck, animation.

"It's getting ready to rain. Those clouds sure did roll in fast. Here." Evelyn walked into the great room and handed Sonja a sandwich and a glass of iced tea.

"Thanks, yeah there was something on the television a moment ago. I'll stick with wine." Sonja sat the iced tea glass aside and bit into the turkey sandwich and moaned.

"This is so good. I didn't realize how hungry I was."

Evelyn walked to the large window overlooking the patio. The winds were growing stronger, but there was no rain yet.

"I hope this rain cool things off a bit, this has been one of the hottest summers in a long time. I should get home before the rain starts." Evelyn turned to look at Sonja.

"Don't rush off. I could use some company, especially a true friend. I need to talk to you about something that's really bothering me." Sonja stood and started to walk towards Evelyn.

The wind was blowing even harder now, Sonja's patio chairs were being rocked and the tree limbs were bending under the force of the wind. Neither woman noticed the sudden change in the atmosphere they knew a very difficult conversation was about to take place. The real storm was in Sonja Davenport's great room. Evelyn pulled up a chair and waited for Sonja to speak.

Walking up to the window, Sonja kept her back to Evelyn. Some how she felt it would be easier to talk to her without looking her in the eyes. Before she opened her mouth, a siren's whine joined the howling winds.

"Oh, it's a tornado warning, let me turn on the local stations and see what's going on," Evelyn explained as she picked up the television remote.

The blond newscaster was reporting major damage to the western part of the city and a funnel cloud was just reported moving northwesterly.

Residents were being urged to seek shelter immediately as power lines, trees were reported down, and structural damage was reported at the new mall as well as to some locations in the downtown area.

Sonja kept watching the storm roll in and by now, her patio furniture was being toppled across the deck. The potted plants outside were already turned over and Sonja was thinking that this was one more mess she would have to clean up.

Evelyn immediately grabbed the phone to call the store to see if there was any damage. Sonja heard the noise first. She and Evelyn both saw the tree leaning, but it seemed to be in slow motion. Evelyn could feel her chest expanding, as though there wasn't enough air to breathe.

By now the noise was at a roar. Evelyn screamed for Sonja to move away from the window, but she never heard her own voice, the roar simply reached inside her mouth, down her throat and tightened its hold on her chest even harder.

Sonja couldn't stop staring at the huge pecan tree next door, as it slowly crashed through the wooden fence, she saw her patio furniture casually swept away and then the roar grew even worse. She caught a glimpse of what liked a very dark cloud, billowing and churning towards her house.

The moment she started to step away from the window, Sonja felt a million bee stings, a trillion pin pricks in her face. She threw her arms up as a shield, but not before she tasted her own blood.

The glass window seemed to shatter in a hail of glass. Sonja sank to her knees, and Evelyn dropped to the floor covering her own head.

Evelyn could see Mrs. Davenport's wheel chair rolling down the hallway towards the great room. The wind was so strong Evelyn knew the disabled woman wouldn't be able to protect herself.

Crawling towards Mrs. Davenport, she tried to hold her back. It was useless; defiance was in those dark Italian eyes as she kept rolling her wheelchair, trying to get close to Sonja.

Evelyn finally grabbed the chair and yelled for her to wait. The great room was a disaster zone, furniture was upside down, half of the roof along with the window was missing, and now rain was pelting down inside the room.

Evelyn was holding onto the wheelchair, but Sonja's mother pushed her hands away, and slowly started to stand up.

Her face was one large painful grimace, as she slowly opened her mouth. "Th...that's my ba..my bay- be." She shuffled her feet towards the spot where Sonja was laying in a fetal position.

Watching Mrs. Davenport fight to get to her daughter gave Evelyn the strength and courage to follow, even though her legs were like water, and she felt that she was going to faint, she kept praying for strength.

"Lord help us... please let Sonja be all right." Evelyn's voiced cracked. She watched Mrs. Davenport slowly turn Sonja over onto her back. Evelyn had never seen so much blood. It was covering Sonja's face and made it hard to tell where the cuts and abrasions started and ended. Her face was like raw meat. Her chest was heaving rapidly and though she was having a hard time breathing and Evelyn thought Sonja might be going into shock.

Mrs. Davenport was wailing and rocking Sonja in her arms as though she was a new born baby.

"She's going to be okay, she's going to be okay." Evelyn kept repeating as she starting tearing pieces of a curtain to make a bandage for Sonja's face. Evelyn started trying to stop the bleeding but the piece of cloth quickly became soaked.

It was raining harder and was starting to get dark. The sirens could be heard nearby, and voices were now audible from the outside of what was left of Sonja's house.

One of the neighbors was shouting to see if everyone was safe.

"We're here! We need help! Please get us some help!" Evelyn could hear her voice shouting, but it seemed so surreal. It was worse than any nightmare she had ever had.

Suddenly a fireman, the neighbor and a policeman came through the gaping hole in the wall. Evelyn wanted to say "thank you", but she couldn't speak. She could see their mouths moving, but she couldn't hear their voices. The room was spinning and the last thing she saw was the huge tree limb covering the roof of the house before everything went dark.

Chapter 11

Gail had coordinated many mock disaster drills for the hospital and she knew all the procedures, but this was real. There were dozens of injured people, several dead and worse, her children were home alone. It was the first time she had ever allowed them to stay home by themselves, but she was scheduled to get off early today. They had made plans to go the movies, get hamburgers and maybe stop out to Maceo's. It had been so hot, she had promised them a swim in his pool.

Most of the phone lines were down and Gail couldn't get through to her house. She kept trying between patching up storm victims and directing fatalities to the morgue. The unofficial death number was already more than 20.

Gail was silently praying that her children were all right, as she repeatedly watched relatives receive the bad news that a loved one didn't make it.

The tornado had been an F5, the deadliest ranking given to tornadoes, Gail heard one of the local news reporters say during a live broadcast from the hospital corridor.

She took a few seconds to review the floor, to make sure her staff was under control. They were. Without panic or confusion, the nurses, doctors and orderlies were administering care, answering questions and dispatching orders. Then Gail noticed Laura wasn't anywhere in sight.

Gail walked through the emergency examination rooms. She walked the corridors which were becoming make shift treatment areas...but still no Laura. She finally made her way to the nurse's lounge. Bingo. Laura was sitting on the sofa, head in her hands, shivering.

"Laura! What in the hell are you doing in here? We need every available person on the floor." Gail snapped.

"I'm sick Gail. I need to go home." She mumbled.

"Laura, I've got people hurt and dying here. We need every available person right now. Don't expect me to go easy on you, not today. I don't need this, not today. My kids are at home alone, I can't even leave to go see about them, and you think I'm going to baby your ass? Pull yourself together, take another pill or whatever the hell you need and get your ass back to the floor. Now!" Gail was trembling with anger.

She no longer valued the friendship, this was a do or die situation and Laura was letting her down. She could no longer depend on her as a friend, and now she was pulling rank as Laura's boss.

She turned quickly and left the nurses lounge. She was worried about Jonathan and Jessica. Grabbing the phone from a nearby nurse's station, Gail dialed her home. The annoying busy signal told her that all circuits were busy or many phone services were still interrupted just made her more nervous. Gail didn't have much time to think, as another crew of ambulances was arriving and paramedics were shouting vital statistics to hospital staff as they wheeled in more victims.

A dazed young woman caught Gail's eye as she rushed past to the first gurney with a badly injured victim. The young woman was holding onto the hand of the victim, who had major cuts and abrasions on her face. Gail immediately started helping the paramedics who had already started an i.v. on the victim. Her friend reluctantly let go of her hand.

"Are you family? Can you tell me how she got hurt?" Gail glanced at the friend.

"G..g..glass...she got cut by glass."

"Are you family? Can you give me some information on her? Is she allergic to any medication? Does she have any existing medical conditions?" Gail was busy cutting away the victims bloody clothing to start examining her for other injuries.

"I don't think so...I'm not sure..."

"I need her name, address and age..." Gail looked at the young woman whose glaze was transfixed on her friend.

"Miss? What is her name? And are you okay? You look like you need medical attention yourself."

"Her name is Sonja Davenport...she's around 30. She was standing in front of the window...and it just..."

"Miss, I'm going to ask you to stand out in the hall. We need you to give us room to work on Miss Davenport and I should really check you over too. You don't look so good." Gail gently took the young woman's arm and led her out of the emergency room area.

They met another crew of paramedics and fire units, bringing in more victims.

"Hey, Gail, we got two d.o.a.'s. You want to do the official notices?" It was one of the fire department's deputy chiefs who had worked with the fire department for more than twenty years.

He and Gail's father had been friends for almost as long, even after her father retired from the department, they still kept in touch. Gail's father was the first black to be hired with the fire department, and it has been one of those defining moments in civil rights history.

Jimmy, the deputy fire chief, had been one of the few firefighters who stood up for and by her father during those turbulent years and she was sure that action prevented him from ever being appointed fire chief.

"My God Jimmy, how many do we have now? What area of town were these located?" Gail sucked in her breath as she turned back the sheet to look at the latest fatalities. She didn't want to hear her neighborhood in that report.

"Last report I heard, twenty-three dead, hundreds injured. These were at that new Marriott on Highway 64. It was leveled."

Jimmy was looking at Gail in a puzzled kind of way. She caught his stare. "What is it?" she asked.

Leaning in closer to her, he whispered. "Don't you recognize her?" Jimmy nodded at the dead woman on the stretcher.

Gail looked a second time and stopped writing the report.

The woman was strikingly beautiful, even with her long red hair matted to her bloody head. The upper torso was badly bruised, but even in its battered condition, Gail could tell the woman had spent a lot of money on cosmetic surgery to achieve the perfect pair of breasts. Folding the sheet down, she noticed a huge ruby and diamond ring on her finger. She then felt a little dizzy, took a deep breath and looked up into the face of Jimmy.

"She was Miss Alabama....married to Simon Parker. She's not a pretty site now huh? First time seeing something this bad?" Jimmy asked and patted Gail's shoulder.

"Yeah, it's my first one," Gail whispered, her tears were distorting her vision.

Jimmy moved closer to Gail so no one could over hear what he was about to say, "You know they found her at the Marriott on 65, naked as a jaybird in a hotel room with Larry Coleman."

Gail looked at the Deputy Chief stunned. He nodded towards the door, "The unit behind me has him. We were told this was serving as the morgue, so they should be arriving in a matter of minutes."

Jimmy then turned back to give Gail encouragement, "You're doing great honey. Your Dad would be proud of you." Jimmy gave her a quick hug and turned to walk down the corridor.

"Larry Coleman? Larry is dead?" Gail hoarsely asked.

"Yeah honey I'm afraid so." Jimmy answered.

Gail's head felt as if it were ready to explode. She had been working since 7 a.m., it was now past 7:30 p.m., and she still hadn't been able to get in touch with her children and now her friend was dead.

She looked around the ward. Most of the nurses were mothers too, but none had asked to leave and she knew they were worried about their families just like she was.

"Gail, phone!" One of the nurses held up the receiver before continuing her conversation with a family member searching for a tornado victim.

"Hello?" Gail was massaging her temples, trying to relieve the intense pain.

"Hey...it's me...I know you're busy...someone wants to talk to you." It was Maceo.

"Mommy! We were so scared! All of the lights are out and the phone too! Jonathan and I hid in the closet and." It was Jessica excitedly recounting every moment of the tornado.

"Honey! You okay? Where's Jonathan?" Gail was laughing and crying.

"Hi Mom. We're fine. We tried to call you but we couldn't get through, so Maceo came over. The tree in the back yard is down, and the fence is real wobbly but we're okay." Jonathan was sounding like a little man, completely unfazed by the situation. Gail knew he was trying to impress Maceo.

"Listen, we're going to my place. I've got electricity and I know you've got a long night ahead of you, so just come here when you get off. When I couldn't get through to them, I figured I should just go and get them, you don't mind do you?" Maceo asked.

"Thank you...thank you. I was so worried. They're both okay?" Gail asked.

"Yeah, Jonathan took great care of Jessica They were both outside in the yard when I pulled up. Overall, your neighborhood fared okay, a couple of downed trees did in the power lines. And don't thank me for doing something that comes naturally. I'll be waiting up for you."

Gail smiled, and turned her back away from the increasing noise in front of her. "I don't have any clothes..."

"I pulled some things out of the trees for you. No seriously, Jessica brought some things for you." He laughed.

"Oh, Lord, I'll be dressed like Hannah Montana!"

"Hurry home. Bye." The kids yelled good-bye before Maceo hung up his cellular phone.

Gail felt a new burst of energy. She knew it would be close to midnight before she could leave. She had to do paper work for at least three death certificates and brief the next shift coming on.

She had just started filling out more paper work when the phone rang again. She answered it. "Hey, it's me again...sorry to disturb you." It was Maceo.

"What's wrong?" Gail asked.

"Nothing, I just wanted to say something and I didn't know if I should wait until you got here, or not. So after thinking about what's happened, you know the tornado, I decided that every minute, every second counts, take nothing for granted. Gail, I love you. Hurry home." He sounded out of breath.

Gail held the phone. She kept waiting for the punch line.

"Well anyway, that was it. So get back to work." He paused for her reaction.

"Maceo, I really needed to hear that tonight. I've seen a lot of pain and suffering. People who seem lost after losing someone they love tonight. Lives have been changed forever, in the blink of an eye. You're right, take nothing for granted. I think I've loved you from the moment you gave me a hard time in this very hospital and I know I love you now. I'll be home soon." Gail's heart was thumping wildly. She felt like she was in love for the very first time.

"Okay...that wasn't so hard after all." He exhaled loudly.

They both hung up and smiled. Gail knew that no matter what time she got to his house, tonight was going to be like no other.

Chapter 12

Evelyn was crouched down in the hallway, watching all of the activity of the paramedics and medical staff at the hospital. They had been working on Sonja for almost an hour and Evelyn still didn't know how bad she was.

One of the nurses had tried to give Evelyn a sedative after the ambulance attendant reported she had fainted, but she refused. She needed to contact Danny, her parents and even Kevin, to let everyone know she was fine.

Numb and still a little dazed, Evelyn stood up and walked to a pay phone in the waiting area. She fished in her jeans pocket and found some change and for a moment, she had a hard time remembering her parents phone number. Slowly dialing the numbers, her mouth became suddenly overwhelming dry. The phone was making a buzzing sound, and finally a recording came on announcing service to that area was temporarily out. Evelyn hung up the receiver and then thought about Kevin. He must have seen the reports on news by now and would be worried.

She dialed the operator and asked for the number for Ritz Carlton in Los Angeles. It was close to ten o'clock in Birmingham and would be around one in the morning on the West coast.

Evelyn heard the hotel desk clerk in a crisp happy voice announce it was the Ritz Carlton, and how could she be of assistance.

"Kevin Williams' room please," Evelyn found the strength to whisper her request.

She heard the phone ringing. On the fifth ring, someone picked up. Evelyn didn't recognize the voice and she thought the hotel operator must have connected her to the wrong room. She was about to apologize and hang up when she heard Kevin's voice in the background.

"Hello, I'm looking for Kevin Williams. Is this his room? This is his wife."

There was a brief hesitation on the other end. The stranger then responded, "I know who you are."

Evelyn shifted her weight to lean against the wall, "Who is this?"

The stranger sighed, "I think you should ask Kevin who I am."

"Is this some sick law school joke? I need to speak to Kevin!"

The stranger met her sarcasm, "Sick? Yes, we are sick. Sick of the charade and frankly sick of you too. I told him marrying you was a mistake, he should be honest enough with an Ellie May like you to just leave you to the simple life. And here you are, tracking him down even after he has told you to get lost. It's over, don't you get it? Kevin is way nicer than I would be. Don't make this a habit of calling him anymore. Bye now." He said.

Kevin picked up on another extension, "What do you want?" He snapped.

"Kevin, who was that man?" Evelyn stammered.

"We'll talk later about that. What do you want Evelyn?" He sounded pissed off.

"I was calling you about the tornado. We had a tornado and a lot of people were killed. Kevin, who was that? What charade is talking about? What is he talking about?" Evelyn's voice started cracking and she couldn't hold back her tears.

"Are my folks okay? Evelyn? Evelyn? Where are you?" Kevin was screaming.

"I'm at the hospital. Sonja was hurt real bad. I can't get my parents because most of the phone lines are down and I haven't called your grandparents yet. I thought you would be worried."

Evelyn shook her head to clear the confusion swirling inside, "I can't believe this is happening…tell me this is a joke. Are you gay? Tell me!" She wiped her face with the tail of her shirt just in time to see a gurney being wheeled past her with a covered body. The only thing showing was the woman's hand and the diamond and ruby ring.

"Oh my God! It's Stephanie! It's Stephanie, she's dead Kevin! I just saw her and she's dead!" Evelyn was cradling the phone with both hands.

She couldn't make out what Kevin was saying on the other end, something about a flight and his grandparents. The shock of the entire day was too much for Evelyn and she was losing control.

Some of the hospital staff heard her wails, and came over to assist her. As they were leading her to one of the emergency rooms, she saw several police officers in distress and visibly upset. She overhead their conversation as she passed by.

"Who's calling Larry's mom? The Chief? One of us should go with him, she's going to take this pretty hard." One of the black officers said shaking his head.

When Evelyn passed one of the treatment rooms, she saw Larry Coleman's body. Bile started to find its way to her throat, he he would no longer be there for her in her time of desperate need. The room started to spin and Evelyn saw the floor coming up to meet her.

Kevin hung up the phone and started throwing his clothes in a suitcase. He never looked at the man sharing his king sized bed, as he barked for him to call the airlines and book him on the next available flight to Birmingham. He then swiftly clicked on the television to CNN to see the devastation.

Evelyn awoke to her hand being stroked by her parents. Her mother was smiling weakly and Evelyn struggled to speak but her lips felt heavy and her throat dry.

"Just relax baby...they gave you a shot to calm you down. Thank God we found you...we were worried sick." Her mother said.

"Have you heard from Kevin? You'd think a man would at least call to check on his family." Her father grumbled.

"Shush! Phones are out Sam. He'll get here when he can. Please don't start this now." Patty whispered.

Evelyn's father turned to walk out of the room, but met one of the doctors at the door.

Evelyn was groggy, but the doctor still looked awfully young to her. Must be a resident she thought. The young white doctor removed his black-rimmed glasses and rubbed his eyes before looking at her chart again.

"I'm Dr. Klein. How you feeling Mrs. Williams?" He spoke slowly.

"I'm tired." Evelyn mumbled.

"Welcome to Birmingham on tornado day." He smiled weakly.

"I examined you and really didn't find any thing major. No doubt you are under a lot of stress. I understand two of your close friends were, well didn't survive. I would suggest you go straight home, go to bed and take one of these mild sedatives I'm going to prescribe. Will someone be home with you?" He started writing on her chart and glanced up quickly to look at her mother.

"Yes. She'll be at home with us." Patty sounded relieved.

"Now, these sedatives are very mild and will just help you sleep, I'm only giving you a few, just take one a day. They shouldn't interfere at all with your pregnancy."

Evelyn thought she misunderstood that last part, until she saw her parent's reaction. Her father spoke first.

"What? You sure got the right chart there?"

"Ah, yes sir. Didn't you know you were pregnant Evelyn?" The doctor looked surprised and then re-read her chart.

Evelyn felt her heart racing and recalled the closet sex episode. She wanted to go to her parents' house, crawl into bed and take the entire bottle of pain pills.

Her mother grabbed her hand, "Honey, a baby! I'm going to be a grandmother! Through all this tragedy, the Lord has blessed us." She smiled.

Evelyn finally found the strength to speak, "I want to go home. Now. Please Daddy, take me home." She was throwing back the bed sheet and swung her legs off the bed to sit up.

Her mother was profusely thanking the doctor and her father was looking at her curiously. He knew something serious was troubling his baby girl.

Chapter 13

Sonja felt as though she was flying in a warm air space with complete darkness. Then she entered a blinding white light, followed by a red glowing light.

She could hear voices but couldn't see where they were coming from. She wanted to open her mouth, but her lips felt too heavy to part. She tried to raise her arms to stop from flying towards the red light, which was starting to burn her face.

Her arms felt too heavy to lift. The red light became hotter and hotter, she could feel the tears rolling down her face, and her heart was pounding in her chest as though it would crack her chest cavity at any moment.

She kept trying to speak, wave her arms for someone to help her, but the voices grew fainter. Then darkness. Complete darkness.

Sonja's mother and Danny kept calling her name, watching as she tried to flail against an invisible monster. The doctors had warned them she would be in extreme pain and the morphine administered intravenously would provide only temporary relief, and force her to sleep to stop her suffering.

Sonja had suffered a fractured left arm, serious lacerations and cuts to her face. A shard of glass had severed her top lip and a section of her nose. It was a miracle she wasn't blinded by the shattering glass in her face. They had bandaged her face after having to give her close to two-hundred stitches, but a plastic surgeon would have to be consulted for reconstructive work.

She would come in and out of consciousness, but the pain was so intense, Danny would administer the pain i.v. pump to spare her suffering.

If there was one silver lining at all to the tragedy, it was Sonja's mother. She had made a miraculous recovery after witnessing Sonja's injury and regained her ability to walk and speak. She kept a vigilant watch over her daughter, refusing to leave for three consecutive days.

Danny, who was beside himself with worry, badgered the nurses and doctors' non-stop about Sonja's injuries and how long the bandages would stay on. He knew she was going to be devastated and he wanted to have answers ready the moment she came from under the sedatives and pain medication.

§§§§§§§§§§§§§§§§§§§§

Evelyn was in her old room, surrounded by her fashion magazines, high school photos, favorite books and favorite music.

Her parents had respected her privacy and let her stay without questioning why she was so upset about the baby. Only her grandmother had ventured into the darkened room to check on her. Each time Evelyn pretended to be asleep.

She hadn't even gone to the hospital to see Sonja. She did call and speak to Danny, who said Sonja was so heavily sedated, she wouldn't know who was in the room anyway.

Three days after the tornado, Kevin came to Evelyn's parents' house. She could hear their voices rising and falling in conversation. First the friendly greeting and then her father's bass voice controlling the rest of the dialog.

Evelyn felt one-hundred years old as she slowly got out of bed and made her way to the kitchen. She could hear her father questioning Kevin.

"Boy, it's been three days and you ain't called, or nothin. What kind of husband acts like that? I don't care if you and Lynn are fighting, she is your wife and for you to just now come traipsing over here ain't right."

"Sam, I understand you're upset, but I had to check on my house and my grandparents had no electricity and needed to be put up in a hotel. I knew Evelyn was okay over here and I'm here to take her home now." Kevin responded in his best attorney's tone. The only thing missing was an introduction that said, *"Ladies and gentlemen of the jury."*

Evelyn walked into the kitchen and sat in a dining chair, "I am not going anywhere with you. Get out." She stared into his face with such hatred that Kevin took a step backwards.

As usual, her mother butted in, "Now Evelyn, you have a lot of hormonal things going on right now. It's normal when you're expecting, to be emotional."

That revelation gave Kevin enough courage to kneel at Evelyn's side, "You're pregnant? Baby, this is great…"

"Great? Great? What's so great about it? That your cover will remain in tact? How will your gay lover feel about a baby? Do you think I'm this desperate to go back to a lying, conniving, cheating queer?" Evelyn turned to face him.

The silence in the room was deafening. Evelyn's father was the first to speak.

"I knew it all the time. All you had to do was ask a few folks and the truth would come out…I knew it all the time."

"I don't believe this garbage. Jealous folks will start a lie and make it stick to your dying day if you let them. Evelyn, I know you do not believe some crazy gossip about your husband," Pat stepped in front of her husband.

"Mama, I don't have to believe anything except my own ears and eyes. I spoke to Kevin's lover on the phone. I called his hotel room the day of the tornado, and his special friend answered the phone. You want to know the truth Mama? Kevin and I were getting divorced anyway. He doesn't love me. He doesn't love any woman. He is a two faced homosexual who needs to keep up appearances."

Kevin stood up quickly, "Stop saying that! We need to talk at our home…not here. You are confused and creating all this drama because I wouldn't support the loan for the dress shop."

"Stop saying the truth? Stop calling you a lying two faced fag?" Evelyn stood up and walked towards Kevin. The right-handed slap echoed in the room.

He took the blow with silence and slowly rubbed the cheek with a handprint left behind.

Suddenly feeling a renewed sense of strength, Evelyn continued, "And I am at home. This is my home. And this is my baby. You are dead to me and this child."

"Evelyn, stop being overly dramatic. Listen to your mother, do you know how many women would love to be in your place? You're throwing this away! We are going to be parents. Get your things and let's go." He reached for her arm, but Evelyn's father intercepted his hand, and held it firmly.

"Evelyn is at home. This is her home, and son I'm only gon' say this once. Get out of my house. If my child says you a fag and I say you a fag, you might as well be one."

Kevin's face started to turn beet red and he looked at Pat who knew not to contradict her husband on this one. Mama Ree walked to the kitchen door and held it open. Kevin walked out without a word.

It was then that Evelyn allowed herself to completely break down. She cried for being fooled, for being hurt and for having to raise a child alone. She cried for Stephanie and Larry and Sonja. She cried because she had no words to explain how she felt. Her parents held her and told it was going to be fine. And she believed them. Everything was going to be fine.

§§§§§§§§§§§§§§§§§§§§

It had been seven days since the tornado and Sonja was slowly being weaned off the morphine drips and would stay awake for several hours a day. She had difficulty speaking because of the swelling of her top lip, and her entire face was swollen. The bandages were due to come off today, and she would get the first look at the damage done to her face. She had wanted no one in the room except her mother, but Danny had insisted on being there.

The doctor and nurse were standing before her; the doctor's face was like a stone wall, so Sonja decided to focus on the nurse's face.

A woman's reaction would tell her all she needed to know before she looked in the mirror. Her mother was to her right and Danny was on her left, holding her hand.

The doctor made three or four quick snips with scissors to start the gauze to unravel. To Sonja, it seemed the gauze never stopped. The doctor silently unwound, snipped, and unwound. He discarded the blood stained gauze in a little metal pan held by the nurse.

Sonja kept eye contact with the nurse. She would catch Sonja's eyes and give her a nervous smile, or an encouraging nod that things were going well.

Finally the doctor spoke as the last piece of gauze wrap fell away, "Let's see what we've got here…umm…not bad…not bad at all. Still some swelling, that's to be expected. I'm sure it's pretty sore, but that will dissipate as well…"

The nurse kept nodding in agreement with the doctor's words. Sonja saw something else in her eyes. Not horror, or repulsion; but pity.

Sonja reached for the hand mirror on the nightstand. She heard the gasp escape from her throat, because she didn't recognize the face staring back at her. There was only a deep purple and red gash where her top lip had been and her eyes were blackened as though Mike Tyson had used her as a sparring partner.

Her cheeks were swollen to twice their size and the stitches covered her face from her forehead to her chin in a zigzag design. Her nose was still covered with surgical tape because parts of her nostril was still missing and would be reconstructed by the surgeon. She couldn't stop looking in the mirror, finding a new bruise, stitch or injured part the longer she looked.

Then she heard her heart beating. She looked at the doctor and nurse, certain they could hear if from where they were standing. Her mother kept whispering in Italian trying to console her, while Danny stood there with tears in his eyes said nothing.

Her breathing became more labored and Sonja knew she was having a heart attack. She tugged at the neck of her hospital gown as the perspiration trickled between her breasts and down her back. The sweat trickled down her forehead, which burned the scarred skin like hell. Without uttering a word, Sonja handed the mirror to the doctor and lay back onto her bed.

The doctor's lips were moving, but she could only hear her heart pounding in her ears, and word "monster' screaming inside her head.

She saw the nurse preparing to give her an injection, saw her rub alcohol on her arm and watched the sliver of a needle quickly disappear beneath her skin. She saw all of this, but she felt nothing.

§§§§§§§§§§§§§§§§§§§§

Gail slept for 12 straight hours and still awoke bone tired. Maceo's large master bedroom had served as community property for all of them the past few nights. Electricity was slowly being restored to damaged neighborhoods but Gail's was one of the last ones to even see a utility company truck. She had made a few trips to her house to get clothes for her and the kids, and to start throwing away spoiled food in the freezer and refrigerator.

With only minor structural damage to her house, the insurance adjusters couldn't promise hasty action. Gail enjoyed the large master bedroom and the even larger kitchen that Maceo was only too willing to share.

She was scheduled to go to work in 24 hours and still had not heard from Laura. Her stomach turned a flip just thinking of what was ahead when they saw each other again.

Gail had placed Laura on medical leave, insisting she get counseling and help for withdrawing from the diet pills. The administrative action kept Laura on the payroll as part of the employee assistance program, but the counseling would have to be documented in her personnel file, in order to save her job.

Laura refused to speak to her and still was not taking her calls. Gail did the only thing she knew, and that was to call Ted. He thanked her and said he would check on Laura. And then he said he would make sure they did counseling together.

Maceo was at his office and Jessica and Jonathan were in the pool. That had become her kids' life; that pool and those dogs. Gail slowly walked to the kitchen and picked up the morning paper while pouring a glass of orange juice.

The tornado victims were featured on the front page. Twenty-three of Birmingham's residents from every walk of life. From the elderly and frail, to the rich and powerful like Stephanie Parker, photographed clutching her roses and Miss Alabama crown from years past.

Fighting back the tears, Gail focused her eyes on Larry Coleman's photo, so handsome in his police officer's uniform.

Funeral arrangements were being finalized, and life was now trying to return to normal in Birmingham.

Chapter 14

Evelyn dreaded what lay ahead. Funerals.

Funerals for Stephanie and Larry.

Pain and suffering. Seeing Kevin at Stephanie's funeral.

Her father had tried to talk her out of going, but she needed closure. She wasn't so sure if the closure was to see Stephanie or Kevin, for the last time.

All of the Southern region's highest society, including the Governor of Alabama was at the First Baptist Church that sat in the town square. Evelyn recognized many of the peroxide blondes and their grim faced husbands as they entered the church.

There was just enough room in the ten-thousand-seat sanctuary, and from her seat in the upper level, Evelyn could see Simon below, his head bowed, his arms linked to his adult daughter and son. She spotted Stephanie's parents and siblings. She saw the law firm's partners and families sharing an entire section.

Then she saw Kevin. Sitting next to one of the partners, constantly craning his neck looking around and periodically whispering something to his colleague.

Probably negotiating if he should jockey for a better seat in the church, surrounded by the most powerful people in the State thought Evelyn.

Evelyn changed her focus and let her eyes fall on the large oil portrait of Stephanie on a gold easel near the closed casket. The portrait had captured the former beauty queen in one of her many designers' gowns looking flawless. Just the way she would have wanted it.

The service ended after forty-five minutes and the sanctuary started to empty. Outside, funeral goers took turns hugging and giving condolences to Simon. Evelyn stood her turn in the long line and suddenly felt a firm hand on her arm.

"Hi, you okay?" Kevin nudged through the crowd, mouthing apologies as he moved around mourners behind Evelyn.

She yanked her arm from his grasp. "I am fine. And I want to speak to Simon alone."

"There is no need for this now. We can go up to him together, he would appreciate it more." Kevin whispered in her ear.

"How do you know what he'd *appreciate*? I've known him longer than you have, I think I know what he'd appreciate. He appreciates honesty and not some fake show of concern." Evelyn walked towards Simon who held both hands out to greet her.

"Evelyn...I was wondering if you were coming. Kevin said you might not because you were sick. Well, I shouldn't say sick, that's such a negative connotation. Congratulations my dear. You'll make a wonderful mother, Steffie thought the world of you, and if she were here now..." Simon's voice trailed.

Evelyn finished his sentence, "She'd be planning the biggest baby shower in all of Alabama. I'm going to miss her so much Simon, and I know saying I'm sorry doesn't start to show how much we all will miss her. She was like another kind of sister to me you know." Evelyn wiped a tear from her cheek and gave Simon a hug.

He clung to her longer than any of the others who had paid their respects. With misty eyes, he whispered. "Take care of that baby and if you need anything, I mean anything, call me first."

Evelyn started to feel weak as she turned to walk away. If only Simon had known about the other side of Stephanie, he would be destroyed. Thank God she had never confided to Kevin about Stephanie's secret life. He would surely blackmail her with the information and use it to leverage his relationship with Simon, just like he tried to do by telling him she was pregnant.

Kevin was waiting at her car. Evelyn clinched her teeth and hissed at him, "Why in the hell did you tell Simon I'm pregnant?"

"Why not? It's good news. We're going to have a family."

"We are not going to have a damn thing. I want a divorce and I want it soon." Evelyn opened her car door, but he blocked her entrance.

"We need to talk. You are about to destroy the best thing you have going for yourself. A successful husband, the perfect society marriage and a beautiful home. All over some bullshit."

"It is not bullshit to me that my successful husband wants to have his downlow life style protected. I hate your guts, you bastard."

"Hey Evelyn. How's it going?" Maceo Sloan suddenly walked up behind Evelyn.

"Hi Maceo, I'm hanging in there."

"You must be Kevin, Evelyn's husband, I'm Maceo Sloan," he extended his hand to Kevin, who took it quickly.

"Mr. Sloan. A pleasure, I've heard a lot about you. The firm considers you one of our best clients. I've been trying to get the opportunity to meet you for a while."

"Well thank you. And thank you for letting your smart wife go into business with me. I think after this tragedy dies down, the shop will take off like gang busters." Maceo gave Evelyn a warm smile.

Kevin tried to hide the surprise at that news. He looked at Evelyn as though he had caught her in bed with another man. She smiled sweetly, letting his sick and suspicious mind do the rest of the damage.

"Yes, this shop has been a dream of Evelyn's for a while...we're very excited about what it will mean for this area." Kevin mumbled out a vague response.

"You should be excited, especially for Evelyn. I love seeing young people attack a dream and refuse to take no for an answer. We need more visionaries like her," he smiled warmly at Evelyn.

"Thank you Maceo, but my husband here doesn't think I have the brains to run a business. That's why I needed you, Danny and Sonja to step up and make this happen. What we need are more people who support each other, not lie, cheat and perpetrate to keep up appearances." Evelyn opened her car door as Maceo cut a sharp glance at Kevin.

"Well, I won't get into this debate. I think I should be going. Nice meeting you Kevin, and Evelyn we'll be talking soon." Maceo turned and walked away as Evelyn started her car and gunned out of the parking lot, leaving Kevin dumbfounded.

The episode at the funeral with Kevin gave Evelyn the energy to go to the hospital to visit Sonja. Mentioning her name as a business partner shot pains of guilt through Evelyn, reminding her that she hadn't been a good friend. Sonja needed her support now. Danny was at wits end trying to figure out how to deal with her injuries. Danny hadn't left her side since the tornado, even though she was so heavily sedated she had no idea who was in the room.

Evelyn slowly opened the hospital room door and saw Danny at her bedside reading the paper. He looked up and gave Evelyn a warm smile.

"Hey, come on in. I didn't think you'd come by so soon. With the funeral and all." He hugged Evelyn.

She glanced at the bed at Sonja and felt her stomach lurch. Sonja's face was swollen to twice its normal size with purple baseball sized bruises. Her breathing was shallow and Evelyn guessed she was in a drug induced sleep.

"How is she doing?" Evelyn asked.

"She was awake for few minutes this morning. The doctors are concerned that the swelling isn't going down as fast as they had hoped. The reconstructive surgeon will be here tomorrow, but there's nothing he can do until the swelling goes down." Danny sounded weary and looked exhausted.

"You should go home and get a real nap, some hot food and let me stay." Evelyn pleaded.

"I'm okay. I'm used to sleeping on the chairs now. I can't leave. If she wakes and I'm not here, she'll freak out. It happened yesterday with her Mother. I'm the only one who can calm her down." Danny took a kleenex and dabbed at the corners of Sonja's mouth as a trickle of saliva started to make its way down her chin.

Chapter 15

S onja was flying through a sky that was bright red. Not a burning hot red, but a warm soothing red. There was no sky, just a vibrating red enclosing her and pulling her faster and faster.

She could hear voices, but couldn't see their faces. She spread her arms open and let the warm red light flutter around her body. She could feel herself smiling as the voices grew louder. She finally saw the outline of the bodies where the voices were coming from. There were so many of them and Sonja wanted to see their faces, but couldn't stop flying long enough to determine who they were.

They kept calling her name, and she wanted to apologize for stopping to talk with them, but she knew she had to keep flying. She was late and didn't want to keep the important person waiting for any longer.

She kept flying as the red light grew brighter and started to fade to a light pink. She knew the special person was just beyond the pink light as she reached her arms in front of her body trying to speed up her flight. The pink light started to glow to a soft creamy white. She could feel the creamy light permeating her pores, going right into her heart, her lungs and her stomach. She could almost taste the light, as though it was cotton candy that melted into on her tongue.

It was the best sensation of Sonja's life. She didn't want it to stop. She kept smiling and flying, and finally saw the shadow of her important friend.

He was tall. He reached out to meet her out stretched arms, and slowly brought her body to his chest. She clung to him and started laughing.

She could feel him shaking his head slowly, letting her know the answer was no. He seemed sad, as he gently took her entwined arms from around his waist. He never said a word, but she knew he was telling her goodbye.

Sonja tried to argue and protest his decision, but he started to back away and no matter how hard she tried, she couldn't walk towards him to stop him. He became a faint shadow and Sonja started to cry.

Her body was violently jerked backwards so fast, her hair blew into her face and there was no more warm red colors, just deep darkness. It was so dark she couldn't tell where she was going, just that she was moving very fast.

Her eyes started to burn and her chest felt as though it was going to explode. She could hear voices again, this time they sounded frightened. They were calling her name with a sense of urgency and fear.

The darkness was stripped away by a blinding blue light. She shut her eyes and tried to scream but something was blocking her throat and covering her mouth.

"Clear! What's her bp?" Dr. Klein was in a near panic as he administered the defibulator procedure on Sonja.

Gail Emerson was watching the monitor for Sonja's vital signs and finally saw the heart monitor line peak after the first electrical shock.

"She's back Dr. Klein." Gail spoke softly to the young doctor.

"I want her closely monitored every 15 minutes. I don't understand what could have created this state. She was recovering nicely." He was muttering to himself as he examined Sonja's chart.

It was only a few minutes later they both remembered they had an audience. Evelyn was whimpering into Danny's shoulder. He still could not speak.

Gail turned to him and touched his arm.

"Are you okay?"

"I..I...just never thought she could die." he stammered.

"I'm Gail. A friend of Maceo's. He told me to look out for you and your fiancée. He is so fond of you… he sometimes forget that looking after patients is my job." She gave him a warm smile.

"You saved her life. I don't know what we would have done if you had not been here." Danny said.

Gail waved off his compliment, "Oh there are plenty of people capable of taking good care of Sonja, and Dr. Klein did all the heavy lifting." She nodded as the doctor walked up.

"I'm just a second year resident, believe without Nurse Emerson I …"

"Is she going to be okay?" Evelyn interrupted.

Dr. Klein gave her a look that acknowledged he recognized her and answered. "We will have to keep a close eye on her blood pressure. Her doctor will be in today to go over her progress. She was scheduled for reconstructive surgery this week and he may want to postpone that. But how are you doing? Getting enough rest?"

Evelyn was caught off guard and embarrassed by his obvious concern. "I'm much better... I am going to start getting more rest. I promise."

"You both look like you haven't slept in days." Gail scolded.

"I'll tell Maceo I met you and you call me if you need anything. While I'm on duty I will personally come by and check on Sonja. Okay?" Gail started walking to the door and Dr. Klein quickly followed her.

After they left, Danny allowed himself to finally fall apart.

The following week Sonja seemed strong enough to undergo her first round of reconstructive surgery to repair her nose and top lip. The doctors warned her mother and Danny that her recuperation would be painful and several surgeries would be needed in the coming eighteen to twenty-four months.

She was writing notes and asking a lot of questions about how she looked and when would she be going home. She had lost weight because of the soft foods, and liquid diet and was adamant about postponing the wedding. Danny kept trying to convince her that in a month she would be able to walk down the aisle just as pretty as any bride could hope to be. He was a man in a desperate situation that seemed to be going from bad to worse.

It started out as a better than normal second week since the tornado. Danny was carefully feeding Sonja a cup of clear broth and wiping away the constant drool that escaped her mouth when her hospital room door opened to a flurry of activity.

A young be speckled Hispanic man walked in and looked from Sonja to Danny.

"May I help you"? Danny asked.

"Sorry. Sorry to intrude. Is this Miss Davenport?" he asked casting a quick look at Sonja.

"Yeah... who are you?" Danny stood up.

The young man quickly extended his hand.

"I'm Jose' Suarez, personal assistant to Senator Raymond Ramos. He is touring the disaster area with Senator Collins, and we understand that one of his constituents was injured. Miss Davenport." He nodded towards Sonja.

"She used to be one of his constituents. She lives here now and she is one of Senator Collins' constituents." Danny snapped.

"Certainly…you are?" The young assistant asked.

"I'm her fiancée."

Without really listening for an answer, the assistant got to the point. "Very good. Well Senator Ramos is here, actually, he'll be coming this way in about 15 minutes and I'm just here to let him know that Miss Davenport has been alerted to his visit. Excuse me," he quickly snapped his blackberry off his belt and read an email.

"The Senator is on the property…" he looked at Danny as though he was no longer asking permission but giving an order.

Danny cast a quick glance at Sonja who was struggling with her pillows, trying to sit up in bed. He saw a look of panic on her face.

"I can't allow him in here. She doesn't want to see him and." Before he could finish the door swung open.

Senator Raymond Ramos was taller than he looked on television, and that surprised Danny. His deep olive skin was darker in person and that surprised him as well.

His tailored black and white thin pin-striped suit fit perfectly and the tailored pristine white shirt practically glowed. His stride was long and he walked with an air of confidence that unsettled Danny. He walked towards him and smiled, held out his hand and shook Danny's the way young boys are taught to shake hands by their fathers.

"You must be Mr. Taylor. It's a pleasure to finally meet you. Sonja speaks very highly of you."

"Senator... likewise." Danny looked him directly in the eye.

Without emotion, Ramos didn't blink, and immediately turned his attention to Sonja. He walked to the side of her bed and reluctantly touched her head, smoothing her hair away from her forehead in a familiar gesture.

"Sonja? How are you? I know you are going to be fine. If you need anything, anything at all I'm just a phone call away," he was obviously uneasy looking at her bruised face, the mutilated lip and nose.

He turned back to Danny. "I'm glad you're here for her. She is a strong woman, a fighter and I know she'll be okay. You do have good doctors?"

"Yeah. The best." Danny dryly answered.

"I mean plastic surgeon? She deserves the best plastic surgeon in the world. She wouldn't settle for less." Ramos was emphatic.

"We're just glad she's alive. Getting her face to look politically correct isn't a priority." replied Danny.

"Of course. I agree. Jose', are we still on schedule?"

And just like that, seconds later, Senator Ramos was onto another agenda and departing the room.

Sonja's eyes said it all. She was embarrassed and sad. She refused to eat for several days afterwards and after the doctor warned her that they would be forced to insert a feeding tube, unless she started accepting food.

The third week after the tornado, Sonja underwent her first round of reconstructive surgery.

Evelyn was battling morning sickness noon and night. She went to the shop and stopped by the hospital to visit Sonja everyday.

She was nervous and excited on this particular day because it had been two days since Sonja's first surgery. The doctors had done a wonderful job and expected her to be able to finally speak.

Danny still hadn't recovered from Senator Ramos' visit and avoided talking about it. Evelyn repositioned the armful of American beauty roses in her arms and as she walked down the hospital corridor.

Mrs. Davenport was in the room, and gave Evelyn a big smile, "Ohhh... look beautiful roses...see Sonja? How pretty."

Sonja had a large surgical gauge covering her nose and most of her cheeks, which was typical for a nose job. Her cheeks and under eye area were the most drastic. The stitches were the give away that she had been in an awful accident and her left eyelid still drooped down a little, but the rest of her face looked like she had a very bad bee sting with lots of swelling. She tried to smile when she saw Evelyn, but quickly winched with pain.

Her words came slowly and sounded slurred.

"Ah asked for Nicole Kidman's nose... but this woss the best they could do."

"You look great. My God, they did an incredible job. How you feeling?" Evelyn whispered.

"Liquid valium is a miracle. Ah highly recommend it."

Evelyn didn't think she had any tears left to cry, but they flowed anyway and she couldn't stop them. In fact, it felt really good to cry. She knew she wanted this baby and with that realization, she was able to release any fears of being a single parent.

Sonja looked puzzled at Evelyn's emotional breakdown, "Whaz wrong wit you?" she managed to ask between dribbles of saliva.

"I might as well tell you now. Kevin and I are getting a divorce and I'm pregnant!" Evelyn put her head in her hands while the sobs racked her shoulders.

"Wha happened?" Sonja propped herself up on one elbow and handed a tissue to Evelyn.

"My God this is too terrible to believe. Sonja, Kevin was having an affair. He's gay. He's been lying to me, his friends, his co workers, probably all of his life. How could he do this me? I want to kill him, I really do!"

Sonja's mother put her arms around Evelyn and looked sadly at Sonja, "Blessing from God, and will give you much joy."

"He's gay? How did you find out?" Sonja asked.

Blowing her nose, Evelyn regained her composure, "Did you suspect anything Sonja, I mean you only knew him a moment but I could tell you didn't like him. Danny never liked him and my father detested him. How could he hate me so much? Was I the only fool here?" she cried.

Sonja shook her head denying any knowledge, "No, I didn't know sweetie. But men like Kevin, have issues that do not involve women like you. He doesn't hate us, he wants to be us."

Evelyn managed to continue, "I called his hotel in California to tell him about the tornado. We had already had a knock down drag out before he left and he asked for a divorce. I was already getting used to that, but when I called his room and this man answers and talks to me like I'm nothing! Kevin didn't deny it either, just did usual selfish, condescending insulting act. I hate him, I really hate him." Evelyn stood up and walked to the sink and splashed water on her face.

"Evelyn? What about the baby? I mean I'm trying to keep it real here." Sonja asked.

"I don't know what to do." Fresh tears started as she faced the question that had been tugging at her heart.

Sonja's mother limped over to Evelyn and repeated her earlier prophecy, "Baby is blessing from God. This baby will bring you much joy."

Chapter 16

anny finally gave into the reality that there would not be a summer wedding. The surgery was taking a tough toll on Sonja and she had sunken into a deep depression after Raymond Ramos' visit.

She was home recuperating but still scheduled for additional surgeries. The tables had turned for Sonja, who was now being cared for by her mother.

Even though the doctors had done a miraculous job on Sonja's face, it was evident she would never be as drop dead gorgeous as she used to be. For Sonja Davenport, anything less than drop dead gorgeous, was unacceptable. She reluctantly agreed to a Thanksgiving wedding date after being badgered by her Mother and Danny, but her heart wasn't involved anymore. She felt empty, hollow and wallowed in her depression.

The wedding invitations, catering, reception and all wedding decisions had been made by Sonja's mother and Evelyn. She felt disconnected from all of her surroundings and spent most of her days at her vanity table examining her face.

The one experience Sonja could not escape was her dream of meeting the mysterious and comforting stranger. Since that dream, she had an overwhelming feeling of loneliness that made her long for his welcoming embrace. For the first time in her life, Sonja Davenport picked up her mother's Bible and started to read.

§§§§§§§§§§§§§§§§§§§§§§§§§

Evelyn was on a mission to coordinate the best wedding Birmingham had ever seen. Morning sickness nor the arrival of her signed divorce papers would stop her from taking charge of the entire nuptials event planning. It was actually a necessity since Sonja had seemed to remove herself from all things associated with the wedding.

Evelyn had just gotten off the phone with Tank Hooks who sheepishly asked if she would take the heavily tornado-damaged boutique off his hands for a lot less than he was asking, and Evelyn said yes, since they had not legally completed the transaction yet. It seemed the same storm system slammed Texas and Hooks suffered extensive personal and professional losses He needed cash before Evelyn reneged on the deal.

Maceo had prepared her for such an offer and told her he his construction firm could make the structural renovations and repairs at a cost savings that Tank Hooks couldn't compete with. Her only requirement was that the store's insurance cover costs for the HVAC, plumbing and electrical damage. Tank sputtered but agreed, which meant Evelyn's final asking price was 40 percent less that original based on the insurance savings Tank would not have to pay out. Maceo had tutored through the entire deal.

Evelyn was leaving her parents home to dash to the florist for a final selection meeting when the phone rang again.

"Hello."

"Hi, is Mrs. Williams in?"

"This is Mrs. Williams, may I help you?"

"Oh, it's Dr. Klein. Matthew Klein. How are you?"

Evelyn sat down and instinctively caressed her stomach, "I'm good. Just busy that's all. Is everything okay with my baby?"

"Oh, I was just calling to see how you were doing. The baby is fine, and so are you. Well not exactly. You are anemic. So you should be feeling a little tired. That's normal for early pregnancies."

Evelyn breathed a sigh of relief, "I have been. But between planning Sonja's wedding and getting ready to open my business, I just thought I was over doing things."

Giving a light chuckle, Klein responded, "Guess what? You are over doing things, so take it easy. I have been waiting to hear from your obstetrician so that I can get your file to him or her. You should have a follow up visit as soon as possible. I saw your mother last week and she said she didn't think you had even found an obstetrician yet, because you're also going through some personal issues."

"She had no right to share that with you." Evelyn snapped.

"No, really it was out of concern for you and the baby. Please don't be angry with her," he soothingly said.

"So what, you're calling to recommend a psychiatrist for me?" Evelyn asked.

Klein hesitated, "No. I'm calling to see if you want me to recommend an ob-gyn for you. And to see if you'd like to go to dinner. Or lunch. Or dessert. A glass of water...should I go on?"

"Sorry Dr. Klein, I don't think that's a good idea. Isn't that against some kind of doctor patient rule? Asking me out?"

This made Klein laugh out loud, "Well technically I'm not your doctor. I treated you in an emergency care situation, and re-

really wouldn't be seeing you again professionally unless you broke an arm or something."

"Well I don't plan on breaking anything, I will get an obstetrician this week, and I am not interested in having a meal or a glass of water with you. I'm a married woman." Evelyn managed to choke that last sentence out as her mother walked through the door.

This caught Klein by surprise, "Oh...I'm sorry, I was under the impression you are divorced. Sorry, really I did not mean to disrespect you. I was asking someone about you, this being a small town and all and everyone knows everyone, so they obviously gave me bad information."

"Yes. They did. I'm really late for an appointment and I have to go. Thanks for calling though." Evelyn hung up while Klein was still apologizing.

"Mama! Why did you tell this man my personal business?"

"What man?" Pat feigned innocence.

"That doctor. How did he know I was getting divorced?"

"But you just said you were married...child you are confusing me." Pat pretended to be innocent.

Evelyn grabbed her purse, "I have to go to the florist. We'll talk later tonight."

"Wait Lynn, I can go with you. We can have lunch downtown and spend some time talking without interruption. Plus you are taking on too much! This wedding is running you ragged. Come on, my treat."

"Mama, the divorce papers came this morning. Kevin has signed them and I'm going to sign today. My mind is made up and so is his. So please don't start on me about this today."

"What did I say?" Pat put her hands on hips, "I said I want to go to lunch with my daughter. That's all."

The flowers were ordered and the final banquet room seating layout was finalized for Sonja's wedding and as much as Evelyn hated to admit it, her mother was a lot of help. The woman knew how to give orders and make decisions.

They had settled in their seats at a quaint Italian restaurant when Pat gave her a huge grin and announced, "I'm having a glass of wine!"

"Okay Ma. Go for it. I think I may join you."

"No, that's not a good idea Lynn. Later in the pregnancy is okay, but it's too early now." She quietly commented.

Evelyn didn't argue and ordered a glass of iced tea. She could feel a serious conversation about to erupt.

Pat continued to chat, "I never treat myself. I am going to start going out to eat more, trying new things even if your Daddy won't go. By the time I started having babies, I didn't have time for nothing but diapers, formula and combing hair."

Pat took a sip her wine and Evelyn pretended to be engrossed in the menu. Pat looked around the restaurant before continuing, "But nothing and I mean nothing, makes me regret having my babies. You girls have been the light of my life. I wouldn't trade you for the world."

"I know that Mama…you don't have to convince me of that."

Grabbing Evelyn's hands, she got to the point, "Lynn. Please have this baby. Don't have an abortion. It would just kill me and your Daddy."

"What are you talking about Mama?" Evelyn whispered to her.

"I know you. I know how you think, what makes you tick. You are my child and I know you. I know why you won't even find an obstetrician, why you acting like you not even going to be a mother. You are ignoring this baby like he's not going to be around," she kept holding her daughters hands.

"Mama, you don't understand. I was married to a man who slept with other men, who degraded me, lied to me, and hurt me. What kind of father would he be to a daughter or heaven help us, a son?"

"It ain't about him. It's about you and this baby. Kevin has to fight his own demons…if it's true."

"I can't believe you still doubt what I am telling you Mama! Why would I lie? About something like this?" Evelyn leaned in closer to her mother as she spit the questions out to her.

"All I am saying is, situations sometimes seem one way when you're mad, or scared. Did he ever hit you?"

"No. He never hit me. But I wish he did, because that is something I could deal with. Talk about with friends, go to a support group for battered women. But this…I feel like the biggest fool in the world. And suppose I have…" Evelyn's throat choked and she couldn't finish.

Pat squeezed her hands and shook her head, refusing to hear the rest of Evelyn's statement.

"You and this baby are going to be just fine. If you thinking about what I said earlier because you scared, you are playing God. Don't try and second guess God. Now I know I meddle. Always have and you know what, I always will where my family is concerned. I didn't want to believe Kevin was that way, because I should have caught it before you. I should have protected you," Pat eyes filled with tears, "Every boy you ever brought to the house, I knew everything about them from their grades, grand parents to where their birthmarks were. How did I let this get past me? How? Sam kept trying to warm me not to be so impressed, but I just wouldn't listen. Sam never liked him."

"Mama it's not your fault. He was charming and he played on it. He was like Prince Charming, and every girl wants a Prince Charming for herself, and her little girl."

"You will be an awesome mother Lynn and you will have plenty help raising that baby. Yes, I will be meddling in that too," Pat laughed and took a sip of her wine.

After finishing lunch and ordering dessert, Pat reached across the table and gently touched her daughters' cheek.

"Please don't get mad at what I'm about to say. You need to see someone and get used to being tested. Honey, it's the reality of what we are dealing with."

"I don't want to think about that now." Evelyn gazed outside the window.

"Well I know someone who is used to …this kind of situation and he wants to help." Pat looked away from Evelyn's incredulous stare.

"Mama please tell me you didn't tell anyone...please tell me." She groaned.

"Dr. Klein worked in a very good clinic in Chicago, that's where he's from, and he's very trustworthy honey, he wants to help. He was going to talk to you himself, but after you blew up"

Evelyn threw her napkin down on the table.

"I can't believe you! You never stop and I will never forgive you for this!" She stood up and ran to the ladies room. The remaining restaurant patrons silently observed the drama.

In the sanctity of the ladies room, Evelyn stared at her reflection in the mirror, and said what had been in her heart and mind.

"God, it would be so easy to just get rid of this baby. It would solve all of my problems. I could go on with my business, I could just focus on my own health if I got sick, I wouldn't have to

worry about a helpless baby. I can't do this. I just can't do this."
She cried.

She was holding her face in her hands and didn't see where the voice was coming from at first. Then she felt a light touch on her shoulder.

"It's okay to be scared. It's a scary situation." The woman was barely 5 feet tall, and had the most incredible blue eyes. Her platinum blonde hair was pulled into a tight chignon and she was smiling at Evelyn as though they were old friends.

"I didn't know anyone was in here. I'm okay, thanks," Evelyn sniffed and ran cold water over a paper towel.

"Yes you will be okay, but you're not okay right now. Just let me say that nothing is too great for God. Things and people are put in our paths to make us stronger and sometimes they serve as a bridge to get us across a raging river. Cross the bridge my child. Cross the bridge and let God work it out for you."

Evelyn looked at the woman and wanted to ask her what she knew about her situation. This was more than a raging river in her life; it was more like Hurricane Katrina.

Before she could offer a sarcastic response, the blonde stranger continued, "May I hug you? And offer a prayer of protection for you and your baby?" Without hesitating and waiting for Evelyn's permission, she gently pulled Evelyn into her arms and held her.

Evelyn felt a wave of warmth and heard herself exhaling as the stranger softly prayed.

"Heavenly Father, Evelyn is worried, dismayed and she's scared. We come to you today offering her heart and soul so that you may remove the fear, replace it with courage. Take away the worry, replace it with faith, and remove that dismay so that she can hear your voice in her times of trials. Let her know that you are with her and her baby always. We know that you have blessed her with this child for a reason, and God's grace and mercy will surely follow the both of them as they fulfill your destiny. Speak to her spirit Holy Father, and let her know that you are God. Amen."

The stranger looked deeply into Evelyn's eyes and smiled, "Feeling better now?"

Evelyn exhaled, "Yes, thank you. I just need to fix my face. Thank you for your kindness."

The stranger took both of Evelyn's hands and simply nodded. She never stopped looking into Evelyn's eyes as though she were looking into her soul.

Without a word, she turned and left the ladies room.

Minutes later Evelyn returned to her table. She glanced around the nearly empty restaurant for the blonde woman, but she wasn't' there.

"Mama, did you see a blonde woman follow me into the ladies room?"

"Blonde? No. After you yelled at me and ran in, no one went in behind you. I can't blame them. Why?"

"A blonde woman prayed for me. Okay, was she one of your agents? Planted in here to work on me?" Evelyn smiled.

"I don't know what you're talking about. I haven't seen a blonde woman in here at all. The restaurant only had a few people seated when we arrived and I didn't see any blonde woman." Pat protested.

Evelyn signaled for her waitress to come to the table.

"Yes Miss?" the young waitress asked

"I was wondering if the platinum blonde woman has left yet? She has blue eyes and was wearing this pale blue suit, a long skirt, she had her hair pulled into a bun."

The waitress looked puzzled and glanced around the restaurant searching for the mystery diner, "No Miss. I'm sorry, but no one has been in here today fitting that description. I would have remembered, because we are short staffed today and have been helping out each other stations, so I either helped serve or took orders for everyone today. Is there a problem?"

"No. Nothing happened. Just bring the check...but could you ask your co workers please, to see if they saw her?"

"Sure Miss...I'll be right back." She gave a puzzled look at Pat and quickly walked away.

"Maybe she was already in the ladies room and left without anyone seeing her. That could have happened." Evelyn reasoned.

"Why, what did she say?" Pat asked.

"She prayed for me and the baby. But Mama, she called my name. I have never seen that woman before in my life."

The waitress returned with the check and seemed hesitant to speak to Evelyn.

"Miss, no one has taken an order for a woman you described, we were short staffed today, so if something happened to upset you, please let our manager know, it wasn't our fault." She stammered.

"Oh, no, nothing bad happened. Just forget I even asked. And I'm sorry about my earlier outburst, I was just a little emotional about something that's all. Everything is fine." Evelyn wanted to put closure on the blonde stranger as quickly as possible.

Chapter 17

Gail was spending most of her days getting estimates from construction companies to repair her roof and the rear section of her home, which received heavy damage. It was still unsafe to return to her home with a partial roof and missing wall section. With so much structural damage in the city, it was hard to even schedule construction estimates and the insurance adjusters were backed up as well.

The kids didn't mind at all. They were becoming spoiled to living on Maceo's sprawling acreage and were in hurry to return to their own neighborhood.

Many local churches were planning a day of healing and thanksgiving at the downtown civic center, and Gails' church was one of the participating houses of worship, which also kept her busy as a committee member. It would be the first time since the 1960's civil rights movement that Birmingham came together, both black and white to encourage and support the community as a whole.

The planned Sunday event was already getting national media attention, with many of the tornado survivors scheduled to speak about their journey to recovery and survival.

With so much going on, Gail didn't have time to check on Laura. She did speak to Ted, who had come back to help look after the children. Laura was in counseling and sent a message that she wasn't ready to see Gail, and she was grateful for the prolonged employee assistance time off that Gail had approved for her to get her life back on track.

As her mind wandered from crisis to task, Gail drove to her neighborhood on this warm and sunny Saturday morning to meet one more contractor who said he felt he could start on her house within a few weeks. She held her breath as she turned onto her street and was met with a sea of blue tarp covering roofs and houses on her street.

She was surprised to see Maceo's Range Rover parked in front of her house. He was in the yard holding a conversation with a few other men and looked like he was giving them hell.

As she parked, a man approached her car from across the street looking concerned.

"Mrs. Emerson?" he asked pushing his cap away from his forehead.

"Yes. What's going on?"

"I'm Craig Stevens, with Stevens Construction and we spoke last week about getting you an estimate today."

"That's right, is there something wrong?" She glanced over to where Maceo was and noticed Craig Stevens was reluctant to move towards her house.

"Well yes Ma'm, we got a problem. Mr. Sloan doesn't think my services are needed and he's over there talking pretty bad about me to your insurance company. Now I got plenty of other work Mrs. Emerson and I don't need to be insulted after you begged me to come out here today. I just want to know what's going on." He shot a hard glance over at Maceo and folded his arms as Gail tried not to look shocked.

"Mr. Stevens, there must be some misunderstanding. Let me go and see what this is about. Do not leave. I'll be right back."

Gail walked over to Maceo who was just finishing what seemed to be a lecture. Her insurance adjuster was looking flustered and had turned beet red.

He seemed relieved to see Gail, "Hi Mrs. Emerson. I just finished looking at your home and it seems like due to the hardship of your family and the severity of the damage, I can expedite your claim. I understand Mr. Sloan's company is going to handle your renovation and we agree, with the amount of water damage, the entire house has to be gutted to avoid any mold risks."

Gail grabbed her chest and looked at Maceo in amazement.

"Gutted? That will take almost a year! Where am I supposed to live and my children have to go to school. I thought you said the roof and the rear of the house could be done in 2 to 3 months."

Before the insurance adjuster could respond, Maceo took Gail's hand in a reassuring manner.

"Baby I do this for a living. Believe me you do not want to rush and do a half-assed job. Now we've done a complete assessment and no insurance company wants to come back in a year and be faced with mold damages and claims, so this is the best. You can get housing as a part of your claim until this place is completely finished."

"But what about Mr. Stevens, he was going to give me a bid and get started next week." She asked.

"You do not want that guy doing this kind of work. He's shady and inexperienced. Send him on his way, I've got this under control. Sir, it's been a pleasure working this out with you and I know you've got a ton of clients to see this morning." Maceo shook hands with the insurance adjuster and steered him away from Gail.

She was still trying to figure out how this had happened without her knowledge or consent when she remembered she had to go and update Craig Stevens.

"Uh, Mr. Stevens, I am so sorry. It looks like my insurance company wants me to consider more extensive work, to avoid the potential of later and more serious claims."

Stevens squinted at her, "Well I would like the chance to bid on that job as well. It don't seem fair that I'm cut out because the work load changed. I can do what ever is needed."

"I am sorry, but I am going to have to look at another company, that has more experience."

"Oh, another company, like Sloan? Another company that happens to be black owned?" he leaned on Gail's car seemingly in rush to end the debate.

"That's not it. This is just so emotional for everybody and I just want my house fixed with the best work possible."

"You want emotional Mrs. Emerson? Let me tell you about emotional. My house was completely destroyed, nothing left, not a wall, a cabinet, a door. My little girl is in the hospital with two broken legs and a punctured lung. The only reason I am out here trying to get work is because I need the money. Yeah I can fix my own house, and I plan on doing that, but right now, I need money for medical bills, because I got crappy insurance coverage. I need all the work I can get. I'm a little company and I cannot compete with the Sloan's of the world who can just pick up the phone and get a million dollar contract. This ain't the first time he's cut me out of a deal."

"Mr. Stevens I am sorry. This is not personal or about your skin color. I am not that kind of person, believe me. I am just doing what is best for my family."

"Sure. Okay, good luck to you Mrs. Emerson." Stevens turned away and walked back to his truck.

Before Gail could recover, Maceo walked over to her looking a little pissed, "Did I hear you apologize to him? You don't have to explain or defend your decisions to him. This is your house and your money."

"I feel bad because I called him to come out here and he has a little girl in the hospital. Maceo he needs the work."

"So? A lot of people have someone in the hospital, some have people in the cemetery because of this storm." He took her arm and starting walking her towards her house.

She looked at Stevens driving away, "How did you know his work was bad? Did you have to tell the insurance adjuster that? He could lose other bids."

"I don't know the first thing about his work. I know he cannot do this job, because I can get someone to do it better. I was thinking of knocking this wall out and creating one huge open living space. Laminate wood flooring, maybe even pitch the roof for a vaulted ceiling. The resell value will jump and you could make a nice profit." Maceo was looking at the damaged roof and living room wall.

"Maceo that sounds way over my estimate, and I can't make up the difference and who says I am going to sell?" She released her arm from his grasp.

Looking down at her with a sly smile, Maceo caressed her face, "I can get this job done under the bid, you can pocket the difference and still sell and make even more money. This is how it's done babe. All day every day. Don't you want a bigger place?

The kids are growing, will need more leg room and you deserve something nice."

"My house is nice. Nice enough for me and the kids and I only owe 10 years worth of mortgage payments. I am not about to get in debt again. I have this all figured out. So please don't plan my life for me." She stepped away from him and looked him squarely in the eyes.

"I am only trying to help. That's all. You know medicine and I know construction, bids and getting jobs done. I was just trying to help."

Gail took a deep breath but her voiced trembled as she spoke, "Maceo I appreciate everything you have done for me and the kids, but I think we should move into a hotel and get our lives back on track before school starts. I need to take advantage of that housing allowance FEMA is offering and start taking care of my business."

"What are you talking about? The kids love my place and there's plenty of room. Why are you over reacting about this?" He asked.

"For one thing, today, just a few minutes ago? I saw that man I met in the hospital a month ago. That mean, snappy, controlling man who had to have his way. I don't know if I can be with that man and its apparent he still exists..."

"Come on Gail! Just because I exert a little confidence and not a sucker for every sob story that comes along, does not make me a bad person and that you and I can't be together. What we have is special and I can feel it." He tried to pull her closer to him but she resisted.

"It's not just today. I should be setting a better example for my children. I have never lived with a man and even though they adore you and you are good to them, I can't let them think, especially Jessica, that it's okay to live with a man."

Maceo chuckled and folded his arms across his chest, "Oh I see where this is going."

"What do you mean? I'm being honest with you because I think we have something special too and I want us to move in the right direction." Gail continued, "Being honest is the only way for people to be who care about each other."

Shaking his head he responded, "You know, I thought you had changed from the needy, calculating and clinging woman I first met. I told you months ago how I was. I was honest. So don't try this with me now. I am not ready to get married and you can't make me feel guilty that you are a bad example for your children. Were you a bad example when you were sleeping around, when your ex-husband was slapping you around in front of them? But I'm worse huh?"

"Married? Negro I do not want to marry you! Is that what you think I was getting at? Please! You are a real piece of work. Everything is not about you Maceo. I have a life and will have a life after you. I made a few mistakes but I don't plan on making another one. We will be out of your house tonight." Gail brushed past him and suddenly turned around.

"Excuse me, could you please leave my property? And do not send your construction crews here. I am going to get Mr. Stevens to do this job."

§§§§§§§§§§§§§§§§§§§§§§

It was an emotional scene at Maceo's with Jessica and Jonathan hugging the dogs and crying, begging Gail to stay. Maceo stayed in his room while Gail threw bags, clothes and their odds and ends into her car.

"Whyyyy? Why Mom? I don't want to leave," Jessica whined, while Jonathan huffed, puffed and rolled his eyes at his mother. When her back was turned.

"I already told you Jess. We need to start getting ready for school, and we have money for a hotel room in the city. It will be easier and Maceo needs his house back, we don't want to wear out our welcome. Hurry up and finish getting your things. I don't want to be out here in the dark."

"But didn't a tornado kill people in a hotel? What if another one comes and kills us?" Jonathan asked with a little bit of sarcasm.

"Stop talking crazy. In fact, stop talking at all. Finish doing what I told you." Gail snapped.

After they finished loading the car, Maceo came outside, "All ready to go huh? You guys be good now and mind your Mom. Call me if you need anything." He shook Jonathan's hand and kissed the top of Jessica's head.

Always the drama queen, she gave him her best teary-eyed look and said in a whisper, "Will we see you at the city wide church services? You can ride with us."

Maceo smiled, "Naw, I'm not much for church. Think I'll pass."

"Let's go guys I've got to unload this stuff tonight." Gail started the car without acknowledging Maceo.

"Sorry we wore out our welcome, thank you for letting us stay with you," Jonathan mumbled as he got in the car.

Gail drove towards downtown Birmingham fighting back tears, while convincing herself she had done the right thing. She mentally drew up a list of what was wrong with Maceo. Like the night she wanted to read the Bible and couldn't find one in his house. After asking him about it, he said he didn't own one.

Luckily she kept one in her car and retrieved it much to his amazement. He even asked why she kept one in her car.

Who doesn't own a Bible she kept asking herself?

Or like when she told him she was on the city wide church committee for the Thankful Celebration. It was the first time blacks, whites, Jewish and several other church denominations were united in worship in the aftermath of the tornado.

Maceo was less than enthusiastic and thought the effort was what he called, "bullshit postering for politicians". When Gail pointed out that the churches, synagogues and temples were leading the event, he laughed and said they were politicians too.

It was a huge event garnering national media attention and even Gail had been interviewed by CNN. Her kids were ecstatic but Maceo just shrugged and said it would take a tornado, a hurricane and a tsunami to get the races together in Birmingham.

He had never recovered nor forgiven the fact that one of his cousins was one of the four little black girls killed in the 16th Street Church bombing in 1963.

By the time Gail and the kids had checked into the Holiday Inn Select, she was dog-tired and simply wanted a hot bath and a good nights' sleep.

While Jonathan and Jessica plopped down in front of the television, Gail let out the sleeper sofa and was about to crash when her cell phone rang. Wearily looking at the caller i.d., afraid it might be Maceo, she stared surprisingly at the phone and saw it was Laura's number.

"Hello."

"Hi Gail. It's Laura. Whatcha' doing?" she sounded like her old self.

"This is a surprise! I'm getting ready for bed."

"This early? Oh, I'm sorry, you still at Maceo's?"

"No. We're at the Holiday Inn Select. Got to get back to life you know? Get the kids ready for school in a few weeks and try to get my house worked on. How are you doing Laura?" Gail sat on the side of the sofa bed.

"I am so much better. I just wanted to call and say I'm sorry for putting our friendship through so much. I have been going to counseling and I can't move on until I ask for forgiveness. I got to tell you Gail, aside from Ted, asking you for forgiveness is the hardest thing I've done in years. I am so ashamed." Laura was sniffling.

After a few seconds of silence, she continued, "I took my marriage for granted and our friendship. I took my family for granted and just wanted to believe that no matter how fat, lazy, mean or hard to get along with I was, everybody would stay with me. Like I deserved some kind of special treatment. I had to realize that folks do leave. Husbands leave wives, best friends stop speaking to each other and your children. Ted and I are in counseling, and he wants to come back to us."

She was openly crying now, "My children had become sad, scared and ashamed that they have a mother like I was. How could I not see that? I didn't want to believe what Ted warned me about."

"Laura, you love your children and you love Ted. Sometimes life gives us a real bump in the road. Looks like you're back on the right track. I'm still you're friend and I forgive you."

Laura blew her nose and gave her familiar chuckle, "Then you and the kids come stay over here. We would love to have you and you'll be closer to your house. You can check on the workers and you can avoid that interstate traffic going to work. Please say you'll come."

Gail said a quick prayer before responding, "Okay. Give us a couple of days here and we'll be there on Friday when I get off. I have a committee meeting that night on the citywide service anyway and didn't want to leave the kids here alone."

"I saw in the paper you were one of the organizers! We can't wait to go. This is a major healing and spiritual awakening for Birmingham. So go to bed and we'll see you on Friday. I'll tell Ted and the kids you guys are coming." Laura happily said.

"Thanks Laura. Goodnight. Love you much."

"I love you too...see ya later."

Seemed like things were returning to normal, but inside Gail still wanted her house repaired as soon as possible. She didn't want to test her friendship with Laura again while staying at her house.

Jessica tapped her on the shoulder, "Mama, who was that?"

"That was Auntie Laura. We're going to be staying with her for a little while until our house is finished."

Jessica's face broke into a wide grin, "Thank you Mama! This is going to be fun."

"And Jessica, I want you and your brother to keep your rooms clean, you hear? And no matter what you see or hear, keep your mouths shut and mind your manners."

The last thing she needed was for Jessica to say something that would insult Laura's housekeeping.

Chapter 18

The RSVP's to the wedding reception were piling up fast and her unconcerned state of mind, Sonja paid little attention to the list of people who wanted to attend what was being called the wedding of the year.

As she flipped through the tastefully done reply cards that Evelyn had selected, an enveloped from Texas caught Sonja's eye. She immediately recognized the handwriting as that of her business partner from the Baron's Club. Sonja ripped open the envelope and was met with the unmistakable scent of Chanel #5, Eva's signature fragrance.

Dearest Sonja,

I got your wedding invitation and you know how much I would love to be there, but things have taken an ugly turn here and the reason I am writing you instead of calling is because I am certain my phones are tapped. I don't even send emails anymore or accept phone calls because of the scrutiny I am under. I know you have been struggling with some serious issues with the tornado, your health and your mother's recovery.

I hate to add to your problems, but I want to warn you. After you left, the club and all of our business trans-actions were hit by the federal authorities. It was a sting operation that had been underway over the last few years.

I just discovered that someone on the inside was fun-neling information to the authorities and that someone was Denise, the newly hired assistant. She was working undercover and I have been advised to expect indictments to be handed down in a matter of weeks, if not days.

The IRS and FBI have already placed holds on the clubs financial bank accounts, we have shut down and in a few weeks the media will no doubt have this information as well.

Since you have relocated, I expect it will take a few weeks for the feds to come knocking on your door. Get a good lawyer. Do not try to contact me or any of the other partners.

I had to have a sales girl at Macy's mail this letter to make sure it got to you. I feel I am being followed every day and couldn't risk this letter being intercepted.

I have to tell you this final thing. My sources tell me this entire sting operation is a way to knock Sen. Ramos out of his presidential bid. This means you are in their sights as a possible link to whatever Ramos has done in the past few years.

I know you are a smart and kick ass woman, but do not call him under any circumstances. I am doing okay, but have to live on the money I had stashed in my house, since my bank accounts are frozen.

Again, get a good lawyer, stay on alert and be ready for the onslaught.

I wish I could see you walking down that aisle! We didn't always see eye to eye, but I did consider you a friend and as someone who needed a friend, whether you admitted it or not. Do not write me Sonja, just pray that this will blow over and we will survive.

Kisses to that gorgeous rich man. (I know he must be both, because you wouldn't have it any other way.) LOL

Love,

Eva

Sonja read Eva's letter at least 10 times, trying to find the missing pieces that would reveal it was a joke or a complete mistake.

She made a pot of coffee, read the letter again and stopped herself from calling Ray Ramos.

Fighting the panic building in her chest, she popped one of her pain pills and with shaking hands turned on her computer. Her first order of business was to check her bank accounts. Breathing a sigh of relief, the money was still there. She mentally put an amount into her mind that she would withdraw today.

She then Googled for any news regarding Ramos.

It was the usual political public relations overload. Campaign swings, fundraising events, the typical family photo op with the adoring wife at her man's side.

The People magazine issue naming him America's sexiest Man Alive; the recent polls naming him the front runner for the party's nomination.

Sonja dashed into her bedroom and pulled on a pair of shorts and a tee shirt. Grabbing her purse, she made her way to the garage.

As she was backing out, Danny was pulling in. Giving her a look of total amazement, he beckoned for her to stop, "Where's the fire?" he asked.

"I have to go into town. I'll be back in a few minutes." Sonja was doing a slow backwards roll, letting him know she didn't have time to talk.

"Whoa…did the doctor say it was okay for you to drive? I can take you, slide over and I'll drive." He was following her slowly moving out the drive way.

"I'm fine! I said I would be right back Danny, God! Just let me do what I have to do, please." Sonja peeled out the drive - way and did a screeching take off down the street.

The Bank of America lobby was practically empty and Sonja walked up to the personal banking desk employee who looked barely old enough to be out of high school.

"May I help you?" Bank of America young person sweetly asked.

"Yes. I want to close my account. And I need the funds in cash." Sonja said breathing hard.

"Okay, I need your account number and identification." Bank of America young person took the account information and Sonja's driver's license and keyed the information into her computer.

She squinted at the screen, cast a sly glance at Sonja, and typed in more information, "Miss Davenport? Is something wrong, I mean did the bank not provide you with the kind of service you needed? We sure hate to lose you as a customer."

"No the bank has been wonderful, I just need to close my account."

"If you could give me a few minutes I need for my supervisor to approve this request and I'll go and get him right now." She gave Sonja a fake smile and printed information off her computer. Walking into a nearby glassed wall office, she handed the computer papers to a balding white man who put on his glasses to get a better look at the information, then peering outside to the area where Sonja was sitting, he spoke briefly to Bank of America young person as he stood up and started walking towards Sonja.

"Miss Davenport? I'm Chester Lewis. Branch manager and I have got to ask you is there anything we can do to keep you as a customer? I see you have a mortgage with us, but we sure want to keep you as a customer if possible."

"Mr. Lewis, I'm getting married in two months and I just need to close this account and merge my funds with my fiancée's account. Unfortunately he is not a Bank of America customer."

Bank of American branch manager Lewis was dogged in his approach, "Well, we would love to have both of you as customers. Maybe you and your fiancée could come in and meet with our financial advisors to review the options we could provide."

Sonja twisted in her seat and between the caffeine and the pain pills, she was starting to get agitated, "Mr. Lewis, I am recovering from injuries from the tornado and I have medical procedures that will cost a lot of money, so if you could just complete my request as soon as possible I'd appreciate it."

Bank of America branch manager Lewis cleared his throat while the young bank employee looked at Sonja with a sense of awe.

"Sure Miss Davenport, sorry to have delayed you. Were you still wanting that in cash? I mean we could do a combination of cd's, cashiers checks, to avoid any possible loss, theft or risk of having to walk around with that kind of money." he laughed nervously.

Sonja was not amused. The bank manager continued, "Okay then. Well we show you have a balance of $438,900.00 in your 401K account and a balance of $178,300.00 in your savings account, and finally in your checking account, a balance of $23,025.00. You understand the 401K withdrawal will have a penalty attached and will translate to income. I have to get the forms and have you sign them and we will need a few minutes to collect your cash. I also need for you sign IRS tax forms and capital gains declaration forms. I'll be right back, would you like something to drink? A coke, some water?"

"A coke would be wonderful. Thanks, with ice." Sonja sat back in the chair as the young employee dashed away to retrieve the soft drink.

Sonja's mind was whirling. There would be a paper trail, the bank would show she withdrew the money but no one would know where she moved it.

Like a homicide, no body, no crime; no money, no seizure.

After thirty minutes of signing forms and continually reassuring Lewis the branch manager that she was not a dissatisfied customer, Sonja walked out carrying $640,225.00 in cash. Every nerve in her body was like an electrical wire. She was shaking so hard it was hard to hold the steering wheel.

Pulling into her driveway, she knew she was going to need help and lots of it. Danny was in the kitchen making a sandwich and still pouting at being snapped at earlier.

Dropping the canvas bag full of money on the breakfast bar, Sonja said breathlessly, "Danny. I'm in trouble. I'm in a lot of trouble."

"Wh..what's wrong? What happened? You hit somebody didn't you? I knew you shouldn't be driving."

Before he could finish his scolding, she opened the canvas bag and held it for him to look inside.

With his eyes bugging, he slowly put his sandwich down and backed away from the bag like it was a bomb.

"Danny, just listen to me. No, just read this, it explains everything." She fished the letter from Eva from her purse.

Danny took the letter and slowly lowered himself into a chair. It seemed like hours as he read and reread the letter several times.

"What am I going to do? I got all this money and I don't know where to hide it. I can't lose my money Danny, it's all I got." Fresh tears started as Sonja paced the kitchen floor.

"Damn. How much is it?" he whispered.

"Over $600 thousand. I got an idea! We can bury it on your ranch you've got lots of land, they would never find it."

"No! That's the first place they would look and how do we know you're not already being watched? Damn! This is unbelievable! I don't know what to tell you. We need to find somebody who understands what this means."

"We cannot go to anyone Danny! We can't tell anyone. I can't risk that." Sonja shook her head emphatically.

"What else can we do? Huh? Just wait for them to kick in the damn door and arrest us? This is some serious shit Sonja and I don't want to get caught up in this. If you have a better idea, then let's hear it." He stood up and stared at her.

"You hate me now. I know you do. You want to call off the wedding. It's okay, I understand," she zipped the canvas bag and wiped her face on her sleeve.

Years of memories came flooding into Danny mind.

The time she was twelve years old and a group of girls were going to jump her after school and he wouldn't let them. How she was crying but not backing down and wiping her face on her shirt sleeve as she dared the group of girls to touch her.

The time she was sixteen and had snared someone else's boyfriend just in time for the Senior Prom. The jilted other girl had decided to beat Sonja down the day before the prom to teach her a lesson, to the approval of many other jilted girls.

The time she was seventeen and was caught shop lifting a lipstick from the Rite Aid drug store. Instead of calling her mother like the manager instructed, she called him. He had to beg and promise the store manager she would never do it again. She gave a less than convincing apology as she wiped the tears from her face on her sleeve.

He saw that scared little girl and that desperate teenager with her back against the wall. He couldn't stop rescuing her now, when she needed him the most.

"We are in this together baby. Okay? Let me figure out what to do, please."

"Okay. Whatever you say." Sonja sat down and put her head in her hands.

"I've got to call Maceo. He might have some advice and can recommend a good lawyer. I know that much, we need a damn good lawyer." He started dialing.

"Maceo, hey man it's Danny."

"Danny. What's going on? You sound a little down." Maceo asked..

"Look, I need to see you as soon as possible. Can you meet me somewhere?"

"Getting cold feet?" Maceo joked.

"Naw...I wish it was something that easy. Sonja and I need your advice on something."

"Okay. Sure. How about the Applebee's on Broadway?"

"See you in about 20 minutes. Thanks man." Danny hung up.

"Why do I have to go? Shouldn't I stay here with the money?" Sonja asked nervously.

"Put the money in my safe on our way to meet Maceo and you are coming in case he has questions I can't answer."

Sonja dreaded being judged by Maceo who she felt never liked her anyway and now he would have all the ammunition he needed to turn Danny away from her.

Chapter 19

Maceo had very few questions, but the ones he asked were biting.

"How does this affect our partnership in the boutique?" He was tapping his ink pen on his desk and staring intently at Sonja.

"I haven't thought that through yet, but I imagine you will have to buy me out so I won't have any legal business ties with any of you." Sonja whispered.

"You know very little surprises me when it comes to business deals and politics, but what I don't get is if the feds are tracking Senator Ramos, why are you involved?" He shot a look at Danny that meant for Sonja to answer and not be rescued.

"He and I are…friends. It's not against the law to be friends with someone powerful." She snapped.

"Exactly, so why are you running around here scared and trying to cover your tracks?" Maceo stood up and walked to his window, turning his back on Sonja and Danny.

"I thought you were going to give me some advice, not interrogate me." She snapped.

"I am giving advice to Danny, not you. And the best advice I can give my brother is get the best lawyer money can buy, someone who can get the real truth out of you and protect the innocent bystanders who will end up as collateral damage."

Danny walked over to Maceo and signaled for Sonja to be quiet, "Who do you recommend?"

"Simon Parker. I'll call him for you but he won't be cheap. He's the best and I doubt if any of this will give him any reason to break a sweat. He's seen and heard it all. Give me a few minutes while I get him." Maceo walked to his desk and looked through his rolodex and Sonja jumped up and left the office.

"Is she worth this man? Do you know what you are getting yourself into?" he looked intently at Danny.

"I know you don't understand this Maceo, but I love her. It's all or nothing."

Shaking his head while dialing his phone Maceo gave Danny a sympathetic glance.

Minutes later Danny and Sonja had an appointment to see Simon Parker.

Sonja complained that she wanted to go home and change, she was still wearing sweat pants, no makeup and her hair was in a ponytail.

"This man is going to think I'm a hood rat. Look at me!" She whined at her reflection in the car's mirror.

"He won't care about that. You will have plenty of time to impress him with your wardrobe." Danny said.

"What did Maceo say about me when I left?" she was nibbling her finger nails.

"Nothing," Danny pretended to be obsessed with the local traffic.

"I'm not a fool. I know he said something negative. I told you he didn't like me and never has." She smoothed her hair away from her forehead and patted her face with a napkin.

"We've got bigger things to worry about now don't you think?" Danny parked in the garage attached to Simon Parker's office.

He turned to look at Sonja, "Listen, if you want to talk to him alone I can understand. You have to tell him the truth, and I mean everything that can do us harm. Understand?"

"I want you there. I need you to stay with me." Sonja grabbed Danny's hand and held on tight.

As they were riding in the elevator, Sonja remembered that Kevin Williams worked for the Parker law firm.

She nervously cleared her throat and touched Danny's arm, "That jerk off Kevin is going to be here."

"Baby he is history. He has moved back to California. Birmingham is way too small for his kind of life." Danny gave a half smile.

Simon Parker's suites of offices were tastefully and expensively furnished. He walked out into the main lobby and greeted Danny and Sonja. He was pleasant and reassuring, only briefly pausing to remind his administrative assistant to bring in a file he had requested.

"So, please sit down. Let's start at the beginning."

Sonja cleared her throat. "I'm not sure how much Maceo told you. But I need your services…this letter from one of my associates kind of explains everything." She handed Eva's letter to Simon who read it while Sonja continued.

"I have not been contacted by the authorities and so far -"

Simon held up his hand for her to stop, "Do you have any funds in the bank?"

"I did. I withdrew it today. I have it in a safe place."

"How much?" he asked.

"A little over $600,000."

"Take this notepad and list all of your debts and expenses. Including any business holdings."

A soft knock interrupted his instructions. His assistant came in with a manila folder and handed it to Simon.

"This is my associate, Miss Timms. If I take you on as a client, she will be working on your case. Whatever you can say to me, you can say to her. Miss Timms, please take a seat."

The pretty petite brunette sat on the sofa and snapped open her portfolio ready to take notes.

Danny spoke what was on Sonja's mind. "You don't think you'll take the case?"

"Well, first of all, there is no case. Second of all, we are in a holding pattern and nothing could come of this, or all hell could break loose."

"I want you to be my lawyer. No matter what the hell happens. I would just feel better if I had a team ready. You know what I mean?" Sonja asked.

Simon smiled, "Smart lady. Okay, at this moment, I am your attorney on retainer. This retainer is for a twelve-month period to legally represent you in all matters pertaining or relating to the claims that may be leveled against you in this investigation. That means this case only…nothing else."

Sonja gave him the legal pad with her debt calculations.

Simon motioned for Miss Timms to take the pad.

"My retainer for the year for this case is $100,000. That amount should be deposited into the firms account today. Looking at your debts, I see your mortgage is the lion's share of your financial commitments.

"You will pay off the mortgage balance and transfer the deed to your mother. In fact, all of your assets, including your car, jewelry, artwork, furnishings and valuables will be legally transferred to your mother. We will wire the mortgage funds to your mortgage holder from here and get the paper work done for the property transfers in a few days." He looked over at Miss Timms for confirmation.

"Yes sir. When can we expect the funds to be transferred to Miss Davenport's retainer account?" Timms asked.

Simon looked at Sonja. As Simon was giving instructions, Sonja was doing the math. By her estimates after paying off her house, the retainer, her car and credit cards, she would have roughly $75,000 left. She quickly opened her purse, retrieved one of the Zoloft anti depressant pills, and popped two into her mouth before answering.

"I can bring it today. I am also a partner with Evelyn Williams in the boutique downtown."

Simon sat back in his leather chair underneath the oil portrait of Stephanie wearing her Miss Alabama crown and sequined gown.

He gave brief thought to the information shared by Sonja.

"Okay, Evelyn will buy you out and you will have no legal rights to that business."

Danny spoke up. "Can't I buy her out instead? I don't think Evelyn can afford to do this."

"She can afford it…I will make sure of that. No need to worry. The remainder of your funds will be secured in an account with this firm, that will provide you with a living allowance, monthly expenses for bills and normal personal cash needs. These funds will be available to you simply by contacting Miss Timms and telling her how much you need. You will have an accounting of your balance each week. We don't want any of your money being locked down. They can't track it to the firm, because I'm your counsel.

"Danny, if you and Miss Davenport still plan on getting married, you could be implicated by helping her hide assets. We'll get to that later on. Now since I am officially serving as your counsel, Miss Davenport, tell me about your relationship with Senator Ramos.

"And any other high profile individuals who may become part of this investigation. I have a preliminary background file on you, so please be honest and forthright...no surprises." He opened the manila folder and started making notes as Sonja started from the beginning.

§§§§§§§§§§§§§§§§§§§§

Evelyn didn't notice at first when Dr. Matthew Klein's phone calls became a daily routine. At first it was once a week to just check up on her and then every other day and now it was daily and the conversations ranged from her preoccupation with planning Sonja's wedding to his application to work with the Doctors Without Borders initiative.

Evelyn had started looking forward to his calls and when he worked the late shift at the hospital, she suggested he call her at home on those long and uneventful nights.

This was one of those nights. She had showered and was just climbing into bed when her mother tapped on the bedroom door.

"Lynn, the phone's for you. It's Dr. Klein."

Evelyn winched at knowing she was going to be given the third degree by her mother after this call and reached for the extension next to her bed.

"I've got it Mama...thanks!" she yelled.

"Are you okay? Should I fix you something for your nausea?" her mother asked as she gently opened the door peeking inside.

Cradling the phone to her chest, Evelyn shook her head. "No Mama, I'll be okay. It's okay." She gave a fake smile.

After her mother closed the door, Evelyn answered the phone.

"Hi. How are you?"

"I told her you had called earlier about nausea. She was asking so many questions I just didn't know what else to say." He laughed.

"Yeah she can be tough. I am sure I will get the third degree questions in the morning."

"Sorry it's so late…are you in bed?" Klein asked.

"Just got in and about to get comfortable. You must be exhausted."

"You know this may sound awful, but working the midnight emergency room shift without emergencies is brutal. I think we had one sprained ankle tonight. I've been pouring coffee down my throat to stay alert. I won't keep you, just wanted to say goodnight."

"Do you call to tuck all of your patients in Dr. Klein?" Evelyn joked.

"Sometimes. When they seem to need it. Evelyn?" he sounded serious.

"What."

"Will you go to dinner with me.?" He held his breath as she took a few minutes to process what he asked.

"I don't think that's a good idea. My life is too complicated right now and I've got this wedding, this business I'm trying to open and oh yeah, a baby on the way."

"It's just dinner. And maybe a movie. Just friends going to eat and see a movie. How complicated can that be?"

Evelyn gave his logic some thought. Then she reminded herself she had a father who was old fashioned as they come and would think she was having a complete breakdown going out with a white man.

"Matt, I don't think so. Surely there are some cute nurses who would love to go out with you."

"Do you think I have a hard time getting a date? I don't want to date a cute nurse, I want to date a cute woman named Evelyn."

The years of insecurity flooded Evelyn's mind like raging waters, "Why? Why do you want to date me?"

"I like you Evelyn. I thought you liked me too."

"Oh God what are we? Twelve years old?" she laughed loudly. Remembering her parents' house had ears, she cut her laughter short and lowered her voice.

"Just say yes. It would be fun. Don't you need to have fun?"

Evelyn examined her slightly rounded belly and laughed again, "You do remember my condition don't you?"

"I knew about it before you did, remember? How about next Saturday, seven o'clock. I'll pick you up."

"No! I'll meet you. Just give me the name of the restaurant and I'll meet you there." She insisted.

"Is there a problem? I'm sure your mother will be thrilled."

"Did she put you up to this? Because if she did, I don't ever want to talk to you again." She snapped.

"I don't need your mother to suggest I take you out Evelyn. I wouldn't do that to our friendship." He gently responded.

"Okay. But it's not my mother, it's my father. He wouldn't be so happy. I am supposed to just be getting rid of a son-in-law he couldn't stand and now I flounce around town with a white man? I don't think he could take that. I'm sorry but it's the truth. This is still the deep south and race matters in just about everything here."

"So it's a no then?" he sounded disappointed.

"I think so. I mean it's just too--"

Klein finished her sentence, "Complicated. I know. So I won't flounce around town with you. What if I cook dinner for us? We could rent some movies, kick our shoes off and just relax. Does that work"?

Evelyn patted her stomach and suddenly felt more relaxed than she had in months.

"Okay Dr. Klein. That works. Give me your address."

"Dr. Klein's address is at the hospital, Matt's address is downtown at the Brick Street Lofts. Apartment 1C." He quipped.

"No stairs or elevators? God bless you Matt. So Saturday at 7 p.m. And I'll bring the movies."

"Oh, is there anything you don't like to eat? My specialty is grilled salmon." He asked.

"Salmon sounds good. I do have the traditional cravings though, right now I'm going through my ice cream phase. Chocolate, please." Evelyn swung her legs out of bed and headed for the kitchen to clean out the rest of the chocolate ice cream in the freezer.

Matthew Klein wanted the next 48 hours to speed up so he could finally see Evelyn again. He hadn't felt this excited in a long time about a woman. He hung up the phone and headed towards residents shower and locker room. He opened his locker, took out the photograph of the striking platinum blonde woman with the smiling ocean blue eyes, and gave it a quick kiss.

"Well Mother, this could be the one. Send me some luck and guidance. See you in my dreams."

§§§§§§§§§§§§§§§§§§§§

The Brick Street downtown section of Birmingham was the fastest growing residential area of the city. Urban professionals were flocking to the area to rent and purchase renovated lofts and newly constructed townhomes.

Restaurants and entertainment businesses responded to the urban renewal and just about every block had sidewalk dining, quaint shops and coffee houses.

Evelyn found a parking spot just a half a block away from Matt's building. She buzzed the call button next to apartment 1C and he answered instantly.

She only had to walk a few feet before coming to the door marked 1C and softly knocked.

Matt Klein quickly opened the door and greeted her with a huge smile and light hug, "Did you find a good parking place?" he asked.

"Yeah I did…just at the corner. I guess most people are out tonight. Wow this is a great space." Evelyn looked around the spacious apartment with its dark stained concrete floors and tall ceilings.

"Thanks. Here let me show you around." He gently took her elbow and walked through the spare bedroom that doubled as his office, the hallway leading to his master bedroom and bath with tastefully selected furniture and a huge walk in shower with rain showerheads.

"Very nice. I'm impressed…so neat and clean too." Evelyn smiled.

Looking around the apartment Matt sheepishly confessed, "Merry Maids. I just couldn't' do it all you know? Cook, work and clean? How my mother did it all and worked and raised me, I never know."

Evelyn was walking around his bedroom and peered out the window that overlooked one of the downtown parks.

As she was turning to leave, her eye caught a glimpse of a photo in a silver frame on his nightstand.

Evelyn caught her chest and bent down for a closer look. The platinum blond woman with the ocean blue smiling eyes looked back at her.

Matt was still talking about the apartment, how he had only lived there a year, it was the first time he had bought property and how much he enjoyed it when he noticed her expression.

"What's wrong? Are you feeling sick?" he walked over to her and eased her onto the side of the bed.

She looked up at him and her mouth felt like it was full of cotton, "This woman in the photograph. Who is she?"

Matt picked up the photo and smiled, "This is my mother. Why?"

"Does she live here with you?"

"Evelyn my mother died three years ago. Breast cancer." He quietly answered and replaced the photo on the nightstand.

"No. No. I saw this woman last week. I spoke to her, she prayed for me." She insisted.

"Evelyn, maybe it was someone who looked like her. It happens you know. Come on, let's sit in the living room and I'll fix you a nice glass of wine. Just one though, doctors orders." He smiled.

Vehemently shaking her head, Evelyn took his hands into hers and looked intently into his eyes.

"Matt. It was her. Those eyes only belong to one woman and it's your mother. I don't understand this. She told me a story, wait, let me see. She said for me not to give up on this baby. She told me when she was pregnant she was told by doctors to abort her baby because of birth defects but she didn't," she stepped away from him, "Matt are you that baby?"

The blood drained from his face. He sat on the side of the bed to steady himself.

"My father left her because he didn't want to care for a handicapped child. He said she was trying to ruin his life and he left before I was born. She would always tell me that God holds the future for us. Every birthday, she would tell me this story. How after I was born she was so scared to look at me not knowing what she was going to see." His voice broke and tears welled in his eyes.

"But I was okay. The doctors couldn't explain it. I had defied every test and seemed to be fine. My mother refused to even to look for my father and tell him. I never met him and sometimes I used to get so angry with her for denying me that right." His voice regained some of its strength.

"When I was in college, I decided to look him up and find him. I wanted him to be proud of me. I didn't tell her that I found him and called him. He had a whole new family of course. He was so cold on the phone. You know what he asked me?"

Evelyn squeezed his hand for him to continue.

"He asked me if I was a cripple. That's the word he used. A cripple. I just hung up. That was almost 10 years ago."

"Why would she come to me? I mean I don't know her."

"She comes to me sometimes. Mostly in my dreams. We were very close Evelyn. She always knows when I'm facing a crisis or when I'm getting ready to celebrate. When I was doing work with the Peace Corp in Somalia, she came to be almost every night. Encouraging me or warning me about steps to take for my future."

"But why me? I can't understand this. I'm just confused about her coming to me."

Matt looked at her and gently touched her face.

"Maybe it's because you've been on my mind since the first day I met you. I think about you all the time. You looked so sad in the hospital when I told you that you were pregnant. I just couldn't imagine why you would be so sad, and then I noticed there was never a husband around, and I wasn't sure if he was killed in the storm or if you were still married. Although, that huge diamond was quite intimidating." He picked up her hand with the brilliant diamond.

Evelyn twirled the ring around her finger, "So I guess my mother filled in the blanks for you huh?"

Matt confessed, "She told me you were getting a divorce and that you didn't seem to want the baby. She was concerned you would try to lose the baby on purpose. Your Mom really loves you and I promised her I would keep watch on you and even contact your obstetrician. When you never made an appointment with the o.b., I called your mother to see if there was another doctor you were using. She said you never mentioned going to a doctor at all. That was the day she said you guys were going to have lunch and she would ask you"

"That was the day your mother came to me at the restaurant," Evelyn whispered.

"A restaurant? Mother talked to you at a restaurant?" he shook his head and chuckled.

"Yeah, in the ladies room. I was upset and crying and she walked in and just started talking. What is going on here?" she stood up.

"Let's eat and talk. The salmon is ready, the ice cream is good and creamy"-

She interrupted him, "Wait Matt. This is just going too fast. I'm scared. I don't understand any of this and you seem like it's practically normal."

"It is normal. When people pray they expect results. It's called faith. That's normal right? Sometimes we ask God for answers, and I don't think he's going to call me on my cell and tell me what to do. He answers us in the most comfortable way for us. Maybe it took a stranger for you to listen in that bathroom, because you didn't want to talk to your family or friends. I'm glad Mother visited you. I'm glad she let me know she heard my prayers about you and took care of you." He stood up to face her. Evelyn was speechless. He took her silence as a sign of agreement and he slowly kissed her cheek and pulled her closer for a comforting embrace. They held each other for several minutes before walking into the living room.

"So where are those movies?" he asked as he piled their plates with grilled salmon and tossed salad.

Chapter 20

Amazing Grace

Amazing Grace, how sweet the sound that saved a wretch like me.
I once was lost, but now I'm found.
Was blind, but now I see.

T'was Grace that taught my heart to fear,
And Grace my fears relieved.
How precious did that Grace appear the hour I first be-lieved.

Through many dangers, toils and snare .we have already come.
T'was Grace that brought us safe thus far,
And Grace will lead us home.

It was going to be the largest gathering of multi-racial, religious and diverse Birmingham residents in over 50 years. The convention center seating was too small and organizers moved the Unity Sunday event to commemorate the deadly tornado to the University of Alabama at Birmingham football stadium.

National media converged on the city days earlier, gaining insight on how the tornado had torn the historic city apart, and how the historic Unity Sunday was going to put it back together.

The event was a memorial to the victims and a celebration for the survivors who were rebuilding.

Simon Parker had announced a memorial fund in his last wife's name for emergency and educational support for the victims' families as they tried to rebuild without adequate home owners insurance or emergency housing funds.

Maceo Sloan was sitting in his den watching the television coverage of the thousands of event goers filing into the stadium. CNN, MSNBC, NBC, CBS, FOX and ABC were all represented. He was impressed with the show of unity and for a brief moment felt some of the hostility fading he had always harbored since the 1963 bombing of the 16th Street Church bombing.

He was rethinking his decision not to attend when the reporter introduced one of the local organizers.

"This event is being called one of the models for community unity and one of the organizers is Gail Emerson. Miss Emerson, tell us how you got involved."

Gail looked relaxed and started giving the details of her involvement and Maceo felt a strong surge of pride and had to smile to himself.

It was then he decided to fight the traffic and the crowds and attend. Even though seeing her there was slim given it was a stadium and over 20,000 people were expected.

Just as he tossed the remote control and stood up, he felt the first tinge of numbness in his left shoulder. Rubbing his arm to increase the circulation, he started walking to the door when the numbness caught fire and moved to his chest, knocking him to his knees.

He struggled to the house phone and managed to dial 911.

"911 Emergency. What is your emergency please?"

"I think I'm having a heart attack." He said hoarsely.

"Sir, are you alone and can you confirm your address?"

"I'm alone...it just started. My address is---76. 76 Alabama Road." He was finding it harder to breathe and his vision was becoming blurry. He could hear the operator asking him to describe his symptoms and tell him an ambulance was on the way to stay on the phone. He tried to tell her he couldn't breathe, but nothing came out and his chest felt like it was exploding. Before he completely blacked out, he could hear his dogs barking and the distant wailing of sirens.

§§§§§§§§§§§§§§§§§§§

Danny and Sonja's mother were leaving Danny's house to head to the stadium. Danny yelled upstairs for Sonja to hurry.

There was no response. He called her again and still no response.

Finally taking the stairs two at a time, he dashed up to her room to find her in bed, "Baby? What's wrong?" he sat next to her.

Sonja tightened her hold on the covers and mumbled, "I don't want to go. I just want to stay in bed."

"But your mother and Evelyn will be there. It will be good for you to get out. We have a lot to be thankful for." He patted her shoulder.

Pulling the covers over her head, she moved away from him, "Thankful? I have no money. I have no property and I may be going to jail. Wow, let's bake a cake!"

"Sonja, you have money left and the house and car in your mothers name is just a legal move. It's still your house and your car. And you can walk, talk and get around. A lot of folks would gladly change places with you today."

"Well let them take my place at the prayer vigil or what ever it is. I'm staying home." She sarcastically answered.

"Okay. Whatever. We'll see you later." Danny exhaled and walked out, slamming the door closed.

With so many local churches participating in the citywide event, it took on an almost festive atmosphere with friends sitting in groups and neighborhoods reserving entire sections to sit together.

Evelyn used her cell phone to call Danny and guided him to where she and her family were sitting. She looked puzzled when it was apparent Sonja was not with them.

"Where is Sonja? I know she's coming." Evelyn asked.

Danny shrugged his shoulders and took a seat next to Evelyn, "She's in one of her moods. I think she's dreading having to tell you something about the business."

Evelyn leaned in closer, "Our business? What's going on?"

"I wanted her to tell you before Simon Parker did. But you are buying her out. She is facing some potential legal troubles." He whispered.

Evelyn's face registered shock and bewilderment, "I can't buy her out!" she tried to whisper without her parents over hearing her.

"Don't worry about it. Simon will take care of everything. He will explain it all." He patted her arm.

Evelyn looked at Danny trying to see if he seemed worried. He looked worried to her.

Before she could say anything more, the first choir took the stage and started singing. It was Evelyn's church choir, so she couldn't talk anymore. Her church members were standing and applauding and she joined in.

§§§§§§§§§§§§§§§§§§§§

Sonja tried to pretend she wasn't excited to see folks on television she knew. She could just imagine the pride and excitement that Evelyn was feeling when her church choir finished singing to a standing ovation.

She wondered what Danny told everyone about her absence. The program host broke into her thoughts with an introduction of Simon Parker who took the stage. With a voice trembling with emotion, he announced the Stephanie Parker Foundation for emergency assistance to the thrill of the crowd.

Sonja clicked off the television and walked to the mirror in the bedroom. Wearing no corrective makeup and just plain jeans and a sweatshirt, she grabbed her purse and car keys.

§§§§§§§§§§§§§§§§§§§§

Evelyn was just settling back into her seat from another bathroom break when her cell phone started vibrating. She glanced at the caller identification and saw that it was Matt.

"Hey. You might have to speak up, it's pretty loud in here." She said.

"Yeah I can see that. We're watching on a smuggled in portable tv set at the emergency desk. Looks like a good crowd. Hey I saw your church choir opened things up."

"Yes! They were awesome. We are so proud. Are you busy at the hospital?" she cupped her hand on the cell phone to shield the crowd's noise as the next choir started singing.

"Not very. Just had one emergency so far. Looks like God is giving us a break today."

"That is a break huh? Spoken just like a doctor. What time will you get off?" she was surprised that she really missed him.

"Aw, I hope around 11 tonight. This guy has a heart specialist who just showed up so I have to go in and observe…he's a pretty powerful guy I hear. Maceo Sloan." Matt gave the nurse a signal that he was on his way to check on another patient who had just walked in.

"What did you say? Matt, what did you say?" Evelyn asked.

"I said I get off at 11 tonight."

"No! Who had a heart attack?" She looked around to get Danny's attention.

"Ah, Sloan. Maceo Sloan, you know him?"

"Oh my God! How is he…?" she grabbed Danny's arm and shook him. Covering the phone, she whispered, "Maceo's had a heart attack! He's at the hospital."

§§§§§§§§§§§§§§§§§§§§§

Sonja drove like a woman who was on her way to put out a fire. In a way she was. She was trying to save her life. She knew if she stayed home alone on this day, her life was going to head in a very scary and dangerous direction. She could feel the heavy burden lift from her shoulders the moment she turned the key to her car. She didn't know what she would do when she arrived, but she did know that something was waiting for her at the stadium.

Sonja kept trying to talk herself out of going by using rational arguments: the traffic would be murder; she would never be able to find her mother or Danny; she looked pathetic without make up and folks were sure to stare at her scarred face.

One by one, those arguments faded like a weak smoke screen. The interstate was practically deserted even for a Sunday in Birmingham. Police directed traffic flow into the stadium with ease and she only had to wait a few seconds before her lane of cars smoothly entered the stadium parking.

Loud speakers set up at the perimeter of the stadium grounds piped the program activities into the parking lot for a few creative folks who thought tailgating was the order of the day. Amid the smells of bar- b- que and roasted corn, someone shouted to her.

"Good morning! Want something to eat?"

She shook her head and waved before finally letting curiosity get the best of her.

"Excuse me. But tailgating?" she smiled as she walked over to the group of about 20 people. They were a diverse group of Hispanics, Asians, blacks and whites.

"Why not? We tailgate at football games all the time, we wanted to share the good feeling of being together in praise in worship." A young black guy answered.

A pretty Hispanic girl walked over to Sonja, "We're all in grad school together and our apartment complex was destroyed in the tornado, so since we used to all tail gate at the games, we decided to start this day of celebration off with a party. You were hurt in the storm?" she looked at Sonja's droopy eyelid.

Sonja's hand quickly moved to cover that side of her face, "Yeah…okay, have fun." She turned and walked away.

Someone in the crowd yelled after her, "Jesus loves you no matter what. Your scar is a testament to a miracle. You're alive!"

Now she was really beginning to rethink her decision to come. There were already kooks in the parking lot, who knew what she would find inside the stadium.

Entering the stadium tunnel Sonja could see thousands of people standing and singing. Some were holding photographs of people as they silently wept. She let her eyes follow the sound coming from the stage where a young black girl was singing.

As she sang, the minister next to her kept motioning for the crowd to come down front to the bottom of the stage. As the seats emptied, Sonja effortlessly moved in the direction of the ground level seating. She started walking with the thousands of others, not exactly knowing why, but just that she had to go.

Someone next to her grabbed her hand. She looked at the stranger who smiled warmly at her as they continued to walk.

The girl singer on the stage closed her eyes and began to sing another verse.

"Amazzzzing grace. How sweet, the sound."

Sonja looked to her left and her right and realized she was surrounded by thousands of people, yet it was a peaceful and serene gathering. The minister was speaking as the singer lowered her voice.

"Someone here needs to tell God thank you! Someone who has been touched by this tragedy but is not defeated. We lost loved ones, but we are not defeated. We lost our homes, our jobs, all of our possessions. But we are not defeated. This day we are declaring war on depression, anger and hopelessness. This day we are recommitting our lives to Jesus Christ."

"That saved, a wretch like me. I- -I-I-I once, was lost, was blind but now....I see."

Sonja and the crowd stopped as a priest, a rabbi, and several other clergy took the stage and started praying in silence. Many in the crowd knelt and others swayed as the young singer continued.

"Twas grace, that taught my heart to fear, and grace my fears relieved. How precious was that grace, the hour I first believed."

Sonja slowly put one knee on the ground and realized that no one was noticing her. She then put her other knee on the ground and just waited. She whispered to whomever was listening, "I don't know how to pray."

A soft voice instructed, "Just tell him what you want, what you need and that you will do his will."

She snapped her head around to see where the voice came from, but everyone was in their own moment of prayer.

She swallowed hard before whispering again, "I want to be beautiful again. I want to have money again. I want to be happy."

"You are beautiful. You have the riches of the world when you have my love. You receive happiness so you can share it with others. Look to Matthew." The soft voice seemed fainter now.

"Who is Matthew?" Sonja whispered. There was no reply. "Who is Matthew?" Sonja asked again, her voice rising a little. She stood up as the prayers ended and people started hugging each other. She felt a slight tap on her shoulder and turned to see the smiling face of the young Hispanic girl from the parking lot.

"Hi! Did you enjoy the program?" she cheerfully asked.

"Oh. Hi. Yes, it was uplifting." Sonja turned to leave.

The young girl caught up with her, "I wanted to say that I was sorry if I embarrassed you earlier. About your face."

"No. It was okay. Well you better get back to your tail gate party. Take care." Sonja started walking faster.

The young girl kept pace with her, "I just wanted to say that I used to look like you. I was in a very bad car wreck when I was a senior in high school and they thought I was going to lose my eye.

Bet you can't tell which one can you?" she did a campy mug smile with an ear to ear grin for the full effect.

Sonja stopped and peered closely into her perfectly round face. She couldn't see any signs of a scar or the aftermath of injuries.

"It's this one." She perked up and pointed to her left eye.

"Wow. I still can't see any difference. You look great. I'm glad things worked out for you. I really gotta go, traffic is going to be crazy." Sonja turned to walk away.

"My name is Moira. If you'd like, I can get you in touch with my doctors. They are great and very understanding about cases like ours."

"Like ours?" Sonja kept walking as Moira sped up to keep pace with her.

"Yeah you know. Our looks are our life. Looking good is everything. In high school I was always crowned Most Beautiful. But boy that senior year, I thought I would die when I saw my face for the first time after the accident. Never mind that my best friend was killed in the accident. It was all about me. Know what I mean? What's your name?" Moira looked at Sonja.

"I'm Sonja. What is this really about?" she asked suspiciously.

"I want to study you. I want you for my thesis. I'm a psych major. I decided I wanted to study the minds of challenging folks like me…after the accident, I found I no longer wanted to be an actress, but I wanted to help people like my doctors helped me. They are a team who do a lot of pro bono work in third world countries, but they are based on the principles of the Bible. They don't do cosmetic surgery for the Hollywood effect. I had a great psycho therapist who worked with me before and after my reconstructive surgery. Have you done that yet?"

"I don't need a shrink." Sonja retorted.

"Yeah, I know. You need to be beautiful, have money and be happy. Right?" Moira responded.

Sonja stopped and gave her a wide-eyed look, "Was that you? Back there in the stadium, whispering to me?" Before Moira could answer, she continued, "Who is Matthew? What was that about?"

Moira smiled, "Information will cost ya. You haven't agreed to let me study you for my thesis."

"I'm getting married in a few weeks, I don't have time to play head doctor with a little girl. No matter how much you think we have in common. You really don't know anything about me." Sonja measured her words carefully, trying not to become agitated.

"That's why I want to work with you. I want to get to know you. I promise not to interfere with your wedding plans. This would be a very therapeutic process. I'm not trying to treat you, I mean, I can't can I? I'm not a doctor yet, I just want to use your experience as part of my research. You know they do studies all the time on self-image and awareness when it comes to obesity, eating disorders and stuff. I believe beautiful people, especially beautiful women, have some very challenging reality issues. I know I went through them after my accident. I can't study myself, so I..."

Sonja held up her hand for Moira to stop talking, "I am not a science experiment. I have to go."

"I won't use your real name and I'll work around your schedule..." Moira did a little half run fast walk to catch up with Sonja.

"Who is Matthew?" Sonja asked unlocking her car door. The parking lot traffic had diminished a lot by now and she was eager to get back to Danny's house.

Moira rested her small frame against the drivers' door making it impossible for Sonja to leave.

Crossing her small arms in front of her chest, Moira tilted her head and looked carefully at Sonja before giving her an answer.

"Matthew was one of Jesus' disciples. Some Christians thought the Gospel of Matthew is one of the most important writings in the Bible. You decide for yourself. Read Matthew, chapter 6, verses 19 through 24. It has a message I think you need to hear. So how can I stay in touch with you?" she asked sweetly.

Sonja felt set up, but she gave Moira her phone number.

§§§§§§§§§§§§§§§§§§§§

Gail and her kids were sailing down Interstate 65 laughing and reliving some of the funny moments of the unity celebration when her cell phone rang. Looking at the caller id name, she saw it was Laura.

"Hey, how you feeling?" she cheerfully asked amid Laura's coughing.

"This flu virus is not playing…I'm still a little weak but I did watch the celebration. You did a great job! Girl Birmingham looked like a real city on CNN." Her raspy voice started fading as another hacking cough attack returned.

"Listen Gail, I got a call from work. Actually they were looking for you and figured I knew how to get in touch with you."

Gail shushed the kids to be quiet, "Why? What's going on?"

"Maceo was brought into emergency about an hour ago. He had a massive," Laura stared coughing again before she could finish her sentence.

Gail nearly dropped the phone and the kids sensed something was terribly wrong. Their eyes were glued to their mothers face trying to gather a hint as to what was happening.

"Jesus no...please noooo." Gail wailed.

"Attack...he's alive, but he is having surgery tomorrow..." Laura was resuming her conversation but Gail had already started towards the hospital while Jonathan and Jessica kept begging her to tell them what was wrong.

She struggled to say goodbye to Laura and regain her composure, but her hands were trembling on the steering wheel.

"Mama, what's wrong? Why are you crying? Mama?" Jessica was crying now, not used to seeing her mother visibly upset. Even after the tornado, she seemed to have everything under control.

"Don't cry baby. Maceo is sick. I've got to go the hospital...shoot! I need to take you guys to Laura's," she started looking for the next exit to get them to the other side of town.

Jonathan protested immediately, "We want to go too! Ma please...we want to see Maceo...please, Ma let us go." His voice started to tremble. Glancing at her son in the rear view mirror, she saw his genuine concern and emotional attachment to Maceo.

"Okay...okay. Everybody just calm down. We can't go in there all upset. We have to be strong, okay?" she did a weak smile and as they mumbled in unison, a weak 'okay.'

They entered the familiar emergency wing of the hospital and Gail went to the nurse's station. Betty Dickson, one of the nurses looked surprised and somewhat puzzled looking at Gail and the children, "Hey! What are you doing here on your day off?"

"I need to see a friend who was brought in about an hour ago. Maceo Sloan." Gail tried to seem professional but her eyes immediately filled with tears. How many times had she stood where Betty was and had to give a friend or family member information that their loved one didn't make it?

She bit her bottom lip to stop it from trembling waiting for Betty to answer.

"Sure. Let's see where he is." Betty was looking at her computer screen and stealing glances at Gail and her little family. The computer page took forever to load and Betty tried to make small talk with Jessica and Jonathan.

"Oh you must be so proud of your mother. She did a great job with the celebration today...we watched it on television...Gail you were so good." Betty was furiously typing on the keyboard.

"Well it was a whole committee. I didn't do anything really. Did you find him?" Gail tried to peek around the counter to see the computer screen. Betty exhaled and looked up, "He's on seven. ICU, but his triple bypass is scheduled for first thing in the morning."

"Thanks!" Gail sprinted to the elevator with Jonathan and Jessica on her heels. The elevator ride took much longer than Gail could have imagined and she kept pushing the number seven button as her nerves started to unravel.

Mouthing a quiet prayer, she kept trying to calm herself down at least before Maceo could see how scared she was.

The seventh floor ICU was quiet compared to what she was used to in emergency. Spotting an empty corner in the waiting area, she walked the kids to a brown leather sofa. "Just sit here until I come back for you okay? I'll be right back."

Maceo's room was directly across from the nurses' station and his door was slightly open. Touching her cheeks to wipe away any traces of tears, she put on her best Miss America smile and went in.

His eyes were closed, but his breathing was rhythmic, almost keeping beat with the heart monitor that was filling the room with a beeping signal. Gail walked to his side and touched his hand. His eyes opened with a start and focused on her face.

"Come here often?" she smiled, taking his hand now into hers.

He swallowed hard before answering, "Yeah, I hear it's the best place for picking up sexy women."

"You don't look sick. Why are you wasting some poor doctors time huh?"

"What I have can't be seen with the naked eye. My heart is broken." He squeezed her hand.

"Well, I guess that means you did have one after all…and here I was thinking you were heartless. How you doing, seriously?" she pulled up a chair as close as she could to his bed.

"Surgery in the morning…that can't be good. According to the experts, I've got seventy-five percent blockage of my arteries. Too much bologna I guess." He laughed but it wasn't natural. Gail could tell he was scared.

"Tell you what, I am on duty tomorrow anyway, so after you get out of surgery, I'll stay with you for the night. Did you call your kids?"

"Yeah, funny thing is that they seem a little busy. Remember, I told you my son wants to be the next Spike Lee? Can you believe it? He finally got his meeting with Spike and it's tomorrow and he can't change it so he may show up later in the week. My baby girl's sorority has some national convention, she's running for office. Of course, she can't miss that. So she may show up in a few days. No big deal…" he turned his face towards the window to avoid Gail's eyes.

"By that time you will be fine and I'll be here and you will have the best doctors in the state. Do you need anything?" she looked around his room and found the small plastic hospital water pitcher. Shaking it, she found it nearly empty.

"Yeah, some water would be good. Thanks. You looked good on tv," he said with a wink, "that's what gave me my heart attack you know, seeing you again."

Gail stood , "I'll be back with your water. The kids are outside, they wanted to see you. Are you up for it?"

He immediately perked up and tried to sit up in bed. Gail helped him scoot up and fluffed his pillows.

"Great! Yeah send them in. I could use some cheering up. How do I look?" he rubbed his hands across his light beard stubble.

"Handsome as always. Be right back." She grabbed the water pitcher and made her way to the waiting area.

Jonathan and Jessica stood up the moment they saw her. Questions poured out of both of them at the same time, "Is he awake? Can we go in?"

"Is he going to be okay Mama?"

"Slow down. He is awake and you can go in for just a few minutes, let me get him some water first." She handed the pitcher to one of the nurses who gave her a kind smile and went to fill the pitcher.

The visit was lively and Maceo found himself laughing to the antics performed by Jonathan as he demonstrated the latest hip-hop dances while watching BET on television. Gail decided to put an end to the stage show as she noticed Maceo's energy level getting low.

"Okay guys, we need to let Maceo get some rest. He's got a big day tomorrow."

"Can we come back tomorrow after his surgery? We can bring him some flowers and books." Jessica begged.

"I don't know about tomorrow but later in the week might work. You guys go out in the waiting area and wait for me I'll be on out later."

Jessica gave Maceo a quick kiss on the cheek and Jonathan gave him a soul brother hand shake. The little guy rethought his action and then gave him a light hug.

Gail put the television on mute and sat on the side of the bed.

Before she could speak, Maceo whispered, "I really messed things up didn't I?"

"I am still your friend and I care about you Maceo. I am here for you." She gently touched his cheek.

"I don't need anymore friends...I need someone who loves me, as much as I love her." He caressed her fingers and kissed them.

There was a soft rap on the door and Danny and Evelyn walked in.

"Hey man. You'll do anything for attention won't ya?" Danny joked.

Evelyn was taking in the medical equipment hooked up to Maceo and the tears started to flow. She cried at the sight of rain these days.

"Hey Gail. I know he's in good hands with you." Danny gave Gail a hug.

"Surgery in the morning man. I can't believe I let this thing sneak up on me like this." Maceo shook his head.

"Remember when you were here and we met and how unco-operative you were? Wouldn't wait for tests, checking yourself out? That's how it sneaked up on you." Gail fussed.

"Evelyn, don't look so worried. I'm gonna be fine." Maceo reached for Evelyn's hand and she timidly walked towards him.

"What can I do? While you recuperate I mean. Are you going to have someone to stay with you?" Evelyn asked.

Gail answered, "Looks like I'm drafted for that duty. Probably the only one who can handle this man. I'll leave now and take these kids home. I'll see you tomorrow." Gail bent down to give Maceo a brief kiss on the lips, and to her surprise, he held her head and returned a lingering kiss.

"Now you trying to have another heart attack!" laughed Danny.

"See you tomorrow." Gail whispered.

"I'll walk out with you, I need a Sprite. My stomach is doing flip flops." Evelyn said to Gail.

After leaving Maceo's room and making sure they were out of earshot, Evelyn pulled Gail aside, "We have a situation with our business partnership and I'm afraid if this thing gets ugly Maceo might get sicker. What do you think?"

"I think we should keep all upsetting news far away from him. He eats, breathes and lives business. It's killing him. This heart attack may just have saved his life, if you understand what I mean by that."

Evelyn nodded in agreement, "Yes, I do. I'm glad you're here for him. He's really a good person."

Gail's attention moved beyond Evelyn as her face gave way to recognizing someone familiar.

Evelyn turned to see who it was and was met with the kind brown eyes of Matthew.

"I was hoping to catch you before you left. Hey Gail." He smiled at Gail and immediately turned his attention back to Evelyn.

"Hi Dr. Klein. I better get going. Take care you two." She looked warmly towards Evelyn and called for Jessica and Jonathan.

Evelyn touched Matt's shoulder, "We got here late. We had to drop Sonja's mother off at Danny's first. I think we're about to leave. I am so glad you called me. I don't know how we would have found out about Maceo."

"Look, I get off in about 15 minutes, I could drive you home." Matt offered.

"Oh, that's okay. I know you're tired and it's been a long day. Danny can drop me off."

Matt wasn't giving up that easy, "I'm not that tired. I really don't mind."

Before she could continue to protest his offer, her cell phone rang. It was her mother.

"Lynn, how is Maceo? We've been worried sick."

"He is having surgery tomorrow. We were just about to leave."

"Good. Well dinner is ready and tell Danny he can bring Sonja and her mother over to eat with us."

"Okay Ma...I will. Uh, Ma, do you think it would be okay if I bring Dr. Klein to dinner?"

After a few seconds of silence, her mother answered. Evelyn could tell she was walking through the house trying to find a private space.

"Now you know how your Daddy is. I would love for you to bring him. Tell you what, let me butter your Daddy up. So come on and bring him. By the time you get here, it should be alright."

Evelyn snapped her phone shut and gave Matt a mischievous smile, "You're invited to dinner at my parents. It's a Sunday feast with just family."

"Great! I am starved. Let me go and clock out first, and I'll meet you downstairs at the emergency entrance." He was already jogging towards the elevators.

Evelyn would do something her mother had taught her, she would spend the drive with Matt preparing him for her father.

§§§§§§§§§§§§§§§§§§§

Sonja could smell the Italian sausage, green peppers and onions from the garage. Obviously, her mother and Danny were already back from the city wide celebration, but Danny's car was not in the garage.

Entering the kitchen, she saw her mother doing what was routine for much of Sonja's childhood; draining pasta over the sink. Taking in the huge bowl of shredded cheese and fresh tomatoes, Sonja's mouth started watering for her mothers' lasagna.

"Hi Mama, where's Danny?"

"He went to the hospital. His friend is sick. So they dropped me off. Where have you been?" her mother still walked with a slight limp but she managed to maneuver around Sonja to the refrigerator.

Catching the refrigerator door before it closed, Sonja reached for a jar of olives.

"What friend?" she asked before popping the olive into her mouth.

"Mr. Sloan. I think he had a heart attack. Danny was very upset. I am praying for his recovery."

"Maceo had a heart attack? Wow. I'll call Danny to see how he is. Oh, Mama can I see your Bible?" she tried to ask in a cavalier manner, but her mother stopped chopping onions in mid air and looked at her with disbelief.

"My Bible? Why you want my Bible? Are you getting sick again?" she limped over to look at Sonja's face.

"No. I just need to look something up. I went to the celebration and just wanted to look up something in the Bible." She popped another olive into her mouth.

"You went to the celebration? Did you go alone?" her mother was walking towards a closet in the hallway.

"I just decided to go that's all. Where are you going?" Sonja asked.

Her mother was digging in a box in the closet and finally mumbled, "I know I put it in here...I know I did. Oh! Here it is," she turned to Sonja and handed her a white leather Bible,

"I bought this for you when you graduated from high school remember? Look inside, see I had your name engraved in gold letters." She said with pride.

Sonja remembered tossing the book in her closet as she was packing to leave after graduation. Her cheeks flushed red with embarrassment that her mother discovered she had been so disre-spectful.

"I don't know how it got saved during the storm, but it was in the only closet that was still standing. I guess God really does work in mysterious ways." She touched Sonja's cheek.

"I'm sorry you are so unhappy. I am sorry you had to come back here to take care of me and now you are injured." Her moth-er wept.

"Mama, it's okay...you couldn't help getting sick." Sonja hugged her.

"I tried to be a good mother, I tried to give you things the best I could...I know it was hard not being with your father."

Sonja pulled away from her and looked her coldly in the eyes, "I didn't have a father. He is dead as far as I'm concerned." She coldly stated.

"Don't say that. You don't know how life could have been if he..."

Sonja cut her off, "I know he abandoned you and me before I was even born. He is a low downed coward!"

"Sonja! You don't understand what it was like, my Papa would not have him, he was not welcomed. I thought my Papa and my uncles were going to kill him after I told my family I was pregnant. I told him to stay away--- I tried to protect him."

"Protect him?" Sonja screamed, "What about protecting me? I had to hear whispers about not having a father everyday at school...I had to wear hand me down clothes from a Goodwill store, I had to live under someone's roof and not even be able to get a glass of milk in the middle of the night because the kitchen was not ours! You should have been protecting me!"

"Sonja I did the best I could. I do not have good education and spoke little English, we struggled but we survived. I did the best I could!" Her mother raised her voice and trembled as the words got stuck in her throat.

"I know you blame me for not having things like the other girls, but look at you now. You are still so very beautiful, you have a lovely home, clothes and a man who is going to make up for the loneliness in your life." Her mother sat on the edge of the bed.

"Nothing can make up for what he did to us! Nothing! Don't you get it Mama? He used you! He had you like thousands of other American soldiers' overseas do to foreign girls and he left you behind to come back to the states and finish his life with a woman and children he really loved." She spat the words at her mother.

Recoiling from the hostility in Sonja's words, her mother quietly rose from the bed, "He didn't use me. I loved him, and he loved me. I would hope you were old enough to finally understand what that means between a man and a woman."

"I understand one thing Mama. Marry a man who loves you more than you love him and that's what I am going to do. If anyone leaves, it will be me leaving him. I am not going to be a doormat like you. All those years of scrubbing floors, washing dishes, waiting tables and barely getting by you spent and you still love that son of a bitch! You are pitiful!"

The slap across Sonja face cut through the room like thunder. Sonja grabbed the scarred side of her face and felt the stinging effect of her mothers' strong right hand. She had never hit her before. The tears started to roll down her cheeks.

"I am not ashamed of scrubbing floors! I am ashamed of having a daughter who is not worthy of the work I did! There is nothing wrong with scrubbing floors. It is good honest work and I did it with pride. I have nothing to be ashamed of. But can you say the same? You think I don't know what you were doing in Dallas? You think I'm so stupid you can tell me anything and I'll believe it?"

Sonja was speechless and kept holding her stinging red face.

"Wait here...I have something to show you," her mother went into the closet and pulled out a photo album, "Look at this picture! Look at it and tell me what you see." She pushed a faded sepia toned photo into Sonja's hands.

The grainy photo showed a tall dark handsome African-American service man and a beautiful woman with waist length jet-black hair standing on a sidewalk. His arm was draped over her

her shoulder, holding her tightly against him. His perfect smile was disarming and inviting.

Turning the photo over, Sonja read the caption that was in her Mother's handwriting; *Rome, 1969. Sofia and Steven Davenport. Wedding day.*

"It was the day we got married. I was so happy and so afraid at the same time. I knew it would be hard for us to live as husband and wife in Rome and I couldn't go to America with him. I was already pregnant with you. I was just sixteen and was only good at cooking and cleaning. Girls in the old country were only expected to marry and have children. But not with black men. I cannot help falling in love with your father. I fell in love with his boldness, his way of talking about making dreams come true. Where do you think you get your boldness from? His blood! When it came time for me to decide between him and leaving my home, fear paralyzed me. I was afraid, I was pregnant and my family had put the fears of the unknown into my heart and my head."

"Mama, you were so beautiful." Sonja whispered.

"So people tell me. When I come to this country, lots of men try to get me. white men, black men, all kinds of men, but I have a daughter to raise and I am trying to find your father. You think I didn't have choices? Every job I get as a house cleaner, I am either fired by the wife or felt up by the husband. Moving here was a blessing for us. I was proud to have a job that no one disrespected me. I loved working in the restaurant because people were nice to me. Money is not everything and I raised you to see that. What has happened to you? What are you going to do with your life? Can't you see how much Danny loves you? You are going to lose him with this selfish, crazy way of thinking." She gently took the photo back and replaced it in the photo album.

"I am glad you are reading the Bible," she nodded towards Sonja's hand still clasping the unused book, "I hope you find the answers you are looking for."

Sonja's mother left the room.

Clutching the Bible, Sonja plopped down on the floor and started turning pages. Her mothers' words were floating around her brain like an infection. The love her mother felt for her father, the admission of how their lives had been so similar as young women.

She had a newfound respect for her mother.

She turned her attention back to the Bible and found the book of Matthew in a manner of seconds it seemed. *What did Moira say, look to Matthew?*

Without knowing a chapter and verse to read, Sonja felt totally confused. It was like reading gibberish to her. The frustration level started getting the best of her and she fought back tears as she kept trying to read the gospel of Matthew.

"God, I don't know what I'm doing! I need help. This is not telling me anything…why do you have to be so vague and mysterious?" she wailed.

She kept speed-reading through the chapters; one, two, three, four. The sub- titles helped her navigate the topics a little better; fasting, the beatitudes, divorce and finally the Lord's Prayer.

Sonja started to feel a little more comfortable as the words on the page became more familiar.

By the time she got to the 28th verse, *And why take ye thought for raiment? Consider the lilies of the field, how they grow; they toil not, neither do they spin:*

She knew these words were meant for her and her situation. She kept reading until she got to the 33rd verse; *But seek ye first the kingdom of God, and his righteousness; and all these things shall be added unto to you.*

Take therefore no thought for the morrow; for the morrow shall take thought for these things of itself. Sufficient unto the day is the evil thereof.

She kept reading until she got to Chapter 7, verse 7: *Ask, and it shall be given you; seek, and ye shall find; knock and it shall be opened unto you;*

Before she realized it, she had read the entire book of Matthew. Still a little confused about some of the passages, she felt guilty having to ask God to restore her money and keep her out of trouble.

She had never asked God for anything before. Did Matthew mean that even sinners like her had the right to ask so much of God?

Would God feel disrespected for her coming to him now, when she was about to lose everything? Was she worthy to be saved? She thought back to all of those times she was so difficult as a teenager for her mother to deal with. How she refused to go to church or acknowledge God was real.

She was getting ready to be married, become a mother someday and had never been baptized. There were so many questions and she didn't have any answers.

Her heart told her that one way to find the answers was to pray. She quietly closed the bedroom door and moved to the side of the bed. Dropping to her knees, she clasped the Bible to her chest.

"God I don't know what I'm supposed to say. I feel so dumb about this praying thing. I guess the first thing I want to do is let you know I'm sorry for just now coming to you. I want to thank you for saving my life and making Mama well." Before she could continue, she found her words getting stuck in her throat.

Then the words choked her as she fought to control her tears, "I don't deserve any good luck, but please help me. I need my money and my house. I know what you said in the Bible about not worrying about tomorrow but I can't help it. All my life I worked hard to get these things and now they're all gone. I just talked to my mother like she was a stranger, I think I 'm losing my mind. I know I will go crazy if I end up broke. I can't take it....will you help me?"

She heard Danny's voice downstairs and quickly sat up, "Amen."

Chapter 21

"Let me tell you about my Daddy." Evelyn said in a tutorial tone as Matt maneuvered out of the hospital parking lot.

"He is very old fashioned and very protective of his girls. Your visit today will catch him totally by surprise and even though Mama is going to let him know I'm bringing you to the house, he will look at you as though you are crazy. It's not personal. He didn't like Kevin either. And he was black. Well he looked black." She adjusted the seat belt to avoid her small baby bump.

"I know this is the south, I'm prepared to deal with whatever your father wants to put me through. I think he must be an amazing man." Matt smiled.

"Why do you think that?" Evelyn found a small plastic wrapper of saltine crackers in her purse and was tearing into them to fight the queasiness.

"Cause, he has an amazing daughter. He loves you and I can't fault him for wanting to look out for you. That's what good fathers do." He turned up the air conditioner after seeing how perspiration was starting to form on Evelyn's top lip.

Evelyn adjusted the air so that it hit directly in her face, "Thanks. We'll just have to see what happens. God, I get sick all during the day! Why do they call it morning sickness when I get it all day long?"

"It won't last much longer. Just your digestive system adjusting to the extra hormones and a small little person siphoning off your nutrients."

"You know, Daddy might like having a doctor as a friend of the family. How much do you know about bunions? He has been suffering from those things since I was a little girl."

They both laughed and Evelyn munched on her crackers trying the hide her concern. She really wished Danny and Sonja's mother had joined them, the more the merrier.

After navigating Matt to her street, Evelyn started to relax a little. The familiar quiet neighborhood that had been her home for most of her life reminded her of the good times. There was no room for fear or doubt here. The houses had remained the same, the families had decided not to move to the sprawling outskirts of town and everyone still knew everyone. And that was a real rarity these days.

Matt parked curbside and jumped out to open Evelyn's door. She was sure Mama Ree was peering out of the window to assess the situation.

Evelyn reached for the front door knob but the door jerked open before she could turn it. Her mother was standing in the door way with a nervous smile.

Her high-pitched greeting gave her away, "Hi you two! I hope you're good and hungry…my mother decided to throw down today…with the citywide ceremony being so good, she just wanted to do a good old-fashioned Sunday feast. Come on in." Her moth-

mother was speed speaking which was a sure indication that she was nervous and Evelyn knew that was not a good sign.

"Where's Daddy?" Evelyn whispered.

Pat nodded towards the backyard, and to a plume of smoke billowing from the grill.

"Oh I'll go out and say hello. Maybe I can help him out." Matt winked and walked towards the patio doors before Pat could stop him.

Sam Jones was basting ribs, chicken and beef patties in his special sauce that really didn't need anymore basting. He was stalling as long as possible to avoid seeing Evelyn and her new found 'friend' as Pat had called him. He heard heavy steps behind him and knew it wasn't Evelyn so it must have been the 'friend'. He remembered the young doctor from the hospital but he couldn't understand how he had won Evelyn's attention. He was suspicious if his wife had a role in this like she did in convincing Evelyn to marry Kevin

"Smelling good Mr. Jones." Matt walked to Sam's side and extended his hand.

Sam looked at the hand and looked at the smiling freshly scrubbed face of the young doctor. He shook his hand and turned his attention back to his grill.

"I always wanted to learn how to be a master griller. Evelyn says you grill for the entire community on the holidays," he peeked over Sam's shoulder as the fragrant smoke billowed into his face.

Sam Jones slathered on more bar-b-que sauce before answering, "Well ain't much of a secret. It's all in prepping your meat. I marinate mine for at least 8 hours. That's where the real flavor comes from, the sauce is just a little part of good bar- be- que. Hand me that plate." His eyes never left his grill.

Matt picked up the plate and looked Sam in the face for the first time, "Mr. Jones , I want to thank you for inviting me to dinner."

Sam slapped a side of ribs on the plate before responding, "I didn't invite you. But since you brought it up, why are you here? Why are you hanging around Lynn?" Sam wiped his hands on the dishtowel and placed them in his pockets, widening his stance while returning Matt's eye contact.

"Sir, I like your daughter. I like her a lot. She's smart, easy to talk to and I enjoy her company." Matt nervously shifted from foot to foot and was hoping to be rescued by Evelyn or her mother as he held onto the plate of meat.

"Can't find no smart, easy to talk to white girls?" Sam rocked back and forth on his heels.

"Sir, I wasn't raised to see a person's color. I mean I know she's black, and I'm white and that might make some people uncomfortable..."

"I'm one of 'em son." Sam interrupted.

"I know, Evelyn told me you wouldn't be happy and she really doesn't want to disappoint you. We're just friends. Honestly, we talk, watch movies and eat dinner. I wouldn't pressure her or make her feel she needs to get involved with me in anyway."

"So how come you single? Good looking boy, doctor and young." Sam asked.

"I've been concentrating on my studies, my residency and I spent a few years in the Peace Corps. I'm just starting to get settled in one place I guess."

"Well, I don't like surprises. So if you got a wife, a baby or like men, you better come clean right now." Sam took the plate from Matt.

"Sir? Why would I try to hide something like that?" Matt gave a nervous laugh.

"It's been done before. Let's go inside and eat. You hungry?" Sam started walking towards the patio doors.

Matt followed him, "I'm starving! Mr. Jones, I won't disappoint you or Evelyn. I would never hurt her."

Sam stopped and turned to face the young doctor, "Well if you do, let me say this. You the one who gonna need a really good doctor. I don't play about my family son. I don't know about your background or where you come from, but this family is tight. We stick together, no matter what. Now you say you and Lynn just friends. Well I didn't go to college, but I ain't nobody's fool. So don't stand here in my backyard and say to me you just want to be friends. Cause I know better. So what is it? She pregnant, bout to be divorced and getting over a no good lying dog husband. That's a ready made family with a new baby and she is surrounded by her family and we will protect her. So if you think you want to be a part of her and that baby's life, you need to take a hard long look at every body inside that house, because we come with the deal. Every single one of us. You hear me talking to you?" Sam leaned in closer to Matt.

"I wouldn't have it any other way sir," Matt gave a nervous smile.

Pat couldn't stay away any longer. She had been watching the two men from the den the entire time. She could tell from her husband's body language that he was on the verge of issuing a threat and was just about finished talking.

"Okay, every thing is on the table. We got some hungry folks in here!" She walked over to Sam and gently took the plate. He walked ahead of her into the house.

"How bad was it?" she whispered to Matt as Sam walked ahead of them.

Matt shrugged his shoulders and gently took her elbow to guide her inside, "Not so bad really. He's a good man and hell of a father. I look forward to learning more about him. I think I stood my own ground."

Pat jerked around and looked at him, "You think it's over? Child please. Just wait until you have to go through my Mama. That's the main event. Sam was just the preliminary round." She laughed.

Matt looked around the dining room at the Jones family and felt at peace. The table was laden with corn on the cob, peach cobbler, baked beans, potato salad, green beans, chocolate cake, black-eyed peas, broccoli and rice casserole and turnip greens.

"Wow. This looks fantastic. All of this for me?" He joked. Evelyn's sisters giggled and Mama Ree patted the chair next to her for him to take a seat.

Sam held up his hand and the room fell silent.

"Mama Ree, let him sit next to me. I want to hear more about this Peace Corps job he did. And Pat says you from Chicago, we got lots of folks up there. " He pulled out a chair next to him at the head of the table signaling for Matt to sit down.

Mama Ree looked disappointed but didn't argue.

After the blessing, everyone starting passing the platters of their favorite dish.

"Oh, I forgot the macaroni and cheese!" Pat started to get up.

"No Mama I'll get it." Evelyn pushed away from the table,

"Matt can you come to the kitchen with me please?" she asked.

With a mouthful of potato salad, Matt's surprised expression was met with a chuckle from Mama Ree, "I see what's going on here." She said as she continued to serve her plate.

"What are you talking about Mama?" Pat asked.

"Yall trying to keep Dr. Matt away from me. First Sam keeps him outside all the day long and then won't let him sit next to me and here come Lynn yanking him off to the kitchen."

"Mama, that is not true." Pat scoffed and shot a glance at Sam.

"Um uh. Sam remembers how hard I was on him when he started hanging around my house after you Pat."

Sam tried to stifle his amusement but confessed, "Mama Ree I already took everything but the boys' social security number. Just let him catch his breath."

Matt followed Evelyn into the kitchen who immediately wanted a report, "Are you okay? Did Daddy really give you a hard time?" she whispered.

He looked into her eyes and saw the combination of her mother and father; soft, caring, strong, honest and beautiful. At that moment he knew. She would be his wife and the mother of his children and he would be the father of the one she was carrying.

He gently took her chin and lifted her face to his.

The kiss was soft, warm and sent a shiver through Evelyn's body. She held onto his waist to steady herself.

"Do you have room for macaroni and cheese?" she asked, not knowing how to react to his kiss.

"We better get back to the dining room before your grandmother comes looking for us." He gave Evelyn a hug and walked with her back into the dining room.

Evelyn walked to her seat and sat down still dazed.

"Lynn? Where's the macaroni and cheese?" asked a puzzled Pat.

"Oh! Sorry Mama." Evelyn jumped up and returned to the kitchen. Mama Ree quietly took in the way the two young people had reentered the dining room and she knew. She smiled and said a silent prayer thanking God. She knew.

§§§§§§§§§§§§§§§§§§§§

Maceo had been home for three days after his surgery. His entire body was sensitive to the slightest touch and his attitude was even touchier.

Gail alternated with his nurse and shared the duty of caring for him, cooking his meals and making sure he walked at least 5 minutes a day.

It was Gail's turn to take him on his 5-minute walk from his bedroom, down the hallway and into the master bath and back to bed.

With each step he gingerly made, Maceo grimaced. "When did…five minutes, get to be so damn long?" he huffed.

"Almost finished. It's not a race, just take your time." Gail measured her steps to match his.

"God what I wouldn't give for a stiff glass of bourbon." He complained.

"Oh that would be an event, mixed with pain killers. What would you like for dinner? I was thinking asparagus, baked chicken and new potatoes."

Maceo didn't answer immediately. Leaning on Gail's arm, he looked at her with a mischievous smile, "Wild turkey on the rocks."

"No. And stop asking." Before she could finish scolding him the phone rang.

"Here, sit on the toilet while I get the phone." She closed the lid and eased him on the toilet.

She grabbed the phone on the fourth ring. "Hello, Sloan residence."

"Huh..hi there. Are you my father's nurse?" The clipped voice inquired.

"No. I'm a friend taking care of your father. You must be Laurel, how are you doing?" Gail asked.

"Oh. Okay. Great, can I speak to my dad?" The anxious tone increased with impatience.

"Can he call you back, I've got to get him to the bed. Are you coming for a visit? I know he'd love to see you."

"Have him call me in about 15 minutes, on my cell. Fifteen minutes. Thanks." The conversation was over.

Gail got Maceo back into bed before telling him his daughter had called. She was sure 15 minutes had passed.

"That was your daughter. She wants you to call her on her cell phone. It sounds kind of important." Gail smoothed the bed covers around Maceo and handed him the cordless phone.

"It always is where she is concerned." He hit the speed dial and exhaled.

Gail pretended to straighten up the already neat bedroom as Maceo waited for his call to connect.

"Laurel. It's your father."

He reached for his glass of water as the conversation got underway, "Laurel, I'm fine by the way, thanks for asking. You call me to ask for money and not once did you check to see if I was living or dead after surgery. Don't start that baby act with me girl." He touched his incision and grimaced.

"Laurel, I sent you $2,000 two weeks ago. I don't understand how you fail to manage your finances. I don't give a rats' ass about the Delta's. You better get yourself together and fast. This money train is about to end honey." He motioned for Gail to get his pain pills and she checked her watch before shaking her head denying his request.

Gail reached for the phone and Maceo didn't resist.

He looked exhausted. He gave a heavy sigh as Gail started to talk.

"Laurel, this is Gail. Maceo really can't talk anymore, he needs his rest."

"I'm sorry but who are you again?" Laurel snapped.

"I'm a friend of your father's and I happen to be a nurse also. He needs his rest and he needs to not be upset." Gail walked out of the room as Maceo lay back on his pillow.

"I don't know who you are lady and I don't care, I can talk to my father anytime I want. I want to speak to him right now!" She shouted.

Taken aback at the young girl's hostility, Gail spoke in a deliberate manner, "Laurel, there is no need to shout and get disrespectful. You could talk to your father anytime you wanted, if you were here to see about him."

"Bitch don't lecture me about seeing my father…you're just the hired help who thinks you're a friend. Well he has lots of friends but only one daughter. You better be glad I'm not there…"

Gail clicked the phone off. Then she turned off the ringer. She didn't want to curse this child but she wasn't about to take verbal abuse either.

She peeked in on Maceo who had dropped off to sleep.

Gail wondered how his son was if the daughter was this selfish. She never got to find out, because Maceo's son never called.

Chapter 22

Do I Do

My life has been waiting for your love.
My arms have been waiting for your love to arrive.
My heart has been waiting,
My soul anticipating your love, your love, your
lo-o-ove.

Oh, I don't care how long it might take,
'Cause I know the woman for me, you I'll make,
And I will not deny myself the chance,
Of being part of what feels like the right romance.
Girl, do I do, what you do, when I do my love to you

In between bites of saltine crackers, Evelyn gave orders to the hotel staff setting up the ballroom, the confused looking groomsmen and the impatient bridesmaids. Sonja had insisted on having an elaborate wedding reception in the largest ballroom at the Hilton.

She didn't belong to a church and was embarrassed to ask to be baptized as an adult. Danny's minister reluctantly agreed to perform the ceremony before Sonja joined the church, but because Danny had belonged all of his life, he made an exception.

It would be a challenge for the hotel staff to have the formal dinner place settings ready during the ceremony and then on cue start serving the elaborate dinner the moment the newly married bride and groom did their first dance. The best reference Evelyn had in planning the affair was the Golden Globes Award, which used a similar layout, minus the folks getting married of course.

With very little input from Sonja, she had selected the ivory colored table linens with gold-rimmed place settings against an ivory background. Touches of gold leaf did a magical dance on each tables' centerpiece that seemed to explode from the tables three feet into the air.

Easter Lilies were mixed into the arrangement shiny palm leaves dangerously hanging over the centerpieces tall sleek crystal vases.

While the hotel management snapped photos of the transformed ballroom, Sonja kept nibbling on her recently manicured nails.

"What do you think?" Evelyn beamed as she gently removed Sonja's hand from her mouth.

"It's nice. I like it." Sonja absent-mindedly responded. She kept searching the room until her gaze found Danny.

"Okay, I'm supposed to be very sensitive given my condition, but my feelings are really about to be hurt. I wrangled a photo spread for the Friday edition of the paper and had to practically promise my first born child to the chef who had to hire additional staff to make sure the filet mignon's were done on time for at least 50 people." Evelyn pulled one of the ivory satin covered chairs out and plopped down.

"I'm sorry. I'm just a little preoccupied. I can't tell you why but it's something big...but believe me I love it! You have done a fantastic job. There is nothing I would do different." Sonja hugged Evelyn as she kept staring at Danny.

Finally sensing he was being silently summoned, Danny made his way across the ballroom.

"Forty-eight hours and counting. Evelyn you are a miracle worker. This room looks like something from a movie." He gave her a loud smack on the cheek.

He wrapped his arm around his bride to be and guided her out into the hallway.

"What if they come in during the wedding? You know to make a statement. This whole thing is getting too big." Sonja was pacing and nibbling again.

"You've got to stop imagining the worse. You're driving yourself crazy. You're not a fugitive on America's Most Wanted," he joked.

Before she could threaten him, her cell phone rang, "It's Simon Parker," she whispered.

Danny took the phone from her trembling hand, "Hello Mr. Parker."

"No problem, give us about 45 minutes, we're wrapping up our wedding rehearsal." He snapped the phone shut and sat on a bench.

"What did he want?" Sonja asked.

"He wants to see us, as soon as possible."

"Oh my God. Something bad has happened. Why else does he need to see us? I can't take this!" she broke out into hysterical tears.

"Shhh...Sonja..stop crying. Whatever it is we will handle it together. Okay...pull yourself together. Go get your purse and let's go to Simon's office. Don't fall apart on me now. He knows what he's doing. Let's just see what he needs, okay?" he was rocking her in his arms and she started to quiet her crying.

"It has to be bad news Danny. If it were something good, he would have told you on the phone...my life is over...my life is over! Everything I've worked for is gone. I have nothing!" she put her head in her hands and pulled away from him.

Danny grabbed her wrists and sharply pulled her closer, "If you feel that way Sonja then let's call off the wedding! Right now! You think you're the only one suffering in this mess? I'm sick of your whining, selfish attitude. If you only care about the things that you bought, your car, your house, clothes and not the people who have stood by you, loved you and been with you, then forget it! Evelyn is going through the saddest and scariest thing a woman can face and all you care about are material things? You don't deserve friends, you don't deserve a man who loves you. You deserve just what you got. Things that don't last, 'cause you don't know how to care about people. I'm sick of this!" He tossed her cell phone at her and walked into the men's room.

Sonja stood in shock. She tapped on the men's room door and when Danny didn't answer, she opened the door and peeked in. He was leaning over the sink with his head down.

"I love you baby, but I can't keep being the only one in love in this relationship. I can't," he said softly.

Sonja slowly walked over to him and caressed his shoulder, "I'm sorry. I just panicked. I think I'm losing my mind sometimes, but you're the only thing in my life that makes sense. Please come with me to see Simon."

Biting his lower lip, Danny shook his head to deny her, "It's time you took responsibility for this. I think it's best if you go alone. And when you get back, let me know if I should cancel all of the arrangements." He brushed past her and walked out.

§§§§§§§§§§§§§§§§§§§

It wasn't until Sonja was sitting in the swank outer office of Simon Parkers law firm that she realized how pitiful she must have looked. Her hair was in a frazzled ponytail, she hadn't changed the plain white tee shirt and grey sweat pants. She nervously crossed and uncrossed her ankles and avoided the eyes of the smartly dressed receptionist who kept sneaking glances in her direction.

She wanted to scream at the phone answering message taker that she had a closet full of designer clothes, plenty of bling and a Porche' that her sad job could never afford.

But instead, Sonja snapped the rubber band off her hair and let it swing to her shoulders, quickly smoothing the hair around her face into a manageable style.

Replacing the phone into the cradle, the receptionist looked at Sonja, "Mr. Parker will see you now Miss Davenport."

Sonja nearly sprinted to the massive walnut double doors and disappeared from view. Simon was standing behind his desk and gave her a warm smile. She couldn't tell if he was trying to spare her or really had some good news.

"Sonja, sorry to keep you waiting my dear. Here sit, do you want something to drink?"

"I don't know. Will I need a drink?" she asked.

"Perhaps. I'm having a scotch. Want to join me?" He raised his glass. Sonja could tell it was Waterford.

"No." She weakly answered.

He walked to the bar and refilled his glass, "I only drink this scotch when I'm terribly depressed or terribly happy." He took a sip and sat in the chair next to her. After she ignored his attempt at humor, he got to the point.

"Do you know a Senator Earl Simmons?" he asked.

Smoothing the hair away from her face, Sonja turned to look at him, searching for clues to this question, "I do. Why?"

"Well, it seems the good Senator has a grandson who is the political heir apparent and the younger Mr. Simmons was snared in this web that caught you."

"I don't understand." Sonja shook her head.

"Do you know a …Denise…let me check this file." Simon reached across the desk and flipped open a manila folder.

"Okay, a Denise Templeton? She worked as an assistant at the Baron's Club."

"Denise? Oh, her, she was new. Yeah, I remember her."

"She was undercover FBI. She was tracking your movements with Senator Ramos, but somehow, Senator Simmons and his grandson got in the line of fire. The young grandson of Senator Simmons became quite enamored of the little undercover agent. Sure you don't want a drink?" he asked.

"Okay, on the rocks please." Sonja finally sat back in her chair and crossed her legs.

Simon fixed her scotch on the rocks and placed the drink on a side table next to Sonja as he continued to fill her in, "So in her zeal to impress her superiors and make her first big case, our little agent shared her charms with the grandson and gained some pretty valuable information about the Baron's Club." Simon's eyes twinkled.

Taking a light sip of the expensive scotch, Sonja kept trying to think ahead of the information Simon was slowly telling her, to figure out the ending of the story.

"Lucky for us, the young man likes to video tape his escapades, which he shared with the FBI forcing them to conveniently drop him and his granddaddy from the investigation, thereby making her case and her alleged evidence comprised, to say the least."

"What does this mean?" Sonja took another sip of the cool smooth whiskey.

"It means the fed's only link to Senator Ramos was you, and you are no longer a viable target, since the tainted undercover agent was tracking you. So we can thank old man Simmons and his home movie making grandson for wrecking the investigation, which included you. Meaning, Ramos can no longer be a target where you are concerned unless something else emerges minus you and that's his problem." Simon drained the remaining whiskey from his glass.

Trying to hide her intimate knowledge of Raymond Ramos, Sonja willed her face not to blush in front of Simon.

"It's over dear. Congratulations, get on with your life," he opened his arms and embraced her.

"Thank you Simon. I just don't know what else to say."

"Well, if I were you I'd forget about returning to Dallas for a while. That's not the life I meant for you to get on with. I don't know you very well, but I do know Evelyn and she considers you a friend and that's good enough for me. I'm your lawyer not your psychologist, but allow me to advise you that friends like Evelyn are a real blessing. Finding love like you have with Danny, comes only once in a lifetime, don't waste either of them." He gently patted her arm.

Sonja took his cue, "I'll remember that. I'm sorry about your wife. Evelyn really liked her a lot. I'm sorry I didn't get to meet her."

Simon's eyes grew misty and he walked to the door, "Yeah, she would have liked you a lot. She was full of piss and vinegar, a lot like you. She gave me a new lease on life you know. Next week we will get your finances back in order and reverse ownership of your property, stocks and bonds. Oh and have a great wedding. I hear it's the talk of the town." He gave her a brief kiss on the cheek.

"Thank you. I will. You've been great. I couldn't have asked for a better attorney."

With a mischievous grin, Simon said. "I agree."

Sonja drove to the Hilton Hotel where she knew Evelyn would be in the final stages of arranging the reception. The ballroom was completely transformed into an elegant formal dinner affair with a wall of mirrors at the bronze trellis where the vows would be exchanged. The matching bronze eight holder candelabras were already in place.

Evelyn was musing over a clipboard of instructions and event details when she saw Sonja enter the room.

"Well it's about time! Either you really trust me or love is blind and you only see the man you love." She gave Sonja a tight hug.

Sonja looked around the room, "This is incredible! It's everything I imagined. A candlelight ceremony that rolls right into a formal dinner. So where will I stand?"

Grabbing her hand, Evelyn pulled her onto a platform with her back to the mirrors.

"The audience will be looking at the back of your fabulous gown in the reflection of the mirrors, but will actually see your faces as you recite your vows. I call it the Shakespeare effect, like a Broadway play! Don't you love it? Just wait until the lights are dimmed and only candles will be flickering at each table and at these massive candelabras. I can't wait!"

"And did you arrange the baby sitting services? I cannot have children running around here and creating a disturbance, that's why I want two ceremonies, I can't control that church crowd, but this I can." Sonja said while fingering one of the linen napkins.

"Done! I have three childcare professionals and a suite that will hold up to 15 children. So far we have 8 RSVP's for the service." Evelyn put the clipboard down and pulled out a skirted banquet chair.

"God! I must have eaten something too spicy today I have the worse indigestion. What's your problem?" she asked Sonja.

"Me? I'm fine. Did Danny talk to you?"

"Danny? Why would he need to talk to me? Don't tell me I'm supposed to be cutting corners now. I mean this stuff is confirmed and the menu is set and the musicians' contracts are signed, so cheapo just has to suck it up." Evelyn teased.

"No it's more than that. He wants to call off the wedding. I think he's finally tired of me."

"Come on. Stop kidding around, before I go into early labor." Evelyn looked at Sonja and saw she was not joking, "What happened?"

"I just pushed him too far this time, he says he can't take being with me anymore. Ain't that a joke? A man says he's waited his entiret life for me and when he finally gets me he throws me back."

"What did you do? Something must have happened. You want me to call him?" Evelyn ransacked her purse for her cell phone.

"I don't want to make him madder than he already is…" Sonja hesitated long enough to allow Evelyn to start dialing.

"Hey, Danny what's going on?" Evelyn cheerfully asked.

Sonja sat down next to her and strained to read her reactions from his response.

"Well, I mean it's normal for couples to fight right before the wedding. And you guys fight all the time anyway!" she tried to laugh but stopped midway her chuckle, "Danny. Please. You guys belong together. I know whatever it is you will work it out. Sonja loves you, this I know for sure." She shrugged her shoulders and gave Sonja a desperate look that signaled the end of the conversation.

Looking around the huge ballroom with its elegant and expensive decorations, Sonja let her guard down and panicked, "I can't call people two days before and cancel this wedding, let's just have a party. Minus the wedding vows." She tried to sound sane as she waited for Evelyn's reaction.

"Don't you think Danny will want his money back? He paid for most of this. It's unfair not to tell folks the wedding is off, they've bought gifts, made travel plans…" Evelyn started to argue and was silenced by a cold stare from Sonja.

"Damn him. He called it off and he should pay for it. I am having a party. If you want to walk away too, that's fine. I can take it from here." She angrily wiped the tears off her cheek.

"I'm still your friend Sonja, I just don't want you to be any more embarrassed than necessary. We can still do this with class." Evelyn begged.

"It's too late for class. I've been stood up two days before my wedding, the press is supposed to cover it and I'm supposed to just roll over and die? Curl up in a depressive fetal position and refuse to get out of bed? I'm not going to let him get the best of me!"

"All I ever wanted was the best for you," Danny's voice cut through the rear of the empty ballroom. He moved from leaning against the wall and walked through the maze of round tables, careful not to bump into the sparkling glassware, "So damn me huh? Damn the money I've spent, damn the hours, days and months of taking care of you like you were my wife. Damn the folks who care about you." He walked as close to Sonja as possible without touching her.

She instinctively took a step backwards, letting a chair stop her movement. With her voice barely above a whisper, she managed to choke out a retort, "How could you do this to me? I am going to be the laughing stock of this city! Is that what you want? To break me?"

Danny walked closer to her, "Why is everything always about you Sonja? How can you be so selfish every damn day of your life?"

Evelyn stood between them, "You guys please don't fight. It's just nerves. Why don't you go grab a sandwich or something and talk this out?"

He turned to Evelyn ignoring Sonja, "Talking won't work this time. She doesn't love me and never has, it's time I faced the facts and moved on with my life."

Her mothers' words were still ringing in her ears as she grabbed Danny's arm and forced him to face her.

"I do love you! I love you as much as I can possibly love someone...but you feel sorry for me now. That's not love! It's pity. That's not love! Before the storm I was some sort of conquest, a trophy for you to win after 20 years, that's all I've ever been!" Sonja pushed Danny before she realized what she had done.

"I think you've got me confused with the other men in your life! You were not a trophy for me. Do you think I would put myself through this to prove a point? It's about you and me. We're the only ones who matter, when are you going to realize that?" He shouted.

"I do realize that. I don't know how to make it better. I don't know how to take back the hurt I've caused, I just don't know what you want me to do," Sonja cried.

"I want you to tell me I'm the one you want to spend the rest of your life with. I have to know that Ramos is not going to reenter your life, that Dallas is a thing of the past. I have to know that you are not making a fool of me. Again." He answered.

"You are the one I want to spend the rest of my life with. It took me a long time to see the truth, to see how I've been always seeking a man who doesn't remind me what my father must have meant to my Mama. You remind me of what she must have felt for him."

She continued before Danny could react, "I don't, I didn't want to feel that Danny, I am afraid of having that kind of love for a man. A man who can leave and you never get over it." She touched his hand.

"I want to marry you. I want to have your children, I want to have the family I never had. I want to get baptized. I need to do this the right way. I want everything to be perfect, not just the ceremony, but also our marriage and our lives. Would the minister baptize me before the wedding? Right now, we can go to the church," she pleaded.

Just the light brush of her fingers on his hand melted Danny, "God help me..." he moaned and pulled her into his arms.

"No, God help us." Sonja whispered.

THE END